EVANGALINE PIERCE

Sacred Vengeance

First edition

This book was professionally typeset on Reedsy.
Find out more at reedsy.com

In remembrance of my babies Gideon, Hadasa, Joshua, and numerous others I will name in heaven someday.

In honor of my miracle baby, who is all the blessing we could ever need.

Contents

Deleted Scenes and Extra Chapters

There's more… Not everything could fit in the book. I don't want to spoil it before it starts, but if you want deleted scenes, extra chapters, possibly a free book here and there, and certainly the first chapter of book two, get on the email list.

evangalinepierce.com/contact

Chapter One

Alle scrolled through Facebook in bed as her way of waking up. Who needed coffee when the blue light from a cell phone would do the trick? She didn't bother to sit up, though. Snuggling deeper under her cozy grey weighted blanket.

Runar stirred beside her and lifted his head. "Hey, watcha doin'?" he said, rolling over to give her a sleepy peck on the cheek. He flashed his dimples. His smile could melt hearts. She still couldn't believe she got to be married to this man.

Letting the phone fall to her side, she turned to face him. "I'm just scrolling the socials," she said, kissing his lips deeply. They had precious little time to enjoy each other. Life was busy with full-time jobs and a mobile infant to take care of, but it made these little moments so much sweeter.

"Anything good?" He snuggled into the crook of her neck.

"Well, actually, how do you feel about going on a ghost tour?" She smirked, thinking he would say no.

"Sure. I'm up for a little ghost hunting."

She leaned back away from him. "What? Are you serious?"

"I mean, yeah. I like that one show, and it's not like it's real." He continued to caress her arm with his lips.

"Well, ok…. The tickets are only $10 each. I can see if my mom can watch Lani."

"Mmm hmmm." He moved up her neck to that little place behind her ear that always made her melt. "What are your plans for today?" he whispered.

"Hmmm, I plan to snuggle in bed with you all day." The phone fell from her side of the bed to the floor.

"Tempting," he smiled against her skin and let his hands roam over her hips. He continued brushing his lips on her neck again, and she tilted her head to give him more access.

The video monitor beside the bed squeaked with static and a baby cry. They both deflated.

"Later." She patted his back. "We'll have time tonight," she whispered in his ear, running her hand down the sensitive skin on his lower back. She dug fingers through his thick black hair, matted from sleep, and smiled at his bedhead.

"It's ok. I hadn't brushed my teeth anyway," he groaned.

"I know," she smirked and pushed him playfully. "I'll get her. She probably just wants breakfast and a diaper change. You go ahead in the shower." Alle sat up as he rolled off her.

"It will be a cold one," he mumbled as she left the bedroom, pulling on her fluffy robe.

She maneuvered around their crowded living room. The oversized couch and loveseat combination didn't fit the space. But it was pretty, and she didn't want to part with it.

She didn't have to walk far to Lani's bedroom even though it was on the other side of the house. It wasn't all that large, but it fit their family just fine, and it was an upgrade from their tiny two-bedroom apartment. Plus, the schools in the neighborhood had excellent reviews.

"Good morning, baby!" Alle babbled. She lifted her little girl from her crib, "Oh, girl!" and scrunched up her face at the smell. "Mommy loves you, but man, that is rank."

Alle pulled out a new diaper from the top drawer of the white changing table. She pulled a wipe from the warmer at the edge and the red tube of diaper rash cream. Lani started squirming in her left arm.

Alle bounced with her to calm her down. "Shhh, I know, baby girl. Mommy's working on it." She laid Lani on the table and buckled her in. She sang over Lani as she lifted, wiped, and switched out the diaper. They had become pros at working together to get it done quickly.

With the diaper changed, she picked the almost naked baby up and headed to the closet. She swiped her hand past the long-sleeved winter rompers her mother-in-law kept sending and settled on a cute hand-me-down sundress and leggings. It was filled to the brim with sunflowers. She pulled Lani's chubby arms through the straps and smoothed it down. It was October in Texas. Fall everywhere else. But here, summer liked to hang on for all it's worth. It usually didn't even start to get cool until after Halloween. Winter's first cold front was probably two weeks away, so the sundress still worked great.

Alle added a giant yellow bow. At almost a year old, Lani had plenty of dark blond hair to clip in, but she preferred the elastic band. When Lani looked up at her with those baby blue eyes, dimples like her dad, and the giant bow, Alle melted. She pulled out her phone and snapped yet another picture. "You are going to be the cutest baby on the internet today," Alle whispered and swooped Lani off the floor.

Alle returned to the kitchen and handed Lani off to a fully dressed Runar. He was as handsome in slacks as he was in pajamas. Alle gave him a peck on the cheek and ran off to get herself ready.

* * *

Date nights were always special, but this one seemed extra exciting. They were both doing something they had never done before. Life was an adventure with Runar. He loved taking her places he had enjoyed before, but it was more fun when they both were experiencing something for the first time together.

The week before Halloween was filled with so many spooky activities they could do on their date night. Haunted houses and hayrides. They had already taken Lani to the pumpkin patch in her cute little zebra costume. But tonight, it was just the two of them. Lani was with her Grammy.

Runar pulled into the dark cemetery. It was only thirty minutes past sunset, but they could barely see the headstones that rose from the ground. The only light was from the headlights on their silver SUV.

3

It hadn't been a long drive north. They were still in the same county, but it was still in the middle of nowhere. Trusting someone from social media for a ghost tour in North Texas might not have been the wisest move. But they were here now. Nothing could be done but to proceed with caution.

"Do the tickets have an address?" Runar put the car in park to wait for further instruction.

"It's not tickets per se." Alle gently broke the news to her husband. She had paid for the tickets through a social app. "The directions just said to meet them here."

"Well, here we are." Runar turned off the ignition. "I'm just glad this was so close to home. You would think we would have to drive to New Orleans for a tour like this."

"Well, I guess ghosts can be anywhere." Alle shrugged. "Oh, I see them right there." She pointed. Relief flooded through her. Two women with flashlights and a lot of equipment stood at the cemetery gate. "This is already creepy," she said, clapping her hands together.

"I know." Runar rubbed his hands together with a giddy grin.

Alle shook her head. "I'm still surprised you are excited about this." She pulled the latch and pushed open the door. They both emerged from the car and met the woman as she was heading toward them. Her platinum blond hair glowed against the darkness of the cemetery.

"I'm so glad y'all could make it," she drawled, pointing toward a folding table. "Head over to that table and grab some equipment. Sue Beth will help ya out." She pointed and walked past them to meet another group pulling into the parking lot.

Runar looked at Alle and grinned. "Her name is Sue Beth?"

Alle just shrugged and giggled. They reached the table where an older pudgy woman explained the equipment. "This is a spirit box. It will tell us if the spirits are sayin' anythang." She picked up another electronic box that looked like a walkie-talkie with lights. "This little do-hickey right here is an EMF reader and lets us know if there is any energy in the area. Of course, the best equipment is just a regular camera. There's also some apps for your phone, like the SLS camera app."

4

Alle pulled out her phone and downloaded the suggested app. Runar slung his DSLR camera around his neck and gave Alle a thumbs up. She grinned. "Honestly, I didn't know you were already so well-equipped."

"Are you kidding? I'm so excited! I want to catch a ghost," he whooped and shoved his fist in the air.

The platinum blond lady clapped behind them. Alle jumped at the sound. Her first fright of the night. She was a little on edge, even though she was skeptical. A crowd of about forty gathered around the tables, waiting for instructions. This lady just made four hundred dollars to walk around and talk about ghosts. "I'm definitely in the wrong business," Alle mumbled under her breath.

"All right, everybody. My name is Linda, but all my close friends call me Lin." She giggled as the crowd pressed in closer. "Before we get started, I just wanted to give you a few ghost-hunting pointers," Lin explained the ghost-hunting game plan. "First, we are going to take a walk through this field behind me." She pointed to the back side of the cemetery. There was a vast field with a path through the middle and tall yellow grass on each side. Hundred-year-old oak trees rose up on every side of the field like guardians. Lynn turned back towards her group and continued, "We'll stop and take a few pictures. Please watch for snakes," she said as if that wasn't the most frightening part of the tour. "Then we'll go down to the bridge where all the best activity is. I'll give you all the gory details as we go!"

Lin held up a finger, "But before we get started on the tour, let me show you some things others have captured on tours." She pulled out some spooky pictures to show the group. She pointed out a few "ghosts," but Alle couldn't make out much more than blurry smudges. A few pictures had scary-looking shadows. Alle was skeptical of all this hard evidence. *It definitely could be camera malfunctions*, she thought.

Lin started her story about the ghosts of the bridge. Hundreds of years ago, there had been murders and treachery in the woods nearby. According to Lin, in the early 1900s, a group of white men killed the family of a black goat farmer. When he returned to find them dead, the men took him and hung him from the bridge. This disruption caused the ghosts to roam around the area. The cemetery also helped to feed their energy.

Lin also explained there was more than one ghost. The goat man, of course, would remain to haunt the bridge where he died. But there was also a little girl and a mean old man. They had named this mean old man Steve. He had been the one to lead the gang of men who killed the goat farmer. Steve had imprisoned the little girl and wouldn't let her spirit go. It sounded very sad to Alle if it were true.

Of course, it sounded like a story told late at night around a campfire. "We'll just be taking a little hike down to the bridge. We've seen quite a few copperheads, so watch your step, and if you see one, just yell, snake, real loud."

"Great," someone in the back said. "How are we supposed to watch for ghosts and snakes in the dark?"

Lin clicked on a flashlight. "We won't be in the dark until we get where we're goin'."

There were plenty of skeptics in the crowd. A few murmured that this had been a waste of money. A few others were just there for the thrill. They expected ghosts to jump out at them like at a haunted house.

As they hiked through the woods toward a creek and a bridge, Lin filled them in on some paranormal activity she had experienced. A paranormal team had been to the location, and several of them had been choked by unseen hands. Also, the ghost didn't seem to like pregnant women. Most women who had ventured along the bridge had experienced some sort of activity. One had been scratched. Another wouldn't even talk about what happened to her, and one other woman said that it felt like an unseen foot had kicked her in the stomach.

Alle rolled her eyes. Each of the instances could easily be explained by normal activity or made up by the people already primed to feel ghosts. Runar snapped picture after picture, pausing every little bit to show Alle what he had captured. Alle nodded along and gave him a pat on the back. She didn't want to ruin his fun, but she didn't see anything interesting in his pictures.

As the group neared the bridge, Alle doubled over and grabbed her chest.

"Alle, are you ok?" Runar asked as he put his hand on her back and stopped. He waved the group around them.

"Yeah. I'm just suddenly out of breath for some reason." Alle hadn't lost all the baby weight yet. She was just getting back to working out but didn't think she was this out of shape. The moisture in the air made it feel like they were walking through molasses, so she was sure it wasn't a big deal. She stood up and put a reassuring hand on Runar's elbow. "I'm fine. Just needed to catch my breath. Are we almost there, do you think?"

"I think it's just around this bend."

"Thank goodness. I was not prepared to walk this far."

The group approached the bridge. Lin had them sit on the rickety wooden thing crossing the shallow creek. It was sturdy for being built in the early 1800s. It wouldn't support the weight of vehicles, but the group of people sitting there probably had nothing to fear. She peered over the side to the murky water below. She's great to take a swim with the snakes.

As Lin continued telling the story of the bridge and her experiences, she guided people to take out their phones and use the equipment she allowed them to borrow. One woman pointed her phone at Alle.

"Oh, my goodness!" She pointed. "There's a little figure sitting in your lap."

Alle looked behind her to make sure the woman was talking to her.

"There's a ghost in my lap?"

"Yeah, when I point this SLS app at you, your frame shows up, and a smaller one appears in your lap. Ha! That's crazy. You have a ghost in your lap."

Alle laughed. She couldn't see the woman's phone, so she had no idea what that even looked like. She didn't feel anything and dismissed the idea of a tiny ghost in her lap.

She focused back on what Lin was saying. Along with the goat farmer, there was also a little girl that Steve's ghost had trapped on the bridge. Alle felt sorry for this little girl ghost who couldn't go to the light. Steve was also accused of murdering his pregnant wife, who was the town's teacher.

Alle thought to put some of her skepticism aside and try to communicate with a few of the ghosts as they did on the shows Runar was always watching. She found a quiet place away from the crowd. "Well, little girl ghost, I would really like to talk to you if you want." Alle waited a few seconds. Nothing happened. She felt stupid for talking to the darkness, so she decided to look for her husband.

She found Runar at the back of the group, taking more photos. He pulled his camera down and gave her a smug little smile. Then, a peck on the lips.

"Look what I got." He showed her the viewfinder on the digital camera. The photo showed the trees they were facing now and three bright dots in the middle. They were different sizes and colors.

"Oh wow, you took a picture of Glinda the Good Witch."

"What?! No, those are ghosts. Lin said ghosts sometimes show up as orbs on camera."

Alle bumped him with her shoulder. "Look at you. Top in the class."

"Shut it." His eyes glimmered with his usual mischief.

She knew from the ghost shows that ghosts might need the energy to communicate. Maybe that was why nothing happened before. "Ok, I want to try something then." She pulled out one of the devices. "Alright, ghost! If your name is Steve, make this device light up." She waited a few seconds, and nothing happened. "It's okay. If you need energy, you can use mine!"

"Alle! No!" Runar yelled at her and grabbed her arm hard. "You don't give your energy to them, ever! Do you understand me?"

Alle looked at him in shock and yanked her arm away. He had never been so harsh with her. "Why would you do that? This is not even real."

"I didn't think so at first either. But it is real, Alle. I'm one hundred percent convinced. I'm just not sure these are ghosts. I don't want you to be hurt." Runar explained himself, but Alle wasn't sure it made her feel much better about being manhandled.

"First. I love you, but never grab my arm that hard again." She pointed her finger toward him. "Second, if they are real and not ghosts, what do you think they are?"

Runar hung his head. He looked genuinely sorry that he had hurt her. "I'm sorry. I might have overreacted. I want you to be careful, ok? If they aren't ghosts, they could only be… demons."

Alle stared and waited for the punch line. He was always joking around, and she wouldn't put it past him to be joking about this. But the look in his eyes told her that he was more serious than he had ever been. She shrugged, "Well, you should show Lin what you found," she said, blowing off Runar's momentary freak-out. He had never treated her like that before.

He took a deep breath and turned away from her for a few seconds. His body movements suggested he was struggling to keep his composure. When he turned back toward her, he was back to normal. "I will show her later. She seems a bit busy right now." He pushed a couple of buttons to take him to the next photo. "Look at this one." Ignoring his outburst, he pointed to the top of the picture. "What does that look like to you?"

"Oh, my goodness! You got a picture of an owl!" She was amazed that he could get a picture of the beautiful bird.

"No! That's not an owl. That's a goat head." He looked skeptical that she could think it was anything other than his ghost. He shook his head as he continued to examine the photo. He zoomed into the picture.

"In a tree?" Alle raised her eyebrows as she looked over his shoulder. Even if the goatman were real, she doubted he would hang out at the top of a tree.

"Yes, a goat head in a tree. I'm sure ghosts and demons can be on the top of trees," he said.

Alle was still skeptical. "It's definitely an owl."

"Ok. Well, let's just see what Lin says." He lifted his chin and walked off through the crowd toward the leader.

"I thought she was too busy," Alle mumbled and followed him through the people milling about talking to spirits and taking pictures of the darkness. The people pushed in behind Runar, and they got separated. As she made it to the other side of the bridge, she heard the excited squeal of their ghost-hunting leader. The picture was a goat head.

"Well, there will be no living with him now," she whispered. As she reached Runar, the handsome devil beamed at her and flashed his dimples. "Ok, ok. You win. It's a goat head in a tree." She tilted her head and peered into the dark sky. "I wonder if someone put a mask up there or something."

With that, Runar deflated again.

"I'm sorry. I'm just having a hard time not rationalizing this." She tried to lift his spirits again. "And you know all the ghost shows have to debunk the obvious before claiming it's a ghost."

"You're right. But I looked at this spot for a long time from many different angles. Without the camera, I can't see anything up there. I don't think this was faked."

"Ok. So, a random goat ghost is watching over a group of ghost hunters. Maybe he was guarding his territory." Alle shivered. "That is creepy."

"Well, if you look closely, it looks like it's looking at something." Runar brought the camera closer to his face. "There's a person in the bottom corner." He squinted and leaned in closer. "Wait, that's you." He shoved the camera back at Alle and suddenly turned serious again.

"If you are trying to scare me, you will have to do better than that."

"I'm not trying, Alle. I want you to stay close to me. We should go back to the car now." Runar scooched in protectively.

"First, how are you going to protect me from a ghost? I think we should stick with professional ghost hunters." She motioned her hands toward the ghost tour guides. "Also, wasn't that like thirty minutes ago? If a ghost or demon were going to attack me, it would have done so by now."

Runar didn't move. "This was immediately before you had that episode where you couldn't breathe. Dang it, Alle! And then you allowed them to use your energy."

Alle froze. That was a little creepy, but she didn't believe in all this spirit stuff. She thought angels might be aliens, but even that seemed far-fetched. Runar left his camera hanging around his neck and slapped his forehead. He started pacing and mumbling something to himself. Alle couldn't make out what he was saying. She huffed at Runar and patted her belly. "That was because Mama is still getting in shape." She linked her arms through Runar's elbow and stretched to give him a little peck on the cheek. "Nothing is going to get me."

He looked ready to throw her over his shoulder and get her out of there when Lin got the crowd back on track to hike further past the bridge to see some lights. Runar looked down at Alle and seemed to make a decision. He grabbed Alle's hand and turned to follow the crowd. Alle smirked behind him, knowing she had won that round.

They passed a witch's ring, which was interesting, but the only lights they saw were from hikers coming up the trail from the other direction. The group turned and headed back. Alle and Runar were now in the back of the group. The group was not moving all that fast, but as soon as they neared the bridge, the tightness returned to Alle's chest. She asked Runar to wait while she sat and caught her breath. She didn't want to worry him again but had no choice. She couldn't take another step until she caught her breath. He stood guard, searching the surrounding trees for threats. He looked murderous and ready to fight.

The group had already left them when Lin appeared to check on them. "Are you ok, hun?"

Alle waved her off. "Oh, I'm fine. Just catching my breath. I didn't expect to walk so much tonight."

Lin just nodded her head. "Well, ok. I don't want to leave you out here."

Alle stood again. "I'm good. Let's go." She couldn't wait to leave the bridge and its possible ghosts behind. Lin struck up a conversation with Runar as they walked over the bridge. Alle fell a little behind. As they rounded the corner without her, she felt prickles on her skin like she was being watched. When she turned, she thought she might have seen glowing orbs in the darkness watching her leave. She hurried to catch up to the group. There were more critters than snakes to worry about in the woods, and she didn't want to be separated from the herd. She ran into Runar's broad chest as she hurried around the path. He wrapped her in his arms.

"I'm so sorry. I got distracted asking Lin questions about the activity here. I shouldn't have left you." He pulled away from her and looked her over for injuries.

She patted him on his arms. "It's ok. I'm fine. Nothing got me. Let's just get home. I've had enough fun for one night." She gave him a weak smile to reassure him that she was ok.

They returned to their car tired and sweaty. Runar cranked down the air conditioning. The adrenaline in Alle's veins depleted, and her body crashed. The drive gently rocked her to sleep. She didn't even remember Runar helping her to bed.

Chapter Two

Alle ran her fingers through her dark hair. Her knee bounced. The polish on her fingers flaked as she wiped her sweaty palms on her pants leg. Surrounded by beige, white walls, she waited for answers. Fortunately, this visit didn't require an internal exam this time.

Two days ago, she sat in a similar room. Her arm extended as a needle punctured her skin. She barely felt the prick when the technician inserted the sharp into her arm. "You're good at that," she mused, watching the deep red liquid rush into the hollow tube. Her thoughts drifted to what revelations waited inside those microscopic cells.

She passed the time by reading the literature stapled to the walls. One was about how nursing is good for babies. Another gave information about breast cancer. The boredom had just set in when the knock came, and the door opened.

"Hi, Alle. It's good to see you again," Dr. Philip said, shutting the door behind him. He took a few steps into the tiny room and sat on the black rolling stool. He held a manila file with all the answers to Alle's problems. "How is your baby girl?"

"She's great. Growing fast. She'll be a year old in a couple of weeks," she said impatiently.

Dr. Philips nodded and pursed his lips in thought. "Why are you trying for another baby so soon?"

"My husband and I are only children; we both wanted a large family. We want Lani to have close siblings."

The doctor nodded, satisfied with her answer. He finally opened the file.

His unruly salt and pepper hair shook as he tilted his head to look through his glasses at the answers it contained.

"It looks like you are having a little trouble having another one."

"Yes, Runar and I have been trying for seven or eight months, and it just isn't happening." Alle tucked her hair behind her ear. Her face reddened. It didn't matter that this guy had seen every part of her anatomy and delivered her only child. She was still embarrassed to talk about sex with anyone other than her husband.

"Well, it does look like your hormones are a little out of whack. We'll give you some treatments and some meds. We'll get you pregnant. Don't worry." He smiled and gave her a chaste pat on the shoulder.

His pen scrawled across a notepad he pulled out of one of the drawers. He handed the paper to her and asked, "Did you have any other questions?"

"No, just the one."

"Ok. Great. You will take the medicine for ten days and then call the office when you start your cycle. We'll start you on the next round of fertility meds. You also need to take the hormones daily."

"Do I have to do this for the rest of my life?" Alle asked.

"Yes, you will likely always need hormone replacement. Pregnancy can do that to you." The doctor looked over his paperwork. After making sure all the boxes were checked, he stood. "Have a great day, Alle. I hope to see you back soon." He held out his hand to her. She shook it gratefully.

As soon as he was out the door, Alle took a deep breath. No biggie. She was just going to pop some pills, and everything would get back on track.

Getting pregnant the first time was so easy. The pregnancy was uneventful. There were no pills, no needles. No month-to-month disappointment when the two pink stripes didn't appear on the stick.

The nurse came in quickly and explained the medicine. She read the results of the urine test Alle had submitted when she first arrived for her appointment. There still weren't two pink lines. She walked to her car in the warm afternoon sun, disappointed but hopeful.

Alle touched the door handle to unlock the car and pulled it open. Her faux leather handbag plopped into the passenger seat. She tapped a few buttons on the center console to call Runar. "Hey, babe. I'm on my way home."

"How'd the visit go?" he asked. She could hear the expectant hope in his voice.

"Eh, ok. I've got some medicine that will hopefully help us out. It's a little complicated. I'll have to explain later."

"Ok. I'm making scratch chicken alfredo. Lani is napping." His voice was muffled like he was holding the phone with his shoulder.

Alle's mouth started watering at the thought of cheesy carb overload. She pictured him in the kitchen chopping the ingredients, grating the cheese, and sliding the pasta gently into the boiling water so that it was the perfect bite. She had often watched him sprinkle in spices and salts so that everything melded together into a flavor explosion. "Oh, man. Your alfredo is amazing, but I wish I could nap too. I don't know if I would rather eat or sleep. I've been so tired lately," she paused, thinking of Lani's sweet, sleeping baby face.

"Alle? You still there? Did I lose you?"

"What? Oh, yes, I'm here. Don't let Lani sleep too long unless you want to be up all night playing," she teased. The phone beeped, indicating another call. "Hey, I have to go. The doctor is calling me for some reason." She hadn't even put the car in reverse.

"Ok, bye, babe. I'll see you when you get home," he said, distracted with his culinary masterpiece.

"Love you, bye," she said as she hit the button to switch the line to the incoming call. "Hello?"

"Hi, Alle. I just wanted to let you know that we are having issues with your new insurance. Unfortunately, we aren't going to be able to accept it in the future."

"Wait, what? They told me everything was fine with my insurance." Alle's face reddened with anger. She could feel the heat sizzle through her veins as the adrenaline dumped to prepare her for the stress she was facing. She gripped the steering wheel until her knuckles were white. She took a few deep breaths to keep from yelling at the office clerk. She flipped the air conditioner to high.

"I'm sorry. The business office changed some things, and we can't accept it."

"We checked the insurance before the visit, and everything was fine." After another deep breath, she felt the heat dissipate enough to talk normally. "So now what? We just decided on a treatment."

"We'll take this insurance for this visit, but we won't be able to accept it in the future. Go ahead and start the treatment. I can give you some recommendations for doctors that will accept this insurance."

Alle sighed and put her head on the steering wheel. She didn't want to switch doctors. Dr. Philips delivered Lani, and she liked him. What else was she going to do? "Ok. I guess that will have to do." She dug through her glove box for some paper and a pen. The receptionist rattled off several names, and Alle scribbled them down. She tapped the end button on her phone and laid it next to the pen and paper on the seat.

This wasn't the greatest time for researching new doctors. School started a few weeks ago. The school had a no cell phone rule. She often forgot to make important calls during the busy day. She rolled her eyes and set a reminder to call during lunch.

Her eyelids drooped while she leaned back against the seat. Tears she couldn't control began pouring from her eyes. *I don't know why this has to be so hard,* she thought.

Late afternoon light filtered in through the driver's side window. Dust danced in the rays of the fading sun. As Alle took a deep breath to clear away the negative emotions, she heard a gentle whisper reminding her this was her choice. It wasn't audible, but it wasn't in her head either. She didn't know what choice she had made that led her to weep in the parking lot of a doctor's office, but she wasn't sure it had been a good one. Still, she wouldn't trade her marriage or her daughter for anything. No matter how hard this life was, they were worth every second.

Finally starting the car and clicking the shifter into gear, she turned toward home. There was nothing to be done until tomorrow. Food and sleep would help her deal with the problem of finding a new doctor.

* * *

Alle walked in the front door and threw her purse in the corner. Lani was awake and playing on the floor. The open floor plan allowed Runar to watch her while he was cooking. She scooped her daughter up and swung her around just to hear the delighted squeals Lani would make. Then she snuggled her and held her as she twirled. The baby cooed and babbled at her.

"Ooh, did I hear you say Mama baby girl?" Alle squealed.

"No, but she did say Da Da!" Runar trotted over quickly and gave Alle a quick kiss hello, then returned to his masterpiece in the kitchen.

"No way!" She looked Lani in the eyes. "I don't care what all the baby books say. There's no way you are going to say dada first."

Drool flowed down the baby's chin. She reached up and put her hands in Alle's mouth. Alle covered her teeth with her lips and pretended to bite the tiny appendages.

"So, what was the doctor calling about?" Runar asked from the kitchen.

Alle sighed again and told him the whole story while she bounced Lani on her hip. He stopped everything he was doing and wrapped her in a hug. His woodsy scent, which she loved, filled her and lifted her spirits. When he pulled back, he looked into her eyes. "Everything is going to be ok," he assured her. He lifted her chin with the crook of his finger and planted a kiss on her lips. Then cupped her face in his strong hand. She leaned into the comforting gesture.

Tears rose in her eyes again, and she snuggled into his embrace. He kissed the top of her head and inhaled deeply. Everything would be ok as long as she was in his arms.

Chapter Three

"Are you sure?"

"Yes!" The creature hunched and looked up at the other. "We caught sight of her at the bridge." He snickered and rubbed his bony hands together in a swirl of giddiness. "So many humans, so willing to give their energy to us. It's the best time!"

"Yes, but you are sure of what she is?" the other barked angrily.

"She offered her energy willingly! I felt it. The rush of power, unlike any human. It was delicious," he rasped.

"And what about the man?"

"He did not offer energy. I do not know him." Disappointment rang through the creature's scratchy voice.

"Unfortunate." The other scratched his chin. "It's distressing that you didn't get the man, Bosch, but since you are now connected with the woman, keep track of her. Report back about her movements. She will be critical in my plans if you are correct about what she is."

The creature hobbled to return to the natural realm through the barrier. It was thin this close to the bridge. Humans continued to perform spells so demons could easily pass through in small numbers.

"Oh, Bosch, one more thing. I need you to cause a little havoc in her life. I want her lost and desperate. Defeated before she even knows there is a fight."

The hunched creature bowed, "Yes, sire!"

Chapter Four

"I don't think this medicine is working. It's been two weeks."

"What makes you say that?"

"Well, cycle day one was supposed to start five days ago. And I have some weird side effects."

Runar sat up and kissed her bare shoulder. "Like what?" He had been overly attentive since the ghost bridge tour. Like he was afraid Alle would be hurt or taken away from him. It was almost overbearing.

"Umm… well, my boobs are tender."

Runar perked up. "Do you think I could have caused that?"

Alle giggled. "What? No! It's like I worked out too hard, but it won't go away."

"Oh." Runar sounded relieved that he hadn't caused her pain. "You should definitely call the doctor about it." He gave her a quick peck on the cheek as he went to get ready for work.

"I'll call on my break today," she promised.

* * *

The phone rang twice before the receptionist picked up. "Yes, this is Alle. I just wanted to leave a message for Dr. Carmichael."

"Are you a current patient?" The receptionist droned.

"Sort of. We spoke briefly last week. Dr. Phillips referred me."

"Ok. What's your date of birth?"

"December twenty-sixth."

Alle heard typing on the end of the phone. She tapped her foot impatiently.

"Ok. I'll transfer you to her voice mail." A sweet orchestral ballad flowed from the phone.

"Thank you," Alle whispered.

When the voice mail picked up, she explained how the medicine had caused the side effects and that cycle day one hadn't started yet. She left her number and date of birth again, as the robotic voicemail service instructed. *It's weird leaving these detailed messages for the doctor, especially a new one,* she thought.

Her lunch was barely warm when the doctor's number popped up on her caller ID.

"Hi, I wasn't expecting a call back so soon," Alle answered.

"I got your message about the weird side effects." The doctor paused. Alle felt she needed to fill in the silence.

"Yes, I just don't know what the cause could be other than the medicine."

"Well, have you taken a pregnancy test?" Dr. Carmichael's voice was sweet. Even though they had never met, she wanted to trust her.

"My previous doctor gave me a test before I started the medicine because the medicine could be bad for a pregnancy."

"Yes, it could. But I need you to take an at-home test as soon as possible. The first test could have been a false negative, or it could have been too early. I will go ahead and call in blood work. You can come by at your convenience."

"Oh. Ok. If that's what you recommend. I don't think that's possible, though."

"We have to rule out pregnancy before we can do anything else."

"Ok. I'll stop by the store on the way home." Alle ended the call, put down the phone, and finished her lunch. She rolled her eyes at the doctor's directions. This was a complete waste of time and money.

Alle shrugged and took a bite of her microwaved leftover chicken alfredo. She pulled out her phone and started reading her latest book download. She blew off the idea she was pregnant, instead getting lost in the fantasy world.

* * *

Alle pulled the pink box from the white plastic bag a few hours later. This little box had cost twelve bucks. It held proof that she wasn't pregnant, so they could move on to what was really going on.

Alle bounced from foot to foot as she hurriedly unwrapped the plastic wrap. She had to go since she left work. Fumbling with the wrap until she finally found the tab to break open the seal. The plastic crinkled.

"Why did they make these boxes so hard to get into?" she grumbled. It was wrapped up like Fort Knox.

Alle got the thing out and sat on the toilet with the stick between her legs, just in time. Rolling her eyes in relief, she capped the test and laid it on the counter.

When she finished and opened the bathroom door, Runar waited patiently, pretending to read a magazine. He looked up and raised his eyebrows.

"We have to wait five minutes," Alle announced. She put her nose in the air and pulled her shoulders back. She walked across the bedroom to her side of the bed.

He threw up his hands and growled at the air. Then jumped up and ran toward the bathroom. Alle was right behind him, grabbing at his waist.

He grabbed the test from beside the sink. "You have to wait five minutes, or it won't be right," Alle said, jumping to try to grab the test from him. Runar simply lifted his hand above his head to keep it away from her. After several tries, she gave up and simply put her hand on her hip. "I peed on that, you know."

He gave her a wink that said he didn't care. "I don't think we're going to need five minutes," he said as he studied the plastic stick.

"Why, what does it say?"

"We're going to have another baby!"

"It does not say that." Runar handed over the test this time, grinning ear to ear. Alle stared at it. There was no way there could be two pink stripes. She had dismissed all her symptoms as side effects of the medicine she had taken. Could it be that she was finally pregnant?

Alle stiffly lowered the lid to the toilet and sat down with the test still in her hand. The two pink lines stared back at her from the plastic strip. *"This can't be right!"*

A few moments later, she stood quickly and stomped over to the 'his and hers' bathroom sink. The pregnancy test box lay open beside her sink. There was one more test. Alle flipped up the box, dumped it out, and unwrapped it, shoving it at Runar. "Here you do it!"

He jumped back. "Me?" He slapped his chest. "What good is that going to do?"

"We can see if these are faulty. If you get two pink stripes, then we know there's a problem."

Runar started to laugh but sobered quickly when he saw Alle wasn't smiling. Her eyebrows were furrowed. She was ready to fight him on this. His shoulders sagged as they traded places in the bathroom. He shut the door behind him.

The floor creaked when Alle stepped away from the door, walked to the corner of the bed, pivoted, and returned to the bathroom door. Her nail beds were going to bleed soon. Finally, the door opened.

"Well, I have weird news!"

"See, I told you they were fa...." She stopped when Runar held up his hand.

"The faucet is not pregnant."

"What? You didn't pee on it? That's a bit unfair," she said, crossing her arms and cutting her eyes at him in a cute pout.

Runar huffed a laugh at her antics. "I think this was a better test. But the point is that the tests are fine, and you are pregnant."

Alle let herself fall on the bed and stared up at the ceiling. The bed dipped as Runar lay beside her. He leaned on his elbow and watched her for a few seconds.

"I'm not sure why you are upset about this."

Tears ran down the sides of her head, wetting the comforter. "I'm not upset. I'm dissatisfied with the service Dr. Philips provided."

"Oh, is that all." He gently wiped a tear with the crook of his forefinger.

Alle rolled toward Runar and propped herself up. "I'm happy. I'm just worried about the medicine that I took. Maybe it hurt the baby."

Runar stroked the hair out of her face and tucked it behind her ear. "Let's take it one day at a time. We'll be happy for today. And we'll look forward to Lani having a baby sister."

She pushed him on the shoulder. "She's obviously getting a baby brother."

Runar laughed. "Mama is always right. I'll buy the paint for the nursery tomorrow."

"I still have to go do blood work tomorrow. So, let's not get ahead of ourselves. One day at a time, remember." Even though she was starting to believe the tests, she didn't want to get too excited until the doctor confirmed it.

"Of course, I won't get my hopes..." He threw one hand in the air. "Who am I kidding? I'm totally getting my hopes up!" Runar could not contain the grin that threatened to make Alle weak in the knees. Good thing she was already lying down. His familiar dimples made an appearance. She loved seeing him so happy. Breathing a cautious sigh of relief, she cupped the side of his face and kissed him in celebration.

* * *

A few days later, the doctor called with the blood work results.

"Hi, Alle. Congratulations, you are pregnant! I just want to do another routine blood test to ensure the numbers are where they should be."

"Sure, Doctor. But I've never had to do two blood tests before," Alle said, confused.

"It's routine. I'm surprised you didn't have to do it with your first pregnancy."

"Oh, ok, thank you."

"Congratulations again. I will call you back when we get the results from the next test."

Alle pushed end on her cell phone and smiled. Excitement finally coursed through her body at the confirmation. "Well, I guess that explains the mood swings and fatigue," she whispered to herself. She let herself believe the good news and was glad she hadn't started with a queasy stomach.

The following day, Alle went by the lab to be jabbed with the needle for what felt like the thousandth time. She watched the vials fill with the red liquid from her artery. She couldn't help but worry again that maybe this wasn't happening. There could have been a mistake. Giving the technician a weak smile as she responded kindly to her chit-chat, she tried to push her worries away.

Over the next few days, Alle looked at her phone every five minutes to see if she had missed a call from the doctor. Her pregnancy symptoms had increased, and she was sure the pregnancy was the real deal.

The doctor's phone number finally popped up in her caller ID. She reached for it excitedly and pressed the green button to accept the call.

"Hi Alle, the results of the second blood test are back." The doctor took a deep breath. "Unfortunately, the numbers are not doubling as fast as they should be. I want to schedule an ultrasound. What would be a good day for you to visit the office?"

"The numbers aren't doubling? What does that mean?"

"It could mean anything. I don't want to worry you, but the HCG numbers should double every two days. They didn't, so I want to check with the ultrasound."

"Oh. I can come by tomorrow evening, I guess. I get off at three, so I can be there around three forty-five."

"That's fine. I'll stay late to make sure we get this taken care of. I'll transfer you to the receptionist to put you on the schedule."

After she ended the call with the doctor, she did what no one should ever do. She searched for her symptoms on the internet. After all her research, she was not getting good news. She didn't call Runar immediately, unable to bear to rip his happiness to shreds.

* * *

Late Friday afternoon, Alle sat alone in an olive-green lobby. The seats were partitioned with pony walls topped with frosted glass. Alle sat directly across from the dark oak door that separated the lobby from the exam rooms. Above the door was an iron decoration. There were no other women in the room. She had the last appointment of the day. The doctor was staying late to get her in.

Runar was working, so she had to face this alone. Even after her search, she refused to think about how a sonogram would explain why the HCG in her blood work wasn't doubling. She prayed that the doctor was wrong and that they would get good news.

The door finally opened. A short nurse wearing green scrubs held an opened file in her hand. "Alle Venega?" she called.

As Alle rose and followed her through the door, she noticed the nurse's name tag said, Trisha. It didn't match her face.

She pointed to the floor. "Step on the scale here, please, Sweetie." Trisha wrote down the measurement and motioned for Alle to continue following her.

They reached the exam room. Alle sat on the bed as the nurse started pulling out equipment. She laid out a paper blanket, lubricant, and a pair of purple gloves, then slammed the cabinets. She handed the blanket to Alle, "Please undress from the waist down and put the sheet over you." Trisha smiled sadly and rushed out of the room.

Alle did as she was told. She swung her legs over the edge of the exam table. She had left her phone in her purse across the room. Now, she was stuck just looking at the wallpaper.

Butterflies took flight in her stomach, and she thought she might be sick. She looked around the room for a puke bucket, just in case.

It seemed like an eternity before Dr. Carmichael finally entered the room.

"Hi, Alle. We will do a little sonogram to see what's going on here. And we'll go from there," she said as she wheeled the machine into the room and dimmed the lights. "The technician isn't here this late, so I will do this myself."

"Ok," Alle responded with a shaky voice.

"Alright, just lay back and try to relax." The doctor's calm voice reassured her that everything would be alright. The doctor positioned the machine, so

Alle couldn't see the screen from where she was. It wouldn't have mattered. No one can tell what is happening on a sonogram.

The doctor poked and prodded. Her eyebrows scrunched together as she studied the screen thoughtfully.

"What's wrong?"

"I'm sorry, Alle." The doctor stopped everything she was doing and put away the probes. She stood beside the bed and placed her hand on Alle's. "There's no heartbeat." Dr. Carmichael delivered the news with as much grace as possible for the situation.

"What?" Alle sat up. "You were telling me congratulations on being pregnant four days ago, and now you're telling me there's no heartbeat. My baby died in four days?"

"I'm sorry. You are far enough along there should be a heartbeat by now. It just isn't there. The baby stopped developing about a week ago."

The silence lingered.

Alle's world had stopped turning. The shock from finding out she was pregnant hadn't even worn off yet. And now she was in shock again in the worst way. Tears wouldn't even form.

She already loved this baby. Already had the future planned out. Where the crib would go and how they would decorate the designated nursery. The swaddling blankets ordered online would arrive tomorrow.

"Let's do this…." The doctor's voice pulled her back to the room. "I'm going to print out a few images for you." She clicked a few buttons on the machine, and little black and white prints of Alle's abdomen popped out of the bottom.

"Then we'll wait until Monday to see what you want to do. I'll have you come in for another sonogram with the sonographer. Since it's still a little early, we'll give it a couple more days to make sure."

Dr. Carmichael patted Alle on the arm. "You can get dressed, and we'll make another appointment for Monday."

Alle heard the soft click of the door. Left alone in the room, the tears finally started to flow as she dressed. This was going to be the worst weekend of their lives. Her shoulders drooped as she walked out of the medical high-rise toward her car. Lost in thought, the drive home didn't even register.

Her family was waiting for her at the kitchen table when she walked through the door. Alle ran to Lani, picked her up from the highchair, and squeezed her tight. Her tears told Runar the story. He wrapped his arms around them, hugged tightly, and kissed Alle on the top of her head.

"We're going to be alright," he whispered sweetly in her ear.

He never shed a tear.

He never fell apart.

Alle did all that for both of them.

Chapter Five

They had made it past the holidays. It had been a mild winter, and they were headed for even warmer weather. Lani had noticed the cows calving in the fields on the way to school. "Baby!" she said, pointing at the cows and giggling. Then, Alle realized that she had been spacing out and not paying attention. She vowed to pay closer attention, but it was easy to zone out, trying to avoid thinking.

Later that day, Alle sat at the table in the lunch room with some of her coworkers. She had water in her hand, sipping slowly, listening to the conversation.

"Hey, Alle," her friend and mentor, Mrs. Jackson, said, laying a hand on her arm. "How are you doing with everything?" Then she gave her the pity stare. The one where a person wants to show sympathy but doesn't understand a thing about it.

Alle smiled for the sake of her friend even though it didn't reach her eyes. Her smiles rarely did these days. "I'm fine. We've moved on."

Mrs. Jackson accepted that answer, although it was far from the truth. Alle was living but barely. The only things that kept her going were Runar and Lani. If not for them, she would have given in to her depression weeks ago. She was living for them now. Adrift and unable to find footing in this new world of grief, she would never be the same as she once was.

Trying to avoid her coworker's questions, Alle looked at her phone. The first time all day. She had to have it turned off and in her purse during work hours. Others wouldn't bother her if she scrolled through social media and tuned them out, but she could still appear social.

There were several missed calls seconds apart from a number she didn't recognize. Then, several calls from her neighbor, John. Runar had taken the day off to help him on his ranch. He had left so early she didn't even see him.

She called him back. John answered on the first ring. "Alle! Thank God you called me back finally. There's been an accident. Runar is in the emergency room."

Alle knocked over her water as she stood abruptly. "What? Why didn't you call the school? What happened?"

"I was trying to get him to the hospital. He was using the chainsaw and dropped it too low. It sliced through his leg and cut the artery. I couldn't get the bleeding to stop. Alle, I don't want to freak you out, but you must get here as soon as possible. They are taking him back for surgery."

"I'm on my way. Tell him to hang on. I'll be there as soon as I can." Alle ran down the hall to her classroom to get her keys. She didn't explain where she was going to anyone. They could deal with her classes. She would call her principal on her way to the hospital to explain.

How could this be happening? she thought as she sped to the hospital. It was going to take her forty-five minutes with traffic. She begged the Most High to save Runar all the way to the hospital, not knowing if her prayers were even heard anymore. The distance between her and the Most High had grown. He seemed silent most of the time, but she prayed anyway. It wasn't like it would hurt, but it might not help.

Not knowing exactly what was happening kept her adrenaline up so she could make it to the hospital without losing her mind. The automatic double doors opened as she approached. She ran past the wheelchairs in the corner to the lobby.

John sat hunched in the corner on the orange plastic chairs near a row of vending machines. He stared at the floor, rocking himself until he saw Alle rush in, looking for him. He stood and wiped his face. As he walked up to her, he steeled himself into a mask of bravery. "Alle, I'm so sorry."

"It's ok, John. Just tell me where he is. I need to see him. I didn't get to kiss him this morning, and I need to see him."

29

"I'm sorry."

"John. Tell me where he is." She clenched her fist around her purse strap to keep herself from slapping him.

"Alle, he's gone."

"No. That's not funny, John. Please don't say that." She backed away from him on stiff legs.

"I'm not joking, Alle. I'm so sorry." John wrapped his arms around her and sobbed into her shoulder. Alle pushed him away and collapsed into a nearby chair, staring blankly into space. She didn't believe this could happen to their family. To Lani. They had already had their bad thing happen. There couldn't be more than one bad thing.

She stood abruptly and crossed the room back to her neighbor. "I need to see him, John. I need to kiss him. I didn't get to kiss him goodbye this morning. It was just so crazy getting Lani ready for school. And he left so early to help you." Her hands started shaking, and the tears she held back began to pour over. She couldn't take any more. She screamed, "Take me to him now!"

John jumped up and went to get a nurse. Alle followed him rigidly.

The nurse took them back to the stark white room where Runar's body lay. The room was cold. The bright white lights cast shadows on the walls, giving Runar a heavenly glow. Alle wiped away her tears and paused at the door. She looked at John. "Can you give me a minute?" He nodded and backed away.

The morgue was cold and sterile. Alle clutched her purse and slowly walked up to the steel table. Her vision swam with tears again, and the sob she had held in finally escaped. She was trying to keep it together and wasn't successful. She looked at Runar's pale face and ran her hand through his thick black hair that he was so proud of. She would never see his pale blue eyes or his angelic smile. His skin was already cold, but she kissed his forehead anyway. "I'm so sorry, baby. I'm sorry I wasn't here to hold your hand as I promised. But I'll take care of Lani. And someday..." a tear dripped onto his pale lips. "I'll see you again."

She stood there for an eternity, weeping over the empty shell that had been Runar. Eventually, she gave his hair one final stroke, wiped the tears from her puffy eyes, and turned toward the door.

* * *

The following days were a blur of funeral arrangements and memorial services. Everyone loved Runar for his humor and selflessness. She had been lucky to be married to him. She heard over and over.

Runar's friend John attended every single event. Alle figured it was just guilt that made him stick around. During the reception after the funeral, she physically ran into him as she made her way through the crowds of people.

"Alle, I'm so sorry," he said, grabbing her by the arms. He pulled her into a hug and started sobbing. Alle stood there stiffly. Arms by her sides, unable to think of words to help him cope.

She patted him stiffly. "I know, John." It's not that she blamed him for Runar's death. She didn't. He was just a reminder of everything she had lost. Unable to bring herself to utter words of forgiveness, the silence lingered between them until John regained some composure.

Then, he spoke with urgency. "No. You don't understand. He made me tell you... but..." he said in a hushed whisper.

"But what, John? You did the best you could. Right?"

John let her go. "Yes, I did everything possible, but Runar didn't die from a..." He stopped short like something out of the corner of his eye spooked him.

"What are you saying? That Runar died in a different way? I saw the cut, John. It was definitely what killed him."

"I... I... can't say any more. Just be careful, Alle. Keep your kid close and be watchful."

Alle was stunned into silence as she watched John sulk out of her house without another word. She couldn't understand what he was saying, so she put it in the back of her mind.

* * *

31

She had given up on getting Lani to sleep in her own bed. She missed her daddy; truth be told, Alle didn't want to sleep alone.

She didn't have to return to work, but everyone told her she needed to. For some reason, she couldn't just lay in bed all day and miss her husband. They said it wasn't good for her or Lani.

Runar had done so much for her, even in death. He made it to where she and Lani could live comfortably for the rest of their lives. He even provided for her to have another baby if she wanted to, without ever having told her.

After days of nonstop tears, the numbness set in. There were no more tears left to cry. She went through the motions of caring for Lani, simply feeding her, clothing her, and ensuring she lived through the day.

Alle went to the bathroom one morning and finally caught a glimpse of herself in the mirror. Dark circles underlined her red-rimmed eyes. Oily, tangled hair hung limply around her face. She had aged ten years in a matter of days. *How has Lani even recognized me?* Alle shook her head and quickly looked away from the mirror.

Her mom had stopped by daily to check on her and help with the basic necessities of life. But most visitors had stopped coming by. At least she didn't have to worry about scaring away friends or family.

The bathtub caught her eye. The large white garden tub invited her in to relax. With Lani asleep in the master bedroom, there was time for self-care.

A few minutes later, the air in the bathroom filled with foggy moisture. Steam wafted above the water. Alle slipped in slowly and let her skin get accustomed to the scalding water. It was the first time she had felt anything since she left the hospital.

The razor and soap lay near the side of the tub. She picked up the razor, contemplating shaving her legs. *What would be the point?* she thought. Instead, twirled it in her fingers. She removed the blade. It was less complicated than she had imagined. Blue veins were visible beneath the milky white skin as she turned her wrist to expose the vulnerable site.

Movies had educated her that cutting vertically and not horizontally was the fastest way. The sharp razor slid smoothly into her skin. There should have been pain, but there wasn't. There was only relief. The sadness of loss and guilt that she couldn't say goodbye was ending.

Watching the deep crimson liquid leak from her arm into the bathwater was fascinating. The blood swirled around her until it was difficult to tell if there had been any water in the tub at all. Her eyelids fluttered shut. *It will be ok. I'll just lay here until Lani finds me in the morning.*

Alle sat straight up in the water. She let the clear liquid dribble down her hands, hugging her knees to herself. She examined her arms where she imagined cutting herself open. It would've been easy to end it all and end the pain.

She couldn't do that to Lani. Couldn't leave Lani without a father and mother. Alle didn't want her to grow up that way. It would traumatize her baby girl to find her mother dead in the bathtub.

Pulling the plug from the drain, she stood. The water swooshed with her sudden movement. Even though she could picture exactly how she could end it all, there was still someone she needed to live for. Wrapping a towel around her thin frame, she ran her brush through the tangles in her hair.

Alle decided to take the advice given by almost everyone. She needed to get back to normal if normal was a thing anymore.

* * *

A few days later, she walked through the hall at the school where she worked. The pity stares were worse than ever. Deciding to avoid coworkers as much as possible, she kept her head down and kept walking. She plastered a happy fake smile for her students that still didn't reach her eyes.

"Where have you been all this time?" a student asked. The tears that had been absent for days made a reappearance. Looking up and blotting her eyes, Alle could hear the pressure of her heartbeat in her ears. She struggled to breathe. One girl who clearly knew what happened elbowed the offending student in the ribs and told him to shut up.

Alle held up her hand to stop the conversation. "It's ok that you asked, but I can't talk about it right now without crying. So unless you want your teacher to be a blubbering mess, you may need to ask your parents. They were all notified about my absence."

Alle managed to get through the day minute by minute. Everyone had said this would help, but after a single day, she wanted to hide again.

* * *

Alle's mom had picked up Lani from daycare, so she drove straight home after school. The afternoon sun filtered through the window of her silver SUV. The SUV Runar insisted she needed it for their growing family. She barely noticed the drive. It was so routine, and her attention was turned inward.

"Why is life so hard?" She screamed at a stop light, gripping the steering wheel harder. Hers had been filled with death and sadness.

As she daydreamed, the numbness took over again. Her thoughts went blank. Staring out the window, she heard someone whisper again, "You chose this."

"What? What did I choose? Did I choose to lose my child? Did I choose to lose the love of my life? Why would anyone choose death?" she ranted. The answer came swiftly and quietly. She almost missed the whisper against her ear.

"You chose a human existence."

She dismissed it as her going out of her mind. A human existence? That was ludicrous. Why on earth would she choose a life of suffering? *No one would choose that unless they were escaping something worse.*

She was so wrapped up in her thoughts she didn't see the tawny deer run in front of her until it was too late. She jerked the car to the right out of instinct and barely missed it. Taking a few deep breaths to calm the adrenaline, she sped up again. The insane creature bounded back into the passenger side of her car and then jumped away toward the original field it had been running to.

She slammed her brakes and jolted to a stop. After she caught her breath again, she pulled over to the side of the road. She slid out to check on the animal and the damage to her car. The deer was long gone and didn't seem to be hurt. Her car hadn't suffered either. The dirt had been brushed away where the deer made contact with the fender.

Woods surrounded this section of her drive home, and she hadn't been paying attention. As she inspected the vehicle, the hair rose on her arms and the back of her neck. She felt the pressure of being watched. She looked around for the threat. She knew the deer didn't need a reason to jolt into oncoming traffic, but perhaps something had spooked it.

A cold shiver ran up her spine. *Someone just walked over your grave,* voices of her childhood friends ran through her mind. The feeling of being watched intensified. She fought the urge to run and jump in her car to escape whatever stalked her. Instead, she turned to see who was behind her. Nothing was there, just an empty forest and the rustling of leaves blown by the wind. She wrapped her arms around herself. Her golden cardigan didn't provide much warmth. She slowly walked toward the driver's side of the car. She didn't want to provoke any predators into bounding after her.

Once back in the driver's seat, she took a few more deep breaths. With both hands on the steering wheel, she focused on slowing her heart rate. She put the car in drive and made a decision.

She needed out of this town. It didn't help that everything about it reminded her of Runar. She needed to have a chance to move on. As much as she loved him, she wasn't going to be able to live with the pity stares. She was going crazy.

She passed a billboard with a realtor's giant grinning face on it. Alle dialed the number immediately.

"Harris Group Realty, how can I direct your call?" Alle rolled her eyes at the cheeriness of the secretary.

"I need to speak with a real estate agent. I don't care which one."

"Yes, Ma'am. I'll send you over to Beth Ann. She's in the office right now."

"Great," Alle droned.

Beth Ann picked up after two rings. "Thanks for calling. How can I help you?"

"I need a new start. We're…" She paused at her mistake and made the correction, "I'm selling my house."

* * *

"She's moving?" the demon prince bellowed.

"Yes, master. It wasn't a move I expected." Bosche kept his eyes on the floor. He expected punishment for letting the woman move away from the bridge.

The demon prince leaned back in his chair. He rubbed his oily chin. "Where is it that she is moving?"

Bosche still didn't lift his head. "A small town an hour south in the natural world."

"Not a difficult distance." The demon prince clicked his claws on his obsidian throne.

"No master, not at all. The barrier may even have a weakness there," Bosch said quietly. There was no hope in the underside, and he didn't bother thinking he could avoid his punishment.

"She will be away from all those that love and care about her. She won't have a support system," he pulled his lips back over his teeth and flicked his forked tongue as if he could taste his victory. "On the contrary, I think this will be advantageous for us," he said, rubbing his hands together. "Follow her to the new town. Try to take a few demons through the barrier and infiltrate the town. I don't want any angels disrupting my plans."

"Yes, master." Bosch backed away from the throne with his eyes still on the floor.

"Oh, and Bosch? Ask the guards for thirty lashes from the flaming whip on your way out." The demon prince dismissed him with a flick of his black bony fingers.

Bosch bowed lower. "Yes, master," he mumbled and turned to leave.

He didn't scream as he accepted his punishment for failure.

Chapter Six

Alle had waited a few weeks until spring to look for a new house. May was real estate season, and it would be the best time to sell her home. She didn't necessarily want to give up the home she and Runar had bought together, but it would always be *their* home. She couldn't live the rest of her life in a house meant for both of them.

She sat in her classroom on her lunch break. Her phone rang. "Hello?"

"Hello, Mrs. Venega. I just wanted to let you know we have taken care of your house, and it is ready to go on the market. I've also found some listings in a nearby town that fit your list of wants and needs. When would be a good time to go house hunting?" Beth Ann always sounded happy and excited. Like every day was the best day ever.

"I either have to wait until June, or I can do this after school or on Saturdays. I think I put that on the forms you had me fill out," Alle said curtly. The school year seemed to drag on, and she was ready to be done. She hated when people wasted her time with forms they wouldn't even look at.

"Oh, yes, sometimes the forms don't come over formatted correctly, so I didn't get all the information," Beth Ann said sweetly. Alle hated wasting her time on things that didn't work even more.

"Well, any day is good for me. I just have to have some advanced notice to find a sitter for my daughter."

"Well, let's schedule for this Saturday. I will send over the listings, and we can make a plan for the ones you want to see."

"That sounds great. I'll see you then. You can just email the time along with the listings."

Just as the bell rang, she ended the call and went back to work. Keeping the kids busy with work while she packed her room.

* * *

Her house was sold four weeks later, and she was closing on a new one in a small town. It was her dream house. It was way too big for what she and Lani needed, but she felt the first spark of joy in a long time when she walked in. She knew it was the one right away.

Finalizing the paperwork for the new house was a long process. Alle sat across a giant mahogany table for the title lawyer. The realtor sat to their left and waited for the lawyer to give Alle instructions. She had gone through the process once before with Runar, but he had taken care of everything. She just had to be there to initial. This time, it was all up to her. She bounced her leg with nervous energy.

The lawyer had five pens ready for signing. She laid them neatly next to the large stack of paperwork and looked at Alle. "Are you ready for your hand cramps?" she laughed.

"Can't wait," Alle said with flat politeness.

"Ok, here we go." The lawyer turned the papers over individually and explained what each page said. "You will sign at the bottom, but leave the dates to me."

"Fantastic!"

Alle repeatedly signed her name and initials as the realtor and lawyer looked on. Once the final page was signed, they all stood and shook hands. "Congratulations on your new house," Beth Ann said with an easy smile and passed her the keys.

* * *

Alle drove down the wide streets toward her new house. Lani was strapped in her car set in the back. She had fallen asleep thirty minutes into the drive.

They drove past the city limit sign. Population 5,392. It was quintessential middle America. There was a town square with an old county courthouse where they held street fairs and fall festivals. The town was cute and cozy. Ancient oak trees lined the streets, and everyone knew everyone else.

The best part was no one knew her. She made a point of not telling Beth Ann why she had moved. It would probably come out at some point, but she was trying to avoid the weird looks for as long as possible. She didn't want to start in a new town with literally everyone giving her the pity stare.

A canopy of ancient oak trees hid power lines. Kids rode their bikes down the sidewalk and stayed out until dinner. The canopy rose over the streets to form a cozy tunnel feel.

The house was just a few blocks from the town square. It had been recently renovated. The exterior was dark blue with white trim. There were technically three stories with the attic. It was an old Victorian style. The previous owners had wanted to turn it into a bed and breakfast. But after all the renovations, it wasn't making the expected revenue. They bailed, and she got a good deal on her childhood dream home. Runar had always said he wanted to do it for her, so she let him do it even though he wasn't here to see her joy. She planned to rent out a room now and then to fill the space.

All about making life easier, she hired movers. They had already brought everything into the house when she arrived in her front drive. She was just left unboxing and putting everything in its place.

Her new neighbors waved and introduced themselves as they walked down the street. She met a lovely older couple that had just retired and moved here for a slower lifestyle. The perfect place for a new start.

"Hello," the older gentleman said as he walked his little black dog and held hands with his wife.

"Hi, there," Alle responded. She was rearranging her patio furniture.

"Did y'all just move in?"

"Just today, actually," she explained.

"Oh, it's so great to have new neighbors," the older lady said. "We like to see young new faces in the town."

39

"Yes, I think we will like it here as well."

"Please come by when you get settled in. We can have pie and coffee."

Lani chose that moment to come running through the screen door and giggling as she tried to escape down the stairs to pet the puppy.

"We'll do that. Thank you for the invitation." Alle grabbed Lani before she could make it to the front steps. She swung her around to keep her from crying. She giggled instead. By the time she looked around, the couple had started moving on. They waved as they continued their walk.

Alle pressed her lips to Lani's cheek. "I think we're going to like this town, baby girl," she whispered.

Chapter Seven

A bodybuilder with angel wing tattoos covering his back over his shoulder blades stood in front of Alle. Her hand hid a smirk at the choice of tats. It was a bit ironic that a tough guy had angel wings. Alle shrugged. *To each his own,* she thought.

It wasn't typical for a guy of his stature to be seen in a fast-food restaurant, but here he was. One bad thing about a small town was the lack of options. Since this was one of the only ones, they were always busy, especially at lunch.

Tanned skin and long dark hair. Every inch of him was perfectly chiseled, and there wasn't an ounce of body fat. Her eyes kept finding their way to those amazing tattoos.

The wings on his back were deeply etched into his skin in a way that made them seem as if they were alive, like real wings waiting to be released from beneath his beautiful skin. She opened her mouth to ask him who his artist was because they had some major skills. Then quickly snapped it closed. *He will definitely think I'm a weirdo.* But something about them made her want to touch them. In a trance, her hand lifted to feel this strange man's back. He moved forward and slightly turned to see her drooling.

Oh my gosh, was I literally drooling? she thought. He smiled a quirky half-smile with amazing dimples. She melted and immediately jerked out of her hypnosis. Her face turned beet red as she tried to recover with a little wave and smile of her own.

What the heck is wrong with me? Continuing her inner dialog.

Looking at her feet and around the room, she made sure her eyes focused anywhere but on him as he placed his order. And finally, thankfully, moved to get his large Powerade from the drink dispenser. *What a freaking stalker,* she scolded herself.

"Next, please," the cashier finally said. Alle huffed a sigh. She could concentrate on her order instead of the physique of the stranger.

She smiled, walking to the counter. The perky teenager with spiky bright red hair and a delicate nose ring didn't return the smile. *Ah, to be young again,* Alle mused. Still, the look was a bit out of place in the small town.

She placed her order and headed for the drink dispenser. Every person in the room was staring at her. Uncomfortably. Alle shook her head and dismissed it. They had undoubtedly seen her embarrassing display and lack of self-control. Tucking a strand of her long chestnut brown hair behind her ear, she visited the drink station and pressed her cup against her liquid selection.

She didn't see *Hercules* anywhere around. *"Hmm? Weird."* She thought. Not that she would have said anything to him. She tried to keep her thoughts firmly inside her head so that she would not cause any further embarrassment to herself.

She found a table in a secluded corner. As secluded as you could get in the brightly lit, one-room restaurant. The other patrons occasionally glanced up at her as they ate their meals. Like they were undercover FBI agents, and she was their target.

There was no reason they would take an interest in her. She was as mundane as they came. Her routine was just that - routine. She went to her office, her daughter's school, and straight home. Ordered her groceries online. Hardly left the house otherwise. It was difficult to do after Runar died.

She took the last bite of her ordinary lunch on her ordinary day when the world turned upside down. The side door in the lobby dinged open, and Alle looked up from her meal. The man she was calling *Hercules* stepped through. *Maybe he forgot his number four entree?* His blue eyes pierced her soul. *Is he walking towards me?* She glanced behind her to make sure he was looking at her.

Hercules held out his hand. "It's time, Alle. Come with me." Something about him was oddly familiar. Timidly putting her hand in his, *I have lost my mind,* she thought, but she made the decision to trust him for now. In her shock, she barely registered that he knew her name.

Once he had her hand, he swung her around behind him. A protective maneuver. As he did so, the people all eating in the lobby rose from their seats simultaneously, like they were one being. She peeped around *Hercules'* broad shoulders to see what might be happening. Maybe she could calm everyone down. She was good at de-escalating fights. It was second nature as a former teacher. But as she looked at their faces, she knew there was nothing she could do to calm these people down. Relief flooded through her body that she wouldn't have to fight them.

As if reading her mind, he said, "You are going to have to fight." He shoved a dagger into her hand. It lay loosely in her open palm. *What do I do with a dagger?* she screamed inside her mind.

Questions zoomed around in her brain. Who was this guy? Why did everyone suddenly want to fight them? Was this some kind of secret CIA op, like the ones her dad told her about? He had said the CIA drugged groups of people with hallucinogens to see what they would do.

Reaching behind him, he closed her fingers around the hilt and squeezed her hand in encouragement. "You can do this." He swiveled his head a bit and spoke out of the corner of his mouth. "You have done this before. Just stay behind me and follow your instincts."

"Follow my instincts? Right, got it," she sighed and hunched to hide, hoping she didn't need those instincts.

"It's time to go." He flicked his right hand, and a flaming sword appeared. She could have sworn his back tattoo glowed a little brighter, too, but no wings appeared. Her psychiatrist was never going to believe any of this. She'd be committed for sure.

He raised his sword, and his chiseled triceps bulged from his arm. *Oh Lord*, she thought, *I'm about to die fighting a horde of angry townspeople in the middle of a fast food burger joint,* but *I'm noticing his muscle tone.* She shook her head and focused on the situation at hand.

43

The people advanced slowly, one step at a time, wary of the flaming sword before them. Each one crouching, they closed in on every side, never taking their eyes off her. Everything was fine until one started climbing the wall to attack from above. That's when she freaked out. These were no ordinary townspeople.

She kept a hand on *Hercules'* back as the horde moved closer. The tension was too much. Butterflies sprung to life in her stomach, but she planted her right foot and raised her arms into a W fight stance, holding the dagger in her dominant hand and closing her other hand into a fist. Her kickboxing instructor would be proud. She leaned and side-kicked the nearest guy. He was kind of scrawny and flew across the room. How *did I just do that?* Alle blinked her eyes in disbelief.

The restaurant burst into action. *Hercules* swung his flaming sword, and person after person went down into a pile of black goo. It reminded her of a steaming pile in a cow pasture and smelled almost as bad. She wasn't shocked, only disgusted. *What is wrong with me?* She continued to punch and kick behind her gladiator rescuer as he slowly cleared the way to the door.

The man crawling on the ceiling jumped down in front of them. He opened his mouth like a snake, farther than any human should. *Hercules* lopped off his head without ceremony. It rolled to her feet as she jumped back with a screech.

Hercules reached back for her as his blade shrunk away. He opened the door and shoved her through. The air was fresh and sweet. The parking lot was blissfully empty of weird people wanting to kill them. "Come on. We have to get to Lani." He pulled her toward the packed lot.

"My car is right over here." She raced toward it and stopped. All four tires were flat. "Who?" she stumbled over her words. "Why?" She looked at him, worry clear in her dark green eyes.

"We can take mine." He yanked her again towards a black Mazda RX7. "It's faster anyway."

"Ok, I have so many questions. Let's start with why you have a car from the 90s?"

"It's a classic. And it goes fast." He opened the door for her and jogged around to drive.

"Yes, of course," she said, sliding into the passenger seat. A pang of sadness threatened her composure as she remembered Runar loving classic cars. "Next question. How do you know about Lani? How did you know my name? Are you a stalker?" she held her index finger up, "I probably should've asked that question before I got in a stranger's car…

"I mean, not that I'm not grateful for your… help back there, and usually stalkers are trying to hurt their marks and not save them," she rambled on, trying to make sense of what just happened, "but this is just weird." Her hands whipped to her face as tears welled up. "Ugh. Sorry. It's been a hard few months." She looked up and batted her eyelashes to keep the tears from spilling over.

"Gabriel," he said. Alle stared at him. "My Name… It's Gabriel. Not Hercules."

Alle's eyes rounded in horror, "Can you read minds?"

Gabriel laughed. "No, you are easy to read, and you sometimes say your thoughts out loud."

"Well, that's embarrassing," Alle murmured, poking her hair behind her ear. She looked out the window at the buildings blurring by.

"Also, your tears don't scare me," his low voice startled Alle. She wasn't sure if he was trying to be reassuring or if he really didn't mind that she cried.

"Good because there's a lot of them. I can't seem to do anything without crying these days."

"So you're more worried about tears than fighting a horde of demons."

"Oh no. I'm freaking out about the demons, if that's what we're calling them. I'm just internalizing that to freak out about later. Hopefully, not in an emergency. Probably in the shower."

They rounded the corner on the street of Lani's daycare. Red and blue lights flashed and prompted Gabriel to slow down. *"Please don't let that be Lani,"* Alle thought. *"I will not live through this again."* She couldn't face more bad news. She wouldn't even be able to handle it if Lani had to witness what she had just seen.

Gabriel pulled the car over behind one of the police cars. The horror etched on her face was evident. Risking a hand on her shoulder, "Hey, breathe! It's going to be ok," he whispered.

Alle didn't say anything but stiffly turned and pulled the door handle with trembling fingers. She pushed the door open, stood, and took a deep breath, straightening her invisible mask of determination used to cover her fear.

Gabriel hurried around the back of the car to walk beside Alle.

The daycare was in a residential neighborhood. They passed four two-story-old Victorian homes before they reached the house turned preschool. The playground in the backyard would be a dead giveaway if there weren't a sign in the front yard. Typically, children's screams of joy could be heard. The school was quiet except for the police and the adults talking. Whatever had happened was over now. Thankfully.

An officer stopped them at the front steps of the school. "I'm sorry, ma'am. I can't let you go in there."

"My daughter. Her name is Lani. She's here. I just need to pick her up," she explained.

Then she saw it. The pity look. She nearly lost it. But stopped herself by taking a deep breath. He might have given her that look for any reason. *Lani is going to run into my arms at any moment. I don't need to freak out.* She continued the mantra to prevent the oncoming panic attack.

"We've been contacting all the parents. You were next on the list. They've taken all the children down the street to the elementary school. She'll be in the cafeteria."

Alle released a deep breath. She turned to go, wanting to get to the elementary school as soon as possible, but Gabriel caught her arm to keep her by his side. "What happened here, officer?" he asked.

"We're still piecing that together, and it's still under investigation, so I can't say much."

"Was anyone hurt?"

"Just the bad guy, as far as we can tell. Fortunately, one of the teachers was trained in martial arts and was able to dispatch him before anyone got seriously injured or killed."

"Thank you for the information." Gabriel looked away from the officer toward the front porch, where Lani's teacher was giving her statement to another officer. Her long blond hair flowed beautifully behind her in the light breeze, and she crossed her arms around her stomach. Her lithe body barely looked capable of taking down an intruder, but Alle noticed muscle tone in her arms that she hadn't caught. The woman noticed them looking, and Alle thought she saw the teacher give Gabriel a barely noticeable nod.

As they walked away, her curiosity got the better of her. "Do you know her?" she asked, wondering where the cold jealousy that filled her chest came from. Her hand swiped absently across her sternum.

"Who?"

"The teacher. It seemed like you knew her."

"She's..." Gabriel paused to find the right word, "an old acquaintance."

"Oh." Alle didn't think Gabriel was being entirely forthcoming about how they knew each other, but it wasn't really her business. She had more important things to worry about, so she put her questions about his relationship status to the side for now.

They made their way to the elementary school cafeteria. It was only a couple of blocks away. Alle produced her ID to the school secretary, and they brought Lani to her.

"The kids were never in any danger," she explained to Alle.

"A man died on the doorstep of her daycare. I feel like there might have been a little bit of danger."

"Oh yes, when you put it that way, I can see your point. But everything is ok now. Mama and baby are back together." She beamed at Lani. Everyone did. She was light and happiness, and giggles.

Lani wrapped her arms around Alle's neck. "Mama! I miss you!"

"I missed you too, baby girl!" she said, burying her face into Lani's neck.

"There was a bad man, but Ms. Jane didn't let him get us."

"I know, baby. Did you see it happen?"

She shook her little head, bouncing her golden curls. "No, we hide."

"That's a good girl, baby! I'm so glad you are safe and sound!" she booped

Lani's nose.

"Daddy always keeps me safe, too. He my angel now."

"Yes, he is," Alle barely managed to keep her tears in check. She smoothed Lani's hair and pushed her head onto her shoulder. She turned to Gabriel, "We'll have to walk from here. We don't have a car seat in your car. It's not far."

Gabriel nodded and fell in behind the mother-daughter pair.

Lani raised her head and asked, "Who is that mama?"

She gave a quick glance over her shoulder. "Just a friend."

"He look like my angel daddy," she babbled in her cute toddler talk.

Alle looked back and cocked her head, "He doesn't look anything like Daddy."

"He has a different face now."

Alle squeezed her tight. She needed to look into child play therapy soon. Lani was adjusting well, but she had often talked about her angel daddy. They would probably have to drive back to the big city to get a good one. There wasn't any doubt the tiny town had few child counseling centers.

Turning the corner to her street, she paused. Gabriel had been really nice and saved them from a lot of things today, but was she willing to show him where she lived? There were still some unanswered questions, and she wasn't sure he was entirely safe. At the same time, she didn't mind having a bodybuilder bodyguard with tats and corded muscle and… She shook her head, "*Stop. Just stop, Alle.*"

She decided to let him walk her home. He already knew the street. It wouldn't be all that hard to figure out where she lived anyway. She wouldn't let him in the door, though. That's where she drew the line.

They walked up the front steps. The navy blue paint had been refreshed and stood in contrast to the white shutters. The sellers had done a few updates before it hit the market. The wrap-around porch and swings had sold her on it. The moment she saw it, she knew this was the one. She hadn't even needed to see the inside, although it was as beautiful as the outside. It was the exact replica of the picture she had seen in a magazine when she was little.

She sat Lani down on the swing and lowered herself beside her. "Thank you for everything you've done today and for walking us home."

"This isn't the end of this struggle," Gabriel said abruptly.

"Don't I know it? It seems to never end."

"They will come again. You and Lani are not safe here."

"We're not safe anywhere. Calamity can find us everywhere. If I've learned anything from the past year, I've learned that."

"This will be worse. And I will not let you risk your life and Lani's life for a house!"

Fury built in her core and burned up through the veins in her neck. "I'm sorry. Who did you say you were?" His tone had rubbed Alle the wrong way.

"Gabriel."

"Yes. I remember you just told me your name about half an hour ago. So you don't get to tell me what you will allow and what you will not allow." Alle stood and stepped toward Gabriel. He hadn't made it past the column by the steps, but he didn't back down. "Now, it's been a very trying day, so please excuse us." Digging her keys out of her pocket, she turned to the door and picked Lani up from the swing. With the toddler on one hip, she opened the screen door and held it with her other. The key was shoved quickly into the lock. As she turned it, Gabriel stepped forward and grabbed her elbow.

"You won't remember any of this tomorrow. You are making a mistake. I need you to come with me now," he growled.

Alle looked down at his hand on her arm. "You are the dumbest person on the planet if you think that tactic is going to work." Alle yanked her arm away, opened the door, and let the screen door slam in Gabriel's face as she and Lani made it through, then she kicked the front door closed with her foot.

"Dumb jock," she said and slapped her forehead when Lani repeated her.

She peeked out the window and watched Gabriel walk away. "Geez, that guy is intense," she said, turning the bolt on the door.

She turned to Lani. "So, little girl, we have a couple of hours until dinner and bath time. What do you want to do?"

"Babies?"

Alle nodded, "Babies, it is!" She followed Lani up the stairs to pretend she was the kid and Lani was the mama.

Chapter Eight

Alle jerked awake and looked at her cell phone. It was three hours before she had to roll out of bed. The witching hour, as her grandmother had called it.

Going back to sleep was an option, but that was usually pointless once she was awake. She hated these mornings, probably spending the rest of the day groggy and in a bad mood. Unfortunately, her brain was on and making checklists, so trying to turn it back off was no use.

This was also a lonely time. Even with Lani sleeping next to her, she still missed Runar. After running her fingers through Lani's baby curls, she slipped out of bed slowly and quietly. Might as well get the benefit of being awake and getting the house cleaned.

She clicked the flashlight on her phone, not because of fear of the dark but because her toes usually thanked her for being extra cautious. There was certainly a fear of breaking that little one on door jams.

After a few weeks, she had finally gotten the new house's layout figured out. They slept on the second floor. The master bedroom had a fantastic en suite with a cute claw-foot ceramic tub. She knew that gem had been hard to find. It reminded her of the old bathroom in her grandma's house.

The other two rooms shared a bathroom. One was kept as a guest bedroom, and one as a playroom. There was a bed for Lani in the playroom, but it would be a while before she used it.

The house had been renovated but still had the original hardwood floors from the nineteenth century. Central heat and air had been added, and the units were in the attic. That didn't leave a lot of room for storage up there.

Most of her boxes were still in the one-car garage that wasn't attached to the house. She'd had to give up some items on her list of wants to get good schools and the wrap-around veranda.

The upstairs rooms were attached by a balcony that overlooked the foyer. The staircase hugged the wall with a slight turn and landing. A large chandelier hung from the ceiling overhead. It had to have been installed when the house was updated for electricity over a century ago. A circular window allowed light to come in during the day and displayed the beautiful light fixture at night. It was quaint, and Alle liked it.

As she descended the stairs, movement to her left caught her eye. She pointed her phone in that direction but didn't see anything. The house was quiet.

Lani needed a little noise to sleep soundly. She had a sound machine, but there was no way Alle could sleep with a lullaby all night. They compromised with a fan. The sound machine stayed by the bed in the playroom for naps. With the master bedroom door shut, the resulting quiet was eerie.

Alle refused to get scared and run and jump back in bed as she had at Lani's age. Contemplating just that, she heard a little squeak. She walked back across the balcony towards the guest bathroom and stopped.

Ever since she was a little girl, she often saw shadows move out of the corner of her eye. She was used to it, but there was a sense of dread in her belly. At any moment, she might be grabbed by the boogeyman.

She hated this. This is why women kept men around. To investigate the things that went bump in the night. Well, that was all done now.

Alle took a deep breath to steel her nerves and softly walked to the guest bath door. She quietly turned the handle. As she opened the door to the bathroom, a shadow moved again to her left, toward the open door to Lani's playroom. Slowly creeping further to investigate, she didn't want to spook whatever it was.

Just as she stepped into the playroom, she heard another squeak. "It's just a mouse. It's just a mouse," she repeated the whispered mantra, unsure whether to hope it was true. Needing to know, she arrived at the door jam to the playroom and slid her arm around the wall to flip the light switch.

As the light came on, a sound blared from across the room. Alle jumped back into the bathroom and, in the process, dropped her phone. Her foot landed on something small and furry. "Holy crap!" she whisper-yelled and jumped back into the bedroom.

After a few seconds, the shock wore off, and Alle realized the sound machine had come on by itself. She ran over to turn it off and returned to the bathroom to investigate the small furry, now squished, mass.

A tiny dark grey mouse lay dead on the bathroom floor. She did not want to deal with this at three o'clock in the morning, but now she knew. A call to the exterminator would be made as soon as they were open. "Great, now we have mice and ghosts! So not fair," she said out loud to herself. Once again, the sound machine blared its lullaby.

Jumping out of her skin for the second time, her body swiveled toward the playroom.

"How could the sound machine come on by itself?" she wondered aloud. She knew a mouse could not have accidentally turned it on. She had a fleeting sadness that maybe Runar was trying to contact them but quickly dismissed that ridiculous idea. His death challenged her skepticism. She wanted to hope ghosts were real and could visit their loved ones, but she hadn't been lucky enough that Runar might.

She picked up the sound machine to investigate. As she turned it over, she realized the switch on the back had gotten set to noise activate. She sighed heavily. She didn't know how the switch got moved, but she was glad she didn't have to deal with ghosts, even if she wished it was Runar.

She cleaned up the dead mouse and turned out the lights. She was surprised but grateful her little one slept through the racket she had made.

Downstairs, she pulled out the coffee pot and yawned. It was definitely going to be one of those days. *I should take Lani to daycare and call in sick*, she thought. Then she slapped her forehead. Daycare was probably still closed from yesterday. Alle tried to focus on what had happened. It was too fuzzy. She couldn't pinpoint the reason why she thought daycare would be closed. It was too early to call and figure that out.

She looked up extermination services on her phone. This was an old house, and she had a lot of work left to do, but she couldn't let vermin live with them.

After just a few clicks, she found a company close by with five stars. She hoped they were actually reputable. The online schedule was open. Looking at the clock on the wall, she clicked the 8:30 time slot. It was enough time to drop Lani off at daycare if they were open and make it back home. "I'll need to call into work, though," she whispered.

She enjoyed her coffee and tried to focus on what had happened yesterday. There was that strange guy with the angel wing tat. *Where did I meet him? He helped her with Lani. He must have a kid at the daycare.*

Alle couldn't picture his face. She knew she went to lunch and had to pick Lani up early, but couldn't remember how they got home or what happened. The memories were there. They were just slippery. Whenever she tried to focus on specific details, her mind would slip around them. It was like selective amnesia. She wondered if someone at the restaurant had put something into her food. Unable to remember, she put the thoughts aside and tried to enjoy her coffee.

Alle didn't clean at all. She sat on the couch and scrolled through social media while drinking her coffee. Creeping through all her friends' lives, she unfollowed all those having babies or getting married. She couldn't deal. It wasn't jealousy. It reminded her of all that had been lost and filled her with sadness.

Just as she was about to get up and wake Lani, a text came through. Daycare was indeed still closed due to the ongoing police investigation. Alle frowned. "Definitely calling into work, but I wonder if there is someone I know to babysit." She didn't trust anyone in this town yet. Her mom wouldn't drive an hour so Alle could nap. Even though she loved her house and the new town, she started questioning her decision to move away. She would have to take care of Lani on very little sleep. Nothing new.

* * *

Later that morning, there was a loud knock at the door. Alle startled awake from the couch and spilled her now lukewarm coffee down the front of her pajama pants. "Holy mama!" she yelled as she jumped up. She looked at her watch and wondered why Lani hadn't woken up yet.

The exterminator was punctual. On her way to let him in, she grabbed a towel from the kitchen.

Turning the antiqued brass knob, she pulled back the white door. There was no glass or peephole. She planned to change it soon, but it went with the house so well that it was hard to decide.

A gangly man stood on her porch. His hair was slightly stringy, and he was wearing a brown jumpsuit. He looked like he had just walked off the set of the *Ghostbuster* movie. The 80s one, not the remake. Alle leaned against the screen door to see if the white station wagon was in her drive. No luck, just a normal Ford Ranger. Over the left pocket, his embroidered name tag read Jed. He had a bit of patchy scruff on his chin. He was certainly trying to look older and more respectable.

"Hello, ma'am." He tipped his imaginary hat to her. "I'm responding to your call for immediate assistance."

Alle looked at the watch on her left wrist. "I thought my appointment wasn't until 8:30. You're a little early," she said, even though she didn't think five minutes was all that early.

"Yes, ma'am. Early is on time, on time is late, and late is unacceptable. You were the first on the list, so here I am." He tipped an imaginary hat, again.

"Oh, ok. Come on in." Alle opened the screen door to let him in. "Can I make you some coffee?"

"You know, you should check identification, ma'am. Anyone could impersonate an exterminator to gain entry into your home," he said matter-of-factly. He continued to stand on the porch. Alle continued to hold the door open. She realized he wasn't going to budge until she asked for identification.

"Oh, you were for real? I just thought, you know... small town. Most people are honest," she said. "But now that you mention it, may I see your identification?"

"Yes, ma'am." He pulled out his wallet and flipped out the ID like an FBI agent on TV. Alle had to hide a smirk as she looked closely at the ID.

"Well, Jed, it looks like you are who you say you are. Will you come inside now?"

Jed nodded and put his ID back in his pocket. He stepped through the open door and looked around the house.

Alle poked her thumb over her shoulder toward the stairs as she returned to the kitchen to refill her mug. "Zuul is upstairs, but I was hoping to wait until my daughter woke up on her own."

"I can only exterminate vermin. I specialize in rodents, but I also treat your house for termites, ants, and other insects. Those are the most common, though. Spiders as well. I can't exterminate daughters."

She laughed, but Jed didn't. "Why are you laughing," he asked.

"You were joking, right?"

"I wasn't being humorous. Zuul is a human being with feelings, probably. I should report this incident to the police. You want her exterminated. That's a capital offense, punishable by the death penalty."

Alle stared blankly. This conversation was going to need more coffee pronto. She moved around him into the kitchen. "Come on, Bill. I need a kick in the pants." Jed followed her reluctantly.

"I assume you don't want me to kick you in the pants."

"This is going to be a long morning," Alle muttered. Thankfully, Jed didn't hear her, or he ignored her. "Ok. First, my daughter's name is Lani. I don't want her exterminated." Jed nodded along. "I don't want to explain who Zuul is because it was a joke, and it's not funny if I have to explain it. Anyhow, the mice I contacted you about are upstairs. Would you like some coffee before you get to work?"

"No, Ma'am. I bring my own special brew. It's in my truck. I don't drink on the job." He patted his stomach. Alle scrunched up her nose in disgust but didn't respond.

The bedroom door upstairs opened, and the little pitter-patter of feet echoed through the house.

"Ok. Well, come on up then." She waved for him to follow.

Jed followed Alle upstairs. She grabbed Lani up as she pointed to the guest bath. "Zuul, the mouse, is just in there, Bill. Don't cross the streams and get us all killed, but go." She shooed him away with her hands. "Do your thing. I have to make a phone call and get Lani dressed." Alle kept going with the joke because it was funny to her. She was the only one in on it, but it didn't matter.

Jed hesitated, still not getting it. He leaned in a little. "My name's Jed, ma'am. Just so we're clear." He nodded and went about his business inspecting the guest bathroom.

Alle got Lani dressed and changed herself into jeans and an old t-shirt. She called into her work. The owners were understanding. News of the death at the daycare had spread all over town. However, they didn't seem to know much more about the incident than Alle.

Administrative duties weren't all that important to the factory. She had suspected they hired her out of sympathy for her situation. They saw a single mom. They didn't know she didn't need to work.

She and Lani were eating breakfast at the kitchen bar when Jed made it back downstairs. "You have a rodent problem," Jed announced. "I have set traps. Some holes need to be patched up. I'm not allowed to do that."

"Ok, Bill." She gave him a thumbs-up and a fake smile.

"My name is Jed. I have other appointments. I will be back tomorrow afternoon to check the traps."

Alle saluted him. "Aye, aye, captain. How much do I owe you?" she said between crunches of cereal.

"You don't pay until the job is done, ma'am." Jed waited at the door. "I will see you tomorrow." He turned stiffly like a robot and opened the door. Alle jumped up to let him out and lock the door behind him. City girl habits that apparently didn't include checking strangers for ID.

As Jed walked out the door, another stranger came up the steps. Both stopped and squared off. Sizing each other up like middle school boys. Alle stepped out the door to see what was happening on her front porch. Seeing scrawny Jed bow up to the mountain of a man on her front steps was a sight. "Wow, it's a busy morning already."

"Hi, Alle. I was coming to check on you." The muscled-up mountain man turned, giving Jed his back. She figured he wasn't worried about Jed jumping him from behind. Alle wouldn't have either if she were built like that.

"Can you tell me who you are?" she asked as Jed walked away from the stranger down the steps. He walked slowly and kept his eyes on the man the whole time. Jed was a little weird, so that didn't alarm her much.

"We met yesterday," he said with a sparkling smile, making his way up the steps. It was disarming. Alle almost asked him in for coffee, but with Jed hanging around, she didn't want his warning to go to waste. She motioned him over to the swing. "One second. Let me check on something, and I'll be right with you."

The stranger sat on the white porch swing. Alle noticed he adjusted the pillows so he wouldn't sit on them and flatten them. She hated it when people sat on throw pillows. *Score one for the hot gladiator.*

She came back out of the house with Lani. Lying a blanket out on the porch, she closed the newly installed baby gate across the front steps and let Lani play with some toys.

"Now, what can I help you with?"

"I'm sorry to disturb your day. I was hoping you might remember me from yesterday."

"You seem familiar. I don't remember much from yesterday. Every time I try to remember details, my memory seems fuzzy. I think I can remember the general event, just not the details. I'm not sure. How would I know if I didn't know something? I might see my therapist later, now that I think about it." Alle paused, realizing she had said the quiet part out loud. "I'm sorry that's too much information."

"It's common to have fuzzy memories after a traumatic event." The stranger remained seated even though Alle stood, watching over Lani. His biceps bulged from his button-down dress shirt. No tie. He was a man who wore a suit. He didn't let the suit wear him. She had the fleeting thought he would look good no matter what he was wearing or wasn't wearing. *Whoa, calm down there, Alle.*

"Then it's surprising I can remember anything about the last year. I do have flashes of memory here and there. Perhaps my brain is trying to compensate and compartmentalize." Alle slumped. "You seem to know my name, but I don't know yours."

The stranger stood. He towered over her by at least ten inches. He held out his hand. She realized at this moment there would be no getting away from him if he wanted to hurt her. But she felt completely at ease with him, like she had known him all her life. Perhaps she had met him before, and her brain wasn't allowing her to remember due to the trauma he had mentioned.

"Yes, sorry," he apologized with a smooth, baritone voice. "My name is Gabriel. There are some things we need to discuss about the incident yesterday."

"Ok. Let's sit, then. Can I get you something to drink? Coffee, tea?"

"No, thank you," Gabriel said politely. He sat back on the porch swing, and Alle sat across from him in one of the white wicker chairs.

"I was hoping this would be easier," he started.

"I guess the easiest way would be to start from the beginning."

"Yes, well, the beginning was a long time ago, and that probably wouldn't help."

"Oooo kay, well, maybe you can start with yesterday."

"Let me start with… this will all seem crazy," he spoke softly.

Jed popped his head back around the corner. She didn't realize he hadn't left yet. He had already said he had other appointments to get to. He appeared just to be hanging out, waiting to see if Gabriel was dangerous to her. He was dangerous. Danger practically rolled off him in waves. She felt deep within her spirit that the danger didn't apply to her. Jed seemed to be waiting to see if she needed some protection. She didn't know what he would be able to do. Gabriel could snap Jed like a twig, but it endeared her to him all the same.

Lani didn't recognize the danger either. She came up and handed Gabriel an imaginary cup of tea. "Drink?" she said. He didn't miss a beat; he just pretended to drink the tea and complimented her manners and how delicious it was. Alle sat back and smiled. She never interfered with Lani's play. If it bothered people, they could break her heart. She wasn't going to be the one to do it.

"Lani, you know what would go great with this tea? Could you make me a big piece of cake and maybe some pie?"

"Yes, pie!" she said, giggling and toddling back over to her blanket to make the pretend pie.

"Gracious, you aren't counting calories, are you?" Alle laughed.

Gabriel smiled and showed the cutest dimples. Alle could feel her own face redden as all the breath whooshed out of her lungs. She needed to calm herself down. She was not ready to move on, even if Gabriel checked a lot of boxes.

He turned serious again. "Alle, please understand I would never do this unless it were absolutely necessary. I don't think you and Lani are safe, so I must explain a few things."

Alle grabbed her forehead and squinted, "Oh yeah, Lani's daycare was closed today because of yesterday's incident. I vaguely remember there was a death at the school. I can't remember the people involved."

"Yes, that's part of it. But I don't think you are safe here." He pointed a giant finger down. "At this house."

Alle leaned back in her chair, a little offended that he thought she couldn't keep Lani and herself safe. "We lock our doors at night, and I keep a pistol close by. Locked and away from Lani. But where I can get to it." Runar would have wanted her to be protected. He had taken her to the range many times. She was a decent shot at a stationary target. She realized too late that she shouldn't be telling a complete stranger her safety measures. There was something about him that caused her to let her guard down.

"That's not going to work, Alle."

"Look, I'm not sure what you're getting at here. I don't need protection, and I'm doing a dang good job of protecting Lani. And while I appreciated my late husband, I didn't need him to protect me either. Although it was nice." Lani brought Gabriel his fake pie. He smiled and played along. Then she climbed into his lap as if she knew him.

He looked at ease with a child in his lap as he had been talking with her.

"Alle, I meant no offense, but it will be more than what you can handle on your own once the rest of the spirit world finds out about you. Plus, the fact you can't remember anything important. You will not be able to handle the war brewing at your door. There is so much I need to tell you, but until you accept what you are, you will keep forgetting. I don't like wasting my time or my breath."

Anger simmered beneath the surface, but she let that last thing slide so she could focus on the main point. "And what am I exactly."

Gabriel looked around to make sure Jed was not listening. Though bless him, he was still around. "You're an angel, the same as me. In fact, I'm your guardian," he said quietly as he held Lani as naturally as if she was his own.

"An angel? Is this a weird pickup line? I'm confused."

"Ok, so not officially an angel. It's complicated, and I would rather not discuss it in the open. But you can't fully comprehend the spirit world until you accept your mantle. Your human brain won't be able to remember anything. As soon as you sleep, the memories will become slippery. It will be like those moments when something is just on the tip of your tongue, but you can't quite remember it. Right now, this is dangerous for you."

Alle stood and took Lani off Gabriel's lap. She feared he had come too close to describing exactly how she had felt all morning. "I appreciate you coming over, Gabriel. I'm not sure what your angle is here. I'm not someone you can hustle, though. Please get off my porch," she said, regretting that she had shared so much information with him.

Gabriel stood and stepped closer. "If you don't come with me right now, you will die."

Alle did not do well with threats. "I'm not afraid of you. While he might not be much, Jed is about fifty feet away. I can scream right now, and he would come to help me."

Gabriel scoffed. "You don't need his help."

"Get off my porch," Alle seethed.

"I'll leave for now. Just remember I'm always watching," he said as he turned, opened the baby gate, and walked down the steps. "If you need me, I'm just a call away."

"I won't need you, creep!" she yelled.

She looked back at where he had been sitting. A white card lay on the porch swing. "Oh, he thinks he's so smooth." She rolled her eyes.

Alle carried Lani down the steps to make sure Gabriel had left. When she got to the street, she didn't see a car or Gabriel. "That was fast. Did you see where that guy went?" Jed was walking up to her.

"No, I was worried about checking on you. Are you ok?"

"I'm fine, Jed. Thank you for sticking around. We'll be fine." She looked at her watch. "You'll be late for your next appointment; you better go."

Jed reluctantly left a few minutes later, and Alle took Lani back into the house to play.

Chapter Nine

After the events of the morning, Alle was too tired to cook. Going out was not in the equation either. Lani's favorite food, cheese pizza, was now on the menu.

There was a loud banging at the door. She pulled back the curtain and looked out the window. A young man wearing black pants, a red shirt, and a red cap waited for the door to open. He looked at his watch and shifted from foot to foot. *Does he have ants in his pants,* she wondered. As he raised his hand to knock again, she moved quickly. The pressure of someone waiting on her always got her moving.

She grabbed her wallet to get cash for a tip and opened the door. Stepping outside to dig out the money, she heard Lani's baby run footsteps into the foyer. She let the screen door slam so Lani wouldn't book it for the street.

Alle looked up to see the pizza fall from the guy's hands. His eyes turned black. Not just his irises, his whole eye was black. Alle stepped back in disgust. His fingers elongated and reached for her. Her skin began to sizzle as he wrapped his bony claws around her arm.

She screamed in agony. The pizza guy pulled his lips back into a gruesome smile. Black teeth hung loosely from his mouth. Saliva dripped from the corners of his lips. Even though his grip had to be causing him immense pain, he seemed to enjoy it.

She shoved him away and grabbed her arm. Scorch marks in the shape of a handprint marked her. She opened the door to get inside. As she swung open the screen door, Lani was waiting to make her escape. She reached up and squealed. "Mama, bad man!"

Before Alle could get Lani back inside, the man had recovered. Instead of attacking, he unhinged his jaw like a boa constrictor and released black smoke. The pizza guy slumped to the ground unconscious. The smoke didn't reach for her. It went straight to Lani and swirled around her. Alle tried to reach in to pull Lani out, but a jolt of electricity ran through her arm every time she touched it. It made her all the more desperate to get Lani out of there. She was about to endure the electric shock for as long as it took when the black cloud dissipated into Lani's body.

For a few brief seconds, Lani looked fine. She was standing there smiling. Then suddenly, her eyes darted back and forth rapidly like she was reading a book really fast.

Alle fell to her knees. "Lani!" Her daughter's name screeched from her throat. She tried gently shaking her out of the stupor, but it didn't work. She was afraid to shake her harder, not wanting to damage her brain. She wrapped her arms around her torso and held her as tightly as possible. She was praying she would come out of it and everything would be ok.

Lani went limp in her arms. "God, no. Don't take her from me, too!"

She checked for a pulse. Lani's breathing was fine, and her pulse was strong. She looked like she was sleeping, but she was floppy. Even sleeping Lani was never floppy.

Alle looked around. The pizza guy lay on her lawn as if he had fallen backward down the steps. He was out cold. She didn't care. She wasn't about to check on a guy who attacked her and her baby.

Cradling Lani in her arms, she ran to her car. She didn't remember driving it home but couldn't focus on that now.

She weighed the options on how to get Lani to the hospital. Did she risk not putting Lani in the car seat or not being close enough to help her and keep an eye on her? Just as she was about to put Lani in the back seat, Gabriel appeared out of thin air. Familiarity tugged at her, but she couldn't remember seeing him appear out of nowhere before. The recollection was there on the edge of her memory. Maybe it was deja vu, and she had dreamed it. She was sure she had seen Gabriel before his visit today. When she tried to focus on where she knew him, the memory slipped away from her again.

Alle shook her head and dismissed the problem. Another thing she couldn't focus on right now. Another thing to freak out about in the shower later.

"What happened?" he asked.

"No time." She sat Lani in the car seat and pulled the keys out of her pocket. "You drive. I'll explain on the way."

"Where are we going?"

"Hospital!" she said as she clicked the harness and climbed over the car seat. "Aren't you an angel? Shouldn't you know this already? And, for that matter, shouldn't you have been there to prevent this?"

Gabriel slammed his finger into the ignition button and put the car in reverse. He ignored her blame game. "I tried to protect you. Although you don't remember, I asked you to come with me yesterday. You used her free will to reject that protection. You did the same this morning. Place your blame where it belongs."

"You think I'm to blame here?"

"No, I think demons are to blame here," he said as he turned back toward the front. He threw the car into drive and sped down the residential street. "Explain what happened." He glanced at her in the rearview mirror.

She told the story the best she could remember. The details were already a little hazy and unbelievable. When she finished recounting the ordeal, they continued in silence. Alle kept a watchful eye on Lani.

She saw the emergency room sign and breathed a sigh of relief. But panic surged through her chest when they kept going. Had Gabriel not seen the sign? He didn't seem to be slowing down.

"Where are you going?! That was the hospital," she yelled, pointing to the red E as they passed it.

"We're not going to the hospital. There is nothing they can do for her there." There was no urgency in his voice. His calm demeanor was not helping Alle remain calm. She needed him to freak out a little.

"She needs medical help," she screeched.

"What you described was demon energy. She needs spiritual help. We have a safe place to take her. There will be a healer there."

Alle didn't know what to do. Frustrated tears immediately ran down her face. Her job was to protect her daughter, and she couldn't do that. She didn't have the expertise to do it.

"No, I want to go to the hospital," she decided.

Panic rose in Gabriel's voice then. "Alle, you have to trust me. Please. I have never done anything to harm you. I've only ever helped you. Please trust me now. If we take her to the hospital, they will only run a bunch of tests and tell you what I just told you. They won't be able to help, and we will be wasting valuable time. You know there is nothing medically wrong with her. You saw what happened."

Alle ran through the scenarios in her head and finally sighed. "Ok, fine, but if she dies, you might as well put me out of my misery. She's the only reason I'm still alive."

"It won't come to that. I promise." Gabriel said solemnly and turned down a residential street. Alle assumed they would go to a church, but they stopped in front of a large two-story home. It was much more modern and fully updated than her recent purchase.

"It doesn't look like anyone is home."

"You likely won't be able to see anyone unless they are directly interacting with you. Although having full spiritual sight would make this so much easier."

Alle gave him the look he deserved as a crazy person.

He turned to look her in the eyes. "Can you trust me to get Lani healed? I'm sure you will be able to see more in time," he said seriously. Alle nodded almost imperceptibly, but it was enough to get things moving.

Gabriel got out of the car as Alle pulled Lani from her seat. Her head was still floppy, and she did her best to cradle the tallest two-year-old she knew. She carried her up the front steps and through the door Gabriel had just opened. There was a sitting room to the right. A hallway led to a staircase to the left.

Gabriel turned right. The tap of his dress shoes hitting the wooden floors broke the unnerving silence in the house.

The sitting room was modestly decorated but looked staged. The house was obviously for sale. The room was painted in a light beige. There was an oversized, comfy couch, a bit lighter in color than the walls, and a fake plant in the corner. Other than a Queen Anne-style dining chair in the other corner, there were no other furnishings. She hoped this wasn't a mistake. *Maybe Gabriel has a real estate friend who let him live in vacant houses,* she rationalized.

"You can lay her on the couch. There is a chair for you there." He pointed to the Queen Anne chair. "I'll get the others."

"The house still looks vacant, by the way," she raised her voice so Gabriel could hear her as he left the room. After laying Lani on the couch, she pulled up the chair and held Lani's hand.

She watched Lani's little chest rise and fall. Her eyes twitched back and forth under her eyelids like she was dreaming. Alle hoped against hope they were good dreams and not nightmares.

After minutes that seemed like hours, a tall woman entered the sitting room. Her long blond hair almost hit the floor in waves, and she glowed. Alle couldn't see her feet, but it was as if she floated into the room. With her ethereal qualities, she seemed like a ghost. She didn't smile or frown, but her face didn't show boredom either. Alle noticed her eyes were pure gold. Not like brown with golden flecks. There were no whites at all. Her entire eye was gold. Alle leaned back and gasped.

"Please don't let my appearance frighten you. I'm simply a healer. I will do no harm." Her right hand raised in an oath while her left hand rested on her chest.

Gabriel followed her in. The tendon at his temple pumped vigorously. He showed no other outward signs of worry.

"This is Asa. She will take care of Lani." He gestured to the lithe woman.

"Please step aside. This won't hurt her," Asa said without inflection.

"I'm not leaving." Alle turned her attention back to Lani. She kept searching for any change.

"I need a fair amount of room to complete my evaluation, but you may stand over there near her feet," Asa said and motioned slowly to her right. Every move this woman made was slow and deliberate.

"Alle, please let her work. She won't hurt her." Gabriel pleaded, putting his hand on her shoulder.

Alle nodded, let go, and complied. She had an innate longing to trust Asa, similar to the feeling she got with Gabriel. There was peace and knowledge that everything would be ok now that Asa had arrived. She stood next to Lani like a statue. Golden eyes began glowing as she meditated over the toddler.

Gabriel moved next to Alle and gently put his strong hand on her back to support her. She calmed further and wondered what magic he possessed that he could comfort her with a single touch.

When Asa stopped glowing as brightly, she paused a moment before she spoke. "The demon tried to possess the human child. But the child is not what she seems. Her spirit was too strong and would not allow the possession. She and the demon are at war inside her little body."

Alle's face contorted into a mask of disbelief, shock, and horror.

Asa continued, "There is no reason to fear. The little one is strong, and she will prevail. I have aided her in her spiritual journey, providing her with the tools she needs to overcome."

"Will she wake up?" Tears threatened to spill over Alle's lashes.

"I recommend we keep her in stasis until we are sure she has succeeded. When she releases the dark spirit, we can capture it and return it to where it belongs."

"When she releases the spirit," Alle repeated slowly.

"The dark spirit is not harming her. She is choosing to hold on to the spirit to protect you." Asa shrugged. "She is wise but young. She will realize you can take care of yourself. But it is better to keep her body stable in stasis so she does not deplete, and you don't have to find alternate ways to nourish her."

"So she will come out of this on her own?" Alle formed a shield with her arms crossed over her stomach.

"Without a doubt," Asa stated.

Trying to gather as much information as possible before making a final decision, Alle asked, "Ok, what and where is stasis?"

"The best way to explain it in human terms is that it is like a cocoon. We will take her to the Hall and put her in a pod. You can visit whenever you like. She will get nourishment, but she will not grow physically. It would be like putting her on hold so that she focuses all her energy on spirit without worrying about her body."

"How long will she be there?"

"She will let us know when she is ready to emerge. It should give you plenty of time to complete your task as well. However, we can hold her in stasis for as long as is necessary."

"My task?" Alle asked.

Asa shifted her focus to Gabriel. He shook his head. "We haven't been able to talk about it yet. I was trying to give her time."

"Time has run out, young angel," Asa replied.

Gabriel bowed slightly as he said, "I understand."

"I don't." Alle put her hand on her hip.

Gabriel's hand moved to her shoulder and squeezed her into a hug. "Let's get Lani situated in stasis, and then I will explain what I can."

She shrugged him off. "Fine." Alle didn't want Lani to suffer any longer than she needed to, and it sounded like stasis would allow her little body to rest for a while. It was her best option. Even though it sounded far-fetched, she decided to follow this plan. None of the so-called angels seemed out to get her. They kept showing up at just the right moments to rescue her and Lani. It was the most help she had gotten since she had lost her baby and Runar. *Or it could just be a mother's intuition,* she told herself. There weren't any other good options. Alle held up her finger. "One more question. Will she remember anything when she wakes up?"

"Lani is a special case. It is hard to tell what will happen. Usually, children wake from this sort of thing and forget it immediately or think it was all just a dream." Asa's sharp features gave no hint of emotion. It made it difficult for Alle to read her. "If there is nothing else, we really must move quickly. We do not want to jeopardize this location."

Gabriel stepped back and peeked out the window. A mailman walked up the front sidewalk. "Asa, is mail usually delivered here?"

"I do not visit this realm often. It would be best to defer to Janet," Asa said without inflection. It was starting to get a little creepy just how emotionless she was. How could she empathize with those she healed if she had no feelings?

Gabriel stayed by the window watching the mailman while Alle moved to pick Lani up. Asa stuck her arm in the way. It was the most Alle had seen her move. "I will move the child. I'm not sure what your touch will do?"

"But I carried her here. Are you saying I might have harmed her?"

"It is not Lani you would affect, but the spirit within may react negatively to your presence. Since I've stabilized her, it's best to touch as little as possible."

Tears stung Alle's eyes. She couldn't imagine not being able to touch her baby. Asa hovered over Lani again, and her body rose off the couch. A soft yellow light wound its way around Lani's tiny toddler body. "What's happening?" Alle asked.

Gabriel was back by her side and gave her a quick side hug. This time, she allowed it. "It's ok. Asa is getting her ready to transport. She will be prepared for the pod by the time we get to the Hall."

Asa began to float Lani and herself into the foyer. Lani hung in the air beside Asa with the golden light surrounding her. She was sleeping peacefully.

Just as Gabriel and Alle stepped out behind them, there was a knock at the door. Everyone froze. Asa still showed no emotion. Her face was a mask of golden light. Lani continued to float next to her.

Gabriel jumped into action as the pounding at the door got louder and more demanding. He flattened his palm and pushed his fingers together. Closing his eyes to concentrate, he reached up as high as he could and sliced his hand straight down through the air. As he did, the air seemed to split open, and buttery light poured through the split Gabriel had made. He wrapped his hand around each side of the opening and pulled it wider.

Alle watched in shock. She couldn't see what was on the other side of this opening in the middle of the air because the light was washing everything out. Gabriel stood aside as Asa stepped through with Lani. Alle intended to stay with Lani every step of the way, but her feet were frozen where they stood, and she couldn't force them to take a step. She feared what she could not see. Gabriel waved her over, but she just stared at the opening and watched Lani disappear into the light. That got her feet moving, then. Whatever was on the other side of this magical opening in space, she would not allow Lani to face it alone.

She looked back at the door just as it busted open. Gabriel grabbed her hand and jerked her through his gateway. She was enveloped in the light as she turned back again to see who had found them. Jed stepped over the threshold. Men with aviator sunglasses, blue hats, and jackets with big yellow letters surrounded him. He had brought the FBI. Just as the gap closed in front of her, she wondered how Jed had known where to find her and if she had made the right decision.

Chapter Ten

"Wait, let me back through." She tried to push Gabriel aside. He politely moved aside because there was no way she would be able to move him. The space they had walked through was gone. "Where is the door? How do we get back? Are you kidnapping us?" She turned around. Jed quickly forgotten. "Where is Lani?"

Gabriel nodded and gestured with his arm. "This way."

She paused for a second but moved in the direction he pointed.

They walked down a long hallway. The buttery yellow light subsided now that she was in it. Her eyes had adjusted. She was surrounded by stark white on all sides. The walls looked glassy like they were carved and polished out of solid white granite. There were little sparkly gems that reflected the light and lit up the hall like a disco ball. The floor and ceiling were the same. There were identical doorways every few feet. The only difference was strange symbols on each that she didn't understand. "I see now why you call it the hall," Alle muttered. Gabriel remained silent.

They walked for what felt like miles. Gabriel didn't offer any explanations. Alle's worry for Lani and eagerness to get to her kept her from asking a million questions that replayed in her mind.

They finally reached the end of the hallway and made a turn. Nothing changed. It was the same white sparkly walls. The same doors. The click, click, click of their footsteps matched the beats of Alle's anxious heart.

Gabriel came to a stop in front of a door. How he could tell it was the right door, she didn't know. He pressed his hand against it. The edges illuminated, but it pressed in and slid to the right instead of swinging open.

Alle shielded her eyes. Something she seemed to be doing a lot when following Gabriel.

"Don't worry. Your eyes will continue to adjust quickly," Gabriel said. He put a hand on the small of her back and guided her through the door.

Her eyes didn't adjust. She squinted her eyes closed tighter to keep from going blind. Alle's chest heaved, and she crashed to her knees. Tiny black dots danced at the edge of her vision. She gasped for air like a fish out of water. Nothing she could do would allow her to breathe.

Clutching her throat, she squinted her eyes open when she began to feel pieces of dark flesh from the burn on her arm float away. In the chaos and worry about Lani, she had forgotten the injury. It hadn't been painful. *Must have been third-degree, she thought.* She had read somewhere that third-degree burns weren't painful because the nerve endings had been cauterized.

Panic seized her, and her ability to breathe suffered further. Where the blackened skin had been on her arm became a dark pink, then turned lighter. Finally, in a matter of seconds, it looked like there had never been a burn.

Gabriel was at her side immediately. Rubbing circles on her back, he cooed, "In through your nose and out through your mouth. Everything will be fine."

"Some. Guardian. Angel. You. Are." Alle wheezed, fully opening her eyes.

"Good. If you can say words, you can breathe. But it might be better if you don't talk for a minute. " Gabriel grinned. Alle stared at those gorgeous dimples. Runar had been buried for less than a year. She wasn't ready to move on. Gabriel took his hand away from her back, and Alle immediately regretted the loss of comfort his touch brought.

"You... could've... warned... me...," she said between short breaths. Gabriel just shrugged. Alle got the impression he hadn't worried about it.

It took way too long for Alle's breathing to return to normal, but she finally stood and followed Gabriel. "What was that?" she asked.

"A combination of an anxiety attack and adjusting to the atmosphere. You don't need to breathe here, so it takes a second for your brain to catch on," Gabriel said unceremoniously. He started to explain further.

Alle stopped him with a wave of her hand. "Nevermind. I just want to see Lani. You can explain all that to me later."

Gabriel nodded and took her hand. Fluttering filled her belly, but she willed the butterflies away. She did not have time for a crush on her guardian angel. She had a lifelong love, even if they were separated by death. Lani was way more important now, anyway. *Besides, how would that even work?* She thought. *Isn't hooking up with angels frowned upon in the bible?*

He led her through what looked like a cafeteria, another hallway, and finally, a large room filled with pods. They looked like golden eggs with lids that were transparent orange. They were lined in neat rows with perfectly even spaces between them.

Gabriel spotted Asa in the middle of the pods. She was leaning over with great care and examining her patient. Alle thought the golden highlights surrounding the woman shimmered a little brighter here than in the living room back on Earth.

"Gabriel, what do you call this place?" Alle whispered.

"This is the stasis room." He spoke reverently.

"I meant the whole thing, the hall, this room." She waved her hands in a big circle.

"We say behind the veil. You can think of it as an alternate universe. I have a unique ability among angels to open the veil and take others with me. It's how we get between realms. Only a few angels can open the veil. Others used a portal system we developed. We recently re-engineered an old system to help protect the veil."

"So, is this heaven?"

"No. This is a spiritual realm. Heaven is the place of human souls. There, they commune with the Most High. They cannot come and go. It's a one-way trip for most humans. But being in the presence of the Most High is the highest privilege." He took her hand and squeezed. "Let's see, Lani. Then we'll get answers to your questions. It's a lot for a human mind to process and make sense of it all. As you stay behind the veil longer, your sight of the spiritual will likely increase. You've always had the ability."

Alle noted it had been the most information he had offered since she met him.

"I've had the ability to see the spiritual?"

"You might describe it as seeing movement out of the corner of your eye. But you can't see anything when you turn to see what's there. You can see only those that choose for you to see them."

Alle's mouth dropped at Gabriel describing her experiences since early childhood. "How did you know?"

Gabriel scowled and crossed his arms over his chest. "First, I'm your guardian angel. I know a lot about you. Second, a lot of people describe it that way. I assumed you might have had the same experience. You'll likely be able to see much more now that you are here, though. I'm not sure about when you return. You will probably remember your experiences for now, even after you sleep." He shrugged. "We'll see."

Alle accepted his explanation and looked around at the stasis room. The ceiling was at least ninety feet tall. It had carved spires similar to a cathedral. She had never visited Notre Dame in France, but she imagined it looked like this, but maybe smaller. The room was darkened and cool. She couldn't see any candles, but the room seemed lit by similar lighting. Alle felt small in the vastness of the room. Yet the room somehow still felt cozy. She expected a sterile hospital but got a cozy, million-square-foot cathedral full of pods with people in stasis. Even so, anxiety threatened to overwhelm her again as they arrived at Lani's gold and orange pod.

"Lani is doing well," Asa spoke as if reading her mind. "She will remain in this place until you come for her. She is well-protected. Her body will not need food or water and will not grow." She reminded her. "When you come to retrieve her, it will be as if she went to sleep, and no time passed at all."

Alle reached up to take Asa's hand, but Gabriel stepped between them. "You cannot touch the healing angels," he warned. Alle took a step back. Her guardian angel could switch moods in a blink of an eye.

Alle leaned around him. "I'm sorry. I didn't know I wasn't allowed to touch you, either. I just wanted to thank you for your kindness and your help. I don't know what I would have done without it today."

Asa still did not smile, but she did bow slightly. Without a word, she turned and floated away.

Alle stood a moment longer, looking over Lani's still body. A single tear dropped onto the pod. Lani did look as though she was sleeping. She just wished she could give her another kiss, hug her, and hold her close. Alle sighed. Worrying about it now would not get Lani any closer to waking up.

She turned to Gabriel. "It's time for some answers."

He nodded without a word and walked toward a door. Alle took one more moment to say her goodbyes to Lani. She laid her hand on the pod. "Hang on, baby girl. We'll get this all figured out in no time," she whispered. "Mommy loves you."

Chapter Eleven

When she turned around, Gabriel awaited her across the expanse. She made her way to him. He took her hand again and opened the door. She thought it was the same door they had entered, but they were not in a hall when they walked through. They were in a library.

"I can see you are trying to figure this place out."

That stopped Alle in her tracks. "This has all been a little much. I want to understand what is happening. I need you to be honest with me and tell me everything. Not with innuendos and guessing games."

"I can't tell you everything. I'm sorry. There are things you will have to discover for yourself. I think this room will help."

"A library?"

Gabriel cocked his head slightly. "That's what humans call them."

"Yes, of course, but it's weird this place has a library, right?"

"Not terribly weird. Where else would you keep records and books of knowledge?"

"But you call it a library?"

The corners of Gabriel's mouth lifted slightly, and the fluttering in Alle's stomach returned. He stepped closer to her, and his scent swirled around her. It reminded her of Christmas and cold nights by the fire. His eyes glimmered as she looked up at him. She was seconds from leaning in to…

He cleared his throat. "We don't call it a library. We call it a warehouse of knowledge. Humans… call it a library," he said, turning on his heel and stalking away from her. "It's best to keep up."

Alle caught herself before she fell in his absence. *What the heck is wrong with me?*

Gabriel sighed, "I will explain what I can, but please don't try to go through the doors without me," he said as she rushed to catch up.

"What does that mean? I can't leave?" she asked.

He led her to a little alcove lined with green velvet couches. Looking around, she realized this was actually her idea of heaven. Gabriel sat. For once, he looked slightly less rigid. Alle crossed her arms and cocked out her hip. "Huh? I didn't realize you could relax even a smidge."

"With you here, instead of the natural world, I can let my guard down... a smidge." Gabriel grinned.

Alle didn't return his grin. "You didn't answer my question. Are we prisoners or what?"

"No, you are not a prisoner. I will explain how the doors work." He leaned forward as Alle sat, uncrossing her arms. "First, you have to find a door. The doors will take you anywhere you want to go. Humans cannot typically do this, but you've adjusted rather well, and your sight is better, so it probably will work for you."

Alle nodded, encouraging him to continue, though she only understood about half of what he was saying.

"Once you find a door, you must touch it and think where you want to be. The hallways are transitions between places. Some doors will only get you close to where you want to go. This way, if there are intruders, we have a way to slow them down before they get too far and a way to detain them from leaving."

"Do I have to have a hat?" she asked mischievously.

"A hat? No, that's ridiculous. Why would you need a hat?"

"Never mind. I probably watch too many movies. Continue." She gestured with her hand.

Gabriel raised his eyebrows and cocked his head but finally continued, "So once you picture where you want to go, you step through. If you are with someone else, you must be touching, and then the doors will take you to the place the host will think of. So that you don't get stuck."

"By host, you mean angelic host, hostess with the mostest, or like parasitic host?" Alle could tell Gabriel wanted to roll his eyes, but that was beneath him, so he gave her a blank stare. "Sorry, was that a dumb question?"

"No, not dumb. Sometimes, I can't tell if you are joking in a human way or actually asking a question."

"Let's assume, for everyone's benefit, that it's actually a question. Even if I'm not and you answer it, I will find it funny, and that's what you were made for…" Alle's eyes widened in shock. They immediately glistened at the memory of what Runar always told her was his purpose in life. To make her laugh. Gabriel stiffened beside her. Alle was sure he was uncomfortable with her tears. "I'm sorry." Alle patted her eyes and thought of a list of grocery items she needed back home. Thinking of mundane things helped take her mind off the sadness and kept the tears at bay.

Gabriel side-eyed her but continued without commenting on her tears, "That's basically how the doors work. If you tried to go through by yourself, you might get close to where you are going, but the halls might not be the same, and you could get lost. I would find you eventually, but there would be a wait. And if you just kept trying doors, it might land you in an unpleasant place. Some of the doors are one-way. You can't go out the way you came, so the only way is through."

"Unpleasant places here?"

"This is typically a place for spiritual beings. Not humans."

Alle shuddered, thinking of all the unpleasant places she could end up in. She did not want that. Then she remembered another question she had. "You told me not to touch. You growled that little warning, and I thought I might lose a hand or something."

"No one can touch the healers. It can disrupt their spiritual healing abilities. Angels often prefer not to be touched unless they initiate it. I am your guardian, so you and I can touch as much as necessary."

Why does that sound so nice… She slapped herself on the forehead to stop the inappropriate inner monologue. Her face often betrayed her thoughts; she did not want to let that one slip out. She needed to change the subject. "Alright, tell me about this place. Behind the veil. Other than I can't touch healers and don't go through doors alone. You said it's like an alternate universe."

"It is a little."

"So we didn't cross space and time?"

"Space and Time work differently here. We are in the same basic area that we left. Like the doors, I can open the veil and end up anywhere I want. I have to picture it, open the veil, and then I'll be there. We call it portalling. Time is similar. I can open the veil to almost any moment."

"Almost?"

He shrugged. "Future is iffy because of its dynamic nature."

Alle nodded, "So why did we have to walk so far to get to the stasis room? You could have just taken us right in there."

"I thought you might need time to adjust. If I had portalled you right into the veil, your head could have exploded."

Alle's face went white with the thought of her grey matter all over the stasis room pods.

Gabriel grinned and patted her knee. "It's a lot to try to wrap your head around. Don't think about it too much."

"Are you saying I can't understand?"

"No. I'm saying if you don't understand, don't try too hard. It is difficult for the human mind to comprehend this… realm. You are doing great so far."

"I'm so glad that I could please you." Alle's words dripped with sarcasm.

"I wasn't sure you would be allowed through the veil. It was a risk that has worked out well."

She squinted at him. "You risked my life?"

"No. It wouldn't have been so dramatic. You wouldn't have even seen the veil open. We would have just disappeared."

"So you risked Lani going through without me. I would have just been left behind." Alle stood in her anger and started pacing and chewing her thumbnail.

"It was a calculated risk for your safety and Lani's safety. If you recall, we were in a bit of a hurry. But I had some evidence that you would be fine.

Even if you can't remember fully."

Alle stopped in front of him and gestured wildly. "From yesterday! All the things I can't remember? That's what you're going on?"

"Alle, you'll have to trust me."

"I'm not sure that I do."

"You have so far."

"I've had a choice?"

Gabriel leaned forward, put his elbows on his knees, and steepled his pointer fingers. "There's always a choice," he said in a low voice.

Alle took a deep breath to keep the frustration from building. She started pacing again. "Ok. So now what? We hang out in the library until Lani gets better?"

Gabriel leaned back. "I don't think that's going to work. You've been attacked more than once, and we need to find out exactly why the demons are coming for you."

"Ok, but you have some idea, right?"

"Yes. But this is your journey. If I dump all the information on you immediately, I'm not sure what will happen."

"Like my tiny human mind could literally be blown?"

"Something like that, yes."

"So how do I keep from having a mind melt?"

"We take it slow and leave it open to providence."

"You mean fate?"

"No. I mean providence. Fate isn't real."

"It's the same thing."

"This is what you want to argue about?"

Alle sat on the edge of the soft green couch and tucked her hands under her legs to keep from chewing her thumbs anymore. "Where do I start? I need to get going so we can get Lani home." Her knee bounced in anticipation.

Gabriel nodded thoughtfully. "Well, I'm hoping the warehouse helps. It usually leads us to what we need to know. Eventually."

"So we just sit here waiting for the warehouse to shine a spotlight on the information we need?" Alle fell back against the plush velvet, resting her chin on her chest.

"Something like that. In the meantime, we'll get you settled in."

"Settled in? I want to get started, so we can get on with this so I can wake Lani up and go home to my life."

Gabriel raised his eyebrows. "Your life?"

Alle held up her hands. "Look, it wasn't going all that great, I have to admit, but I was figuring it out," Alle rambled, and Gabriel continued his blank stare. "What would you know about it anyway?"

Gabriel hooked a thumb back at himself. "Guardian Angel. I guard things. It's what I do, my sole purpose. I know your life better than you do."

"Well, it sucks you won't tell me anything about it."

"If I tell you, it would make it easier, but it would ruin all you were trying to achieve, and you might hate me. Not to mention, you might go home drooling and unable to think or speak. I don't want you to be a vegetable. And I don't want you to hate me. It makes my job harder. But I promise to help in any way I can."

Alle had the feeling he wasn't telling the whole story about why he wouldn't tell her. "Will I remember any of this when I go back to my life?"

"It's hard to tell. Humans often remember these visits as dreams. With you, it might be different."

"For the same reason the demons are after me?"

"Possibly."

Alle huffed and stood. "Fine. Let's get settled so we can get this show on the road."

Gabriel's lips thinned. It looked like he was about to say more. Instead, he kept the information to himself. Finally, standing, "This way." Without another word, he turned his back on Alle and walked away.

I guess he expects me to follow him blindly. Should I salute and say yes, sir? she thought.

He led her out of the alcove, past several aisles of books, to an iron spiral staircase in the corner. "This is typical of a cozy old library," she mentioned.

"You will find most of the places here familiar…" Gabriel paused, "This world does its best to meet your expectations. It's easier to transition if the places are expected and similar to past experiences. I believe the ware… library is trying to meet your expectations."

"Neat," Alle quipped as she looked around. She hadn't missed his pause and didn't fully buy his explanation.

Gabriel climbed the staircase, and Alle followed. As she put her hand on the banister and took a step up, she caught a familiar shadow move out of the corner of her eye. She turned her head to see what was there. There was no one, per usual. But something else drew her attention past the elusive shadow. A light coming from one of the aisles of books. Light like the ones from the doors before they opened.

She stepped back down to investigate the weird light. Gabriel and settling in were forgotten. She glided toward the strange light in a trance. Gabriel's garbled voice faintly registered, but she was too focused to care. The light was warm and inviting; she had to know where it led. As she walked down the aisle, she felt more confident this was where she was supposed to be. This was the right path.

She finally stopped in front of a shelf of books. The light was no longer bright but pulsed behind one book. The spine was no taller than a greeting card. There wasn't anything that would have stood out to her otherwise. The cover was faded blue but in pristine condition. It reminded her of a diary. There was no title, just a number three stamped in gold leaf along the spine. The gilded edging of the book's pages continued to shimmer for a moment. Then, the light faded as quickly as it appeared. The sights and sounds of the world around her whooshed back into her awareness. Gabriel's warmth startled her, and she stepped away.

"Alle, I need to know what happened just now. You were not responding to me." Worry coated Gabriel's words.

Alle shook her head. "I don't know what happened. I just followed the light to this book." She pushed the book toward Gabriel. He didn't reach for or even look at it but searched her eyes. She felt the weight of his intense stare and looked back toward the book. He took a deep breath and stepped back.

"It seems the library has given you what you need to start the journey. It didn't take as long as I was expecting."

"Well, that's a relief."

"I'm not sure. If the library is hurrying us along, that might mean time is limited to 'Get this show on the road,' as you say."

"I'm anxious to get started." She turned the book and yanked on the edges. "Let's see what this book says."

It didn't open. She tried again. It was firmly stuck. Her face fell. "Why can't I open it?"

Gabriel shrugged. "The library is mysterious. Maybe it's part of the journey or just wanted to see if you would follow the mysterious light." He shook his hand above his head and made the spooky story voice, then turned as he walked back toward the staircase. "Keep up."

"Oh, now he has jokes," Alle muttered, rolling her eyes.

She tried to open the book again. But it still wouldn't budge. Looking up toward the unadorned ceiling, she gave a frustrated grunt.

"Come on," Gabriel broke in. "You can keep the book. It might be something you need at a later time. There are apartments upstairs you can use and get some rest. Maybe you can solve the mystery after some food and relaxation."

Alle stomped back down the aisle. "A mystery you already know the answer to? I really hate being treated like a child."

"I am not treating you like a child. I don't have all the answers myself. I'm here to protect you. And I will do whatever it takes to do that," he shrugged. "If that means not telling you things, then I won't tell them to you. Right now, I feel the best way to protect you is to let you, the Most High, and the library work this out. I'm here as protection."

Alle narrowed her eyes. "What does the 'Most High' have to do with this?"

Gabriel sighed and continued walking. "Again. That's part of your journey. I am not here to tell you all the information. I'm your protector and, for now, your guide. Nothing more. I've already interfered more than is acceptable, but it was unavoidable. Angels have parameters for interfering with human lives."

Gabriel announcing he was nothing more than a guide and protector stung more than Alle wanted to admit. She had always wanted everyone to like her but always hated feeling like an obligation. Not wanting to explore her emotional trauma, she focused on the supernatural portion of Gabriel's statement. "But you said I was an angel, so interference is not an issue." She stubbornly crossed her arms over her chest.

Gabriel stopped. "You remember that tidbit now, do you?"

"It was just this morning. I haven't slept," she said.

Gabriel stared back at her, weakening her resolve enough to get going.

"Fine. Let's get to that apartment so I can be done with you and get this figured out." She stomped past him and up the staircase.

"Agreed." He followed her.

When they reached the top shelves, the books were interrupted every few feet by doors. "Do these doors do the same thing as the other doors?" Curiosity interrupted her bad mood.

"No. The portal doors will look a little different." Gabriel explained. These doors just looked like regular old doors.

"Which one is mine?"

"You pick. These are guest apartments."

"Wow, ok. I guess I'll just go here." She reached for the nearest door. Gabriel followed her in as her mouth dropped open.

Floor-to-ceiling windows with a forest view greeted her as she walked in. The room was spacious. There was a kitchenette with a small granite top island. Red popped here and there through the sea of neutral greys. "Modern chic meets rustic forest? Nice." She nodded in admiration of the interior designer.

"As I said, the library tries to meet your expectations."

Her feet sunk into the plush carpet as she investigated the rest of the room. "The library knows me well, then," she murmured as she continued to explore. A white sectional sofa was placed along the wall with a boxy coffee table in front of it. The other wall held an electric fireplace and a mounted TV.

"Do you get cable here?" she asked. Gabriel just grunted. She had used up all his good grace today, she supposed.

A door beside the television was opened. She could see a large master suite with an en suite. Her spirits immediately lifted, and she hurried to investigate. Every surface was white or grey. The bed looked like the display at her local department store but one thousand times better. It was so fluffy she instantly knew it would be like sleeping on a cloud. She felt her body relax just looking at it.

The bathroom was just as luxurious. There was a full-on jacuzzi tub and a separate shower with nine nozzles. Water shortages were apparently not a problem behind the veil.

"I'm done. I'm just going to live here from now on." She plopped on the bed and focused on the white ceiling. For the first time in a long while, a genuine smile formed. She felt like she could truly rest in this place. She was safe. Lani was safe for now.

She kicked off her shoes and scooted around so her body fit on the bed. She put the book on the dark oak nightstand.

"Don't go anywhere. We have things to do tomorrow," she said to the book. She was so tired suddenly that she didn't even care that it was weird to talk to inanimate objects. Grabbing the edge of the blankets, she pulled them over her. "You can show yourself out, right, Gabriel?" she mumbled. Would he want to stay with her to protect her?

The weight of the world finally transferred to someone else's shoulders. For the first time in a year, others were sharing her burden.

She heard a door close. "Mmmkay. Goodnight. We'll figure out all the things tomorrow." She said sleepily as the lights dimmed on their own, and she drifted off to sleep.

Chapter Twelve

Alle sat up in her bed. She was drenched in sweat, the thin sheets of the bed twisted around her torso. The room was still dim but not dark, and she looked around to get her bearings. The dream had been real. And now she needed answers.

She jumped out of the bed and rushed to get dressed. There was a tiny wardrobe in the corner of the room. Although she hadn't brought a bag, she thought some clothes might fit her there. She hadn't changed in what felt like days.

She tore open the doors. Three outfits hung on the bar. Fortunately, whoever had used the space before had comfort in mind and was a perfect match for her size. She would leave a little note of thanks and promise to return the items. Not knowing when or how. Gabriel could help her, maybe. With the thought of his name, she remembered the guardian had some explaining to do.

She pulled on the t-shirt, pants, and a pair of comfy walking shoes that would be perfect for exploring the library and researching.

Walking to the door, she threw it open. She poked her head out and saw the broad, muscular back with wing tattoos. He was looking down over the balcony of the upper level. Glad she hadn't lost memories of the day before, she walked right up to him. Lifting on her tippy toes to tap him on the shoulder, she broke the silence of the morning. "Hey, we need to talk."

He turned and flashed her a smile full of charm, but it wasn't the broody angel with the ice-blue eyes that greeted her. This guy could be Gabriel's twin. He had green eyes and smiled easily, revealing a cute dimple on the right side of his face. "Uh. Sorry, I thought you were Gabriel."

"Yeah, I get that a lot." He leaned his elbow casually against the railing without explaining further.

"I haven't met many angels. Do you all look the same?"

He scrunched his face in a silent laugh. "You're funny. Of course, we don't all look the same. I have green eyes," he said and pointed to his eyes.

"Ooo... Kay... Do you know where he is?"

"I'm not my brother's keeper," he said in a deep voice.

Alle's eyes bulged, and she cocked her head. "So, you're brothers? I didn't realize angels had brothers."

"Sorry. Lame joke. I was totally kidding." The new hot angel tried to recover with a grin.

Alle pressed her eyebrows together and squinted her eyes.

"I guess you had to be there." He raised his hands in defense. "Gabe had to go out for a bit. He asked me to watch you... over you. Like a guardian... would." New, dumb, hot angel ran his hand down his face. "This is not going well. Let's start over."

"Let's."

He stuck out his hand. "Hi, I'm Lex. I'm Gabe's friend, mostly. Partner sometimes. Brother, all the time." Alle defrosted and shook his hand. She didn't hold grudges, and at least he was trying.

"Huh?"

"Huh? What does huh mean?" Lex asked.

"I just thought angels all had names that ended with EL. Gabriel. Michael. Ramiel," Alle explained.

"You only know the names of Archangels?"

Alle's eyes bulged again. "Gabriel is an archangel?"

Lex scoffed. "Yeah. And anyway, my name means defender of men. That's what I do." He slapped his chest. "I defend men. So, it works." He shrugged and took up his position, looking over the library.

"Are angels like the seven dwarves?"

He spun back around to face her. "What? No! We are not short men who dig for gemstones."

Alle huffed and waved him off. "Nevermind. I guess you had to be there," she said with a side glance. "Anyway, do you know when Gabriel is coming back? I have an urgent matter to discuss."

"He said he would return before you woke. I wish he had. You are feisty. There is no coffee here. Is that the problem?"

Alle hadn't thought about eating or drinking since she had been here. She didn't even feel hungry or thirsty at the moment. "Coffee might be nice." She sighed. There was nothing she could do until Gabriel returned. She needed answers before she went further. "I'm going to shower. Please don't let Gabriel leave again until I've spoken with him."

"Yes, ma'am. Any other orders?" Lex said with sincerity.

Alle added a please to make herself feel better. She didn't know she had it in her to order angels around.

As Alle closed her apartment door, she heard Lex mutter, "It's good to have you back." She didn't know what he was referring to. She had never been to the hall. But she felt there was more to this situation than she knew.

* * *

Alle almost forgot her name. The shower felt that good. The jets hit every tight muscle group in her body with just the right temperature. There was now no doubt this was heaven. It felt so great she started humming to herself. It had been ages since she felt like humming, but this shower allowed her to put her worries aside for a few minutes and be content. It was a universe all unto itself. And for a moment, she was happy. But all too quickly, it came to an end. She turned the nozzles and stepped out of the shower. She could barely see the sink with all the steam. The fruity smell of her body wash still hung in the air. She wiped away condensation on the mirrors and examined her face.

The dark circles and sallow cheekbones were familiar. It wasn't just because of the stress of the past few days. Just another reminder that her body wasn't capable of producing the needed hormones. She realized it had been several days without her prescribed treatment. She would have to make do. She wondered how to counteract the fatigue and brain fog that would surely come soon.

After dressing and drying her hair, she decided to wait for Gabriel in the library instead of her room. The library was her happy place, and she needed that vibe.

She grabbed the book she couldn't open yesterday and made a mental checklist. Figure out how to open the book, then figure out why the demons were targeting her, then how to wake Lani up. Caught up in her own world, she didn't see the brawny angel standing in her doorway as she swung it open. She smooshed her face right up into his sternum and dropped the book.

"Jiminy Cricket, do you own any shirts?" she said as she jumped back and rubbed her jaw. He was built like a Mack truck. Although she could appreciate his zero percent body fat torso, he needed to wear something besides white lounge pants.

"I own nothing. Angels typically wear armor, but I don't need it in the warehouse."

"What about the suit from yesterday?"

"That was just to impress you so you would come with me."

Alle rolled her eyes. "Great! More manipulation." She threw her hands up and let them fall until they slapped against her legs.

Alle reached down to grab the book just as Gabriel bent to do the same. Their heads smashed together with a loud thump, sending Alle flailing backward. A strong arm came around her waist to keep her from going to the floor. Gabriel set her upright. His hands continued to rest on her hips. "Steady there." Alle looked up at him through her lashes.

She was still unsure if she trusted him entirely but wanted to. Remembering to be angry, she shoved his hands off her hips.

Gabriel cleared his throat. "Lex told me you were looking for me earlier."

"Yes. I had a bad dream."

"A bad dream?" He quirked his eyebrows, following her down the spiral staircase.

"Yes. When I'm stressed, I have them. Recurring dreams. They are usually about tornadoes or snakes, but this one was different." She looked back at Gabriel. He looked uncomfortable. "What's the matter? You aren't afraid of snakes, are you?"

"Of course not," he said flatly.

"Not even because they caused the fall of man."

"He has been overcome."

"Yes, of course," she said as she found the plush green couches from yesterday. She sat on one edge, leaving plenty of room for Gabriel. He remained standing.

"Can you tell me what was different about this dream?"

"Well, sure. It was different because Jed was there. Usually, in my stress dreams, it is an impossible scenario where I'm trying to save everyone I know, but I just can't. Who can stand against hundreds of tornadoes that continually pop up over a city?"

"Yes, I see what you mean." He nodded his encouragement to continue.

"Well, in this dream, I was trying to save everyone. From Jed. I saw his face when we went through the veil, and it just worried me the demons may have gotten to him as they did the pizza guy.

"And then there was this thing where you stepped out of a hole in thin air and saved me from all these people that turned to black goo. It felt very real. More like a memory than a dream."

Gabriel rolled his shoulders and sighed. "Do you remember how I told you wouldn't remember? That your memory would be slippery every time you slept?"

Alle nodded.

"Well, I think this is how you are remembering. It is important for this journey that you know how it started. You need to pay attention to your dreams."

She hugged her arms around herself, "Why don't I remember."

Gabriel met her eyes but looked away quickly.

"Gabriel, what are you hiding? If I'm going to trust you, I need to know." Alle said with a calm she didn't feel.

Gabriel stood with his arms over his chest. His tanned biceps bulged over his perfectly sculpted pecs. It was hard for Alle to concentrate on the matter at hand. But she waited patiently for his reply. He spoke when it was clear that she wasn't going to budge.

"Alle, everything I've done is for your protection. And for Lani's protection. The decisions I've made are the right ones, and I will not have you analyze the situation and my decisions after the fact. You cannot apply current knowledge to past actions."

Alle crossed her legs and leaned forward to rest her elbows on them. She squinted her eyes and waited for him to continue. Gabriel took that as agreement.

"After the incident at the restaurant and Lani's daycare, I felt it best to block some memories." Gabriel didn't look ashamed or even guilty. He said the words confidently that it was the right decision at the time.

"So how would blocking my memories allow me to protect Lani? If I had remembered, I would have gone with you before she was harmed."

"You wouldn't have. You have free will, and I offered to protect you when you were attacked in the restaurant. I came back to warn you there would be more attacks. You refused my offer to help. You didn't trust me."

"Because you blocked my memory," Alle interrupted. Gabriel finally sat beside her on the couch.

"I can't choose which memories to block. I was hoping that you would remember a few things. Like me, for one..." Gabriel paused, looking a little hurt that she hadn't. Alle refused to feel guilty. *He shouldn't have blocked the memory in the first place.*

He sighed and continued, "It was the best decision then. Living with the knowledge of the supernatural can sometimes cause people to have mental breakdowns. No one would believe you when you told them. I was hopeful that we had eliminated the threat. Plus, I wanted to present the danger to you when you weren't fighting for your life. Free will is paramount, and I didn't want you to decide under duress."

"Lani got hurt, and I ended up making a decision under duress anyway. But without all the information, how could I make the right decision."

"Sometimes you have to have faith. You have to trust without seeing or knowing everything. I hoped you would trust me, but I'm not all-knowing and can't see the future."

Alle closed her eyes and sighed. She knew she would get nowhere with this angel who had the spiritual all figured out. There was no changing his mind that he was right. He had already told her. It wasn't going to help Lani to argue with him. She decided to change tactics and ask about her dreams. "What about Jed? I liked him. He was nice, but I had to protect everyone from him in my dream."

"Jed is a demon. I think subconsciously, you knew." Gabriel didn't hide the information from her.

There's no point now, I suppose. Alle thought, looking for reasons not to have blind faith.

Alle deflated against the couch. "So, he played me?"

Gabriel nodded. "He is a low-level demon."

"A demon is a demon."

"Agreed. He was simply a watcher. He could interact, but he simply kept his eyes on you and ensured I didn't disappear with you. His concern was sincere, but he wasn't concerned with your well-being. He probably followed us to the safe house."

"Why did you take us there if you knew he was watching me?"

"It was the quickest way to get Lani to safety."

"I appreciate that. Were there others?"

"At the safe house?" he asked, raising his eyebrows.

"Other angels," Alle confirmed.

"Everyone made it out safely. That location is compromised, and the angels will no longer use it."

Alle's face fell, and her anger faded away. "I'm sorry I'm causing everyone so much trouble."

Gabriel leaned forward, wanting to comfort her with a hug, but settled for a pat on the knee. Alle jerked her eyes to his. Other than keeping her from falling, it was the most he had touched her on purpose since he brought her through the veil.

"This isn't your fault."

"It seems like it is, and now we have to figure out why the demons have decided I'm on their hit list. There's one more thing." Alle wanted to get everything out there so they could move forward together. "I have about twelve more hours before my brain starts malfunctioning. I don't think I should have come here. I need to get back to my things."

"Is this the hormone thing?"

"Yeah. I didn't realize guardian angels knew every aspect of their... ward? Charge? What do you call me?"

"We call you the guarded to make it simple."

"Simple, yes, let's do that. You could tell me everything you know about me. That would make it super simple."

"Alle, we have been through this. It is better to discover these things for yourself, so it is not overly taxing on your human brain."

"Yes, my weakling brain. So why did you tell me about the memory wipe thing? And was that the first time, or were there others."

"I'm sure you have seen many spiritual things you can't remember."

"So, there could have been other times."

"I think you know the answer to that. You've already worked most of it out."

Alle took a deep breath. "We need to move past this. I can't keep being angry about someone messing with my memories."

"Because you are human, I must make decisions without your knowledge to protect you and your free will. The Most High wouldn't have put me in charge of your protection if I weren't trustworthy. If you don't trust me, trust Him.

"That's been hard to do lately."

"I know it seems that way, but suffering produces perseverance. Perseverance builds character..."

Alle held up her hand. "Please don't. I can't take pithy sayings."

Gabriel slightly bowed to her, "As you wish. Everything you need is provided for you. I have had Adriel grab a few things from your home for you and Lani should she wake while we're here. As for your meds, could you not just ask for healing?"

94

Alle squinted her eyes at him. "Don't you think I have asked for healing? The Most High, or whatever you call him here, has not seen fit to provide me with that healing, so I get to be on meds for the rest of my life. Perhaps the meds are his way of healing me. It's pretty dang miraculous I live in a time where we have the medical technology to manage this disease. Imagine if I had been born just one hundred years prior. I would be up a creek without a paddle!"

Gabriel held up his hands in surrender. "I apologize. You are right. I will have Adriel go back for the medicine."

"The sooner, the better."

"She's already on it."

"How?"

Gabriel tapped his temple. Stunned, Alle dropped the book she was holding. She hadn't even realized she had picked it up. "You can speak telepathically?"

"Yes, of course. We're angels."

Alle nodded. "Sure, sure. Can you speak with humans the same way?"

"Sometimes we can hear human thoughts and feelings when there is a great amount of emotion like despair or anger. Fear is a potent amplifier. Guardians can hear these thoughts better because our job is to protect. Positive emotions are more difficult to hear, but we feel them differently. The positive emotions of humans give us a little power boost."

Alle processed the explanation and decided to tuck that nugget away for another day.

"What happens when Lani wakes up, and we return to our lives? Are you going to erase what I learn?"

"I'm going to be honest. It will depend on whether you have or want to have a normal human existence after this. I can make no vows either way."

"I see your point. I don't know how to return to my old life after this. And if I would even want to. I mean, that shower alone is worth dying for."

"Exactly. But I'm hoping there's something worth living for."

"The only thing worth living for right now is Lani," Alle muttered and picked up the book from the floor. "Any ideas on how to open this book?"

Alle turned it over to examine it. She noticed a symbol on the front cover she hadn't seen when she first picked it up. It was a long sword with wings on either side. It was in the same gold leaf as the number three on the spine.

"Perhaps there is a key or some secret words," Gabriel offered.

"And how would I know?"

"If the warehouse gave you the book, either you already have the knowledge to open it, or you will find it here."

Alle began wondering out loud, "If I had written a book, but I wanted to keep the knowledge hidden from certain beings, how would I lock it? As a human, of course, I would use a key." She turned the book over and over. "But there's no obvious place for a key. So perhaps magic words. Maybe…" She turned to Gabriel. "Don't laugh, ok?"

He nodded stoically.

"What was I even thinking?" She rolled her eyes, knowing he barely cracked a smile on a normal day. She turned and positioned her body so he couldn't see anyway. She held the book in her open palms like an offering, "Ok, here it goes… Open says me," she whispered and then waited expectantly. Gabriel smirked but did not laugh.

After a few minutes, she sat back in disappointment. "Ok. Well, I mean, that was a long shot anyway."

He patted her knee. "I think you are on the right track."

"Yes. So this is a book in an angel warehouse. It glowed when it touched it."

"But this houses all sorts of knowledge from the natural world and some items even from the underside of spirit."

"This is not fancy, so that could mean it's from the natural world. But it also has gilded edges." Alle laid the book on the small end table and threw her hands up. "I'm probably way overthinking this."

Gabriel stood. "While you are overthinking, I'm going to walk around the warehouse. If you need anything, you can just shout."

"Shout?!" Alle gasped and laid her hand over her chest, "in a library. Never. Maybe just come check on me in an hour or so." Gabriel nodded and turned to walk away. He stopped when he heard Alle speak again.

"Ok… how to open a locked angel book? Hey, library, got any books on that topic?" Alle murmured.

"It's cute how you talk yourself through difficult problems," Gabriel mentioned casually and continued walking. Alle wasn't even listening to him. She was lost in her own thoughts already.

* * *

Alle continued to work on the puzzle of opening the book until she was out of ideas. The harder she tried to figure it out, the harder it seemed. Like the book was even more locked, as ridiculous as that sounded. Finally, she decided to take a break. She carried the book with her, afraid the library might change its mind about her need for it. Of course, she didn't know what was in the book, but now she had a mystery; she couldn't stop until it was discovered.

She wandered around the library, taking deep breaths and filling her brain with much-needed oxygen. The oxygen would allow for a clear head and more brain power. She thought she might also need a meal to give her some energy to think about this problem. She rounded the stacks and approached a table with breakfast items as if on cue. Food was not typically allowed in human libraries, but the "warehouse of knowledge" didn't mind so much. She wasn't going to complain. The food looked amazing.

She noticed three chairs and lamented there wasn't anyone to share breakfast with. She thought about shouting for Gabriel but took her commitment to quiet seriously. The lack of companions didn't stop her from eating. She had an unhealthy relationship with food. Food, any food, was comforting. It was like being wrapped in a warm blanket. She wanted to change and had tried to change, but it was deeply ingrained. She probably needed to bring that up with her therapist, too.

After a few bites of the heavenly cream cheese and strawberry kolache, she heard voices. Lex's dark hair appeared with another pretty blonde angel. Alle wasn't sure about the gender of the angels, but the other angel appeared female. Something was familiar about her, though. They both smiled and seemed genuinely pleased to see her.

Alle waved, "Hi, Lex. Please sit and have breakfast with me." Then she paused, "Wait, do angels eat?"

The angels shared a side glance, and the new angel said, "Yes, we enjoy human food, but we don't need food." She stuck out her hand. "I'm Adriel; I brought your clothes and…."

"You look familiar," Alle interrupted, shaking her hand and feeling a hint of jealousy, although she didn't understand why. Maybe it was her angelic beauty.

"I'm Lani's teacher. And her guardian."

Alle's mouth formed an "o."

"We can't interfere with every aspect of the guarded. We can only protect them and guide them in some ways. The demon attack was unexpected."

"Lani has her own ideas about what's best for her, even at two years old. I don't hold you accountable, but I hope you will help me fix it."

Both angels sat with her. "Yes, of course, we will and are doing everything in our power."

Alle showed them the book. "Any idea how we can open this?"

A momentary shock crossed Adriel's face, but she stilled her expression and explained she had no clue.

Disappointed, Alle shrugged. "Well, at least we can have breakfast together."

The three of them ate and chatted. Conversation and laughter came easy with Lex. He was funny and liked to talk about things that didn't matter. Alle was drawn into his stories of angel wars and helping humans.

* * *

Gabriel watched from the shadows of the rafters. Angels didn't get jealous, but he wished he could be the one getting Alle's smiles instead of her contempt. Still, he had a job and would do anything to ensure Alle was safe.

Chapter Thirteen

Gabriel couldn't provide Alle with the knowledge she needed to open the book, but he could guide her. He sent Lex and Adriel to help. He knew the harder Alle worked on the problem, the worse her mood would get. He was unsure but assumed the book would work like the angel's power. Human emotions would loosen those pages. Positive emotions would open them, while negative emotions would keep the book shut.

He watched as the tension drained from Alle's shoulders. The smile he hadn't seen in months reemerged, even if it was a little sad. He noticed when the stress of the last few days lifted momentarily. He had hoped Lex's easy-going personality would help lift her spirits and Adriel would be there to keep Alle comfortable. Of course, Adriel had wanted to be brought in sooner, but this was the right time.

"Thank you both for having breakfast with me," Alle said. Adriel explained the warehouse cleaned and cared for itself. Alle picked up the book. He thought she would return to their alcove, but she surprised him by heading upstairs. Lex and Adriel both glanced upward and gave Gabriel a quick nod. They would head back toward their quarters until he needed them again. He assumed he would need many more guardians before this mission was over. He might even need some warriors. He was waiting for Alle to discover just what they were dealing with. Although he had some ideas and assumptions, he was still in the dark.

It wasn't until he heard the click of her door that he floated down from the rafters. He didn't have time or need for his wings to release from the tattoos on his back. He still landed nimbly on his feet. He wandered the warehouse himself, hoping it would also have what he needed.

* * *

Alle sat on her bed with the blue book. She hadn't said anything to the angels because she didn't want to get her hopes up, but she had noticed it shimmering a bit when talking with them. She didn't think it was because of the angels. If it was, she could always call them back. Or maybe Gabriel could help? He was too broody, though. Perhaps if she made him laugh somehow. She hoped it didn't come to that. She didn't even know how to make the amazingly gorgeous angel smirk.

She didn't want to think about that now. She tried to think happy thoughts and get this book opened.

She laid the book beside her and plopped back on the bed. She began to think of all the joyous times in her life. She thought about the first car her dad bought her. It was a baby blue Chevrolet Beretta. It wasn't particularly fancy, but she was so proud her dad had given her something. She was one of the first of her friends to have a car. She thought about her time with her friends, singing loudly with the windows down. It had given her a sense of freedom.

She thought about when she met Runar. The memory threatened to make her sad, but she realized she didn't want his memory to be tainted by her sadness. Their memories together should bring her happiness, not pain. So she remembered the moment she saw him. She was in the auditorium at a local church. They weren't close by, and she was about to go on stage to make the announcements. As she walked up the steps, she saw him in the crowd. Their eyes met, and the world fell away. She knew he was the one at that moment. Somehow, from 100 feet away, she could sense he felt the same. She remembered being disappointed she would probably never meet him. Then, after the service, she met up with a friend who told her about the friend she needed to meet. Then, the love of her life turned around. They were inseparable from that moment.

She thought about the moment Lani was born and how much joy that bundle brought to their lives. She thought about the baby giggles and smiles and how bright that little girl was.

A single tear born of happiness slipped from Alle's eye. She wiped it away with a smile. She picked up the book, smearing the wetness across the cover. The edges shimmered slightly, and then it fell open.

Alle sat up immediately. The book was open. She was never shutting it again. She flipped through the pages. It was written in an angelic language she was able to read. She decided not to question her ability to read a heavenly language. It was close to the Latin she learned in high school and possibly Sanskrit, counting her blessing for now. An examination of how she knew could happen later. There was no time to think about it now.

She flipped the pages, realizing this book was part diary and part angelic journal. Whoever had written it had documented their accounts of specific days and times but also included drawings and diagrams of places and artifacts. She flipped through the book as gently as possible since the paper felt ancient. Her eyes snagged on a familiar word. Nephilim. Specifically, the Nephilim prophecy.

She read through the page. There was no specific definition of Nephilim. The prophecy said the Nephilim would break down the gates of hell. She didn't know how that would apply to her or Lani. Neither of them was Nephilim, so she read on.

She continued to skim the pages. She got caught up in a story about an irrelevant angel war and the prince of Persia. She realized after page six the prince was actually a demon prince controlling the human prince. Realizing she needed to move on, she skimmed through a few more.

Then, she came across the fountain of Siloam. She remembered that the pool of Siloam was in the Bible. In the New Testament, during the time of Jesus. The pool of Siloam was used for ritual bathing.

This was a little different. The drawing depicted a fountain with a pool at the bottom, similar to the fountains she had pitched pennies in and made wishes as a child. The explanation said the pool was helpful in revelation.

She hopped up from the bed, carefully keeping the book open and her finger on the right page. She hurried out the door to find Gabriel. After a quick search, she found him on the green couches he favored.

"Gabriel, I found something," she said, descending the stairs.

Gabriel lifted his head. Had he been sleeping? She loved he finally smiled at her again. The flutters had returned to her belly. The ones she was actively trying to ignore.

He was now wearing a shirt. A faded grey t-shirt, which was still too tight to hide his amazing angel physique, but at least he had honored her request and was slightly more covered.

"You figured out how to open the book!" He met her at the bottom of the steps.

"What?" She shook the inappropriate thoughts away. "Oh yes. That seems like ages ago. Was it a long time?"

"No, not all that long. You've been in your room for about eight hours natural time."

"Eight hours! It seemed like no time at all."

Gabriel just nodded. "Remember, time is not relevant here. You won't age; as soon as Lani wakes, we can return to the moment we left. Although we would pick a safer location."

"Yes, right. Ok." Alle walked over to the couches now with Gabriel trailing her.

"How did you open the book?" Gabriel asked.

"Oh! I just thought happy thoughts about times in my life. When I met Runar and Lani was born, I'm unsure if it was thoughts or the happy tears I accidentally wiped on the cover."

"I see," Gabriel shrugged. "It could be either."

"If the book closes again, I will experiment. Hopefully, I won't need to. I'll try to keep it open."

"Good plan. What did you find?" He gestured to the couch. Alle walked in front of him and sat on the green couch. She turned her knees to face him as he sat, ready to listen.

"Do you know what the fountain of Siloam is?" Alle asked, assuming he would have known.

"No. Unfortunately, I am not all-knowing, as I've said." In an instant, Gabriel was back to his default brooding self.

"Right. Add that to the list." Alle made a check mark motion with her hands.

"I have, of course, heard of the pool of Siloam in Jerusalem."

Alle sat and leaned forward, carefully leaving a couple of inches between them. She could feel the warmth from his leg even from this distance and wanted to lean into his body. Restraining herself, she placed the book between them.

"Look at this." Alle pointed to the page with the fountain.

He moved his arm behind her and braced his body on the back of the couch to get a closer look. His smell wrapped around her, and she felt a pang of familiarity. It was like snuggling on the sofa with Runar. It very much felt like a betrayal to him, so she leaned away. If Gabriel noticed, he didn't show it.

"It says the fountain of Siloam provides revelation. Perhaps that could help me understand what is happening to Lani or with the demon attacks ?" Alle explained.

Gabriel nodded. "It sounds helpful. Maybe the elders can help us find it. We'll leave immediately." He stood and pulled her to her feet.

Alle dug in her heels. "Whoa. I wasn't expecting us just to go traipsing around the veil to find the elders." She ran her fingers through her tangled hair. "I need to freshen up a bit. Then we can go."

"You don't need to." He turned again toward the door as if that solved all her problems.

"Gabriel, trust me, I want to get going too. I'm excited to get this information, but I'm human. I have things I need to do. Even beyond the veil where time stands still." She winked and pointed to a nearby column. "You go lean against that post and look handsome. I'll be back down in two shakes of a lamb's tail."

Alle grabbed the book, carefully kept it open, and ran up the stairs again. *At least I'm getting my cardio in today,* she thought, taking the steps two at a time. She jumped in the shower and ran through everything she knew in her head. This was where she did her best, thinking and processing things she didn't have time or energy for during the day.

So, I'm the target of demons. Lani was caught in the crossfire. Gabriel and Adriel are our guardians. They're powered up by positive human emotions, which also helped open the book. I still didn't know why any of this was happening, but the fountain is the key to finding out.

She stepped out of the shower. As she was drying off, she noticed her prescription medicine bottle on the counter. Adriel must have delivered it at some point. She hadn't seen her come or go. Alle got lost in her thoughts, trying to remember where she had seen the angel before. To anyone watching her, it probably looked like she was in a trance. It happened when she hadn't taken her medicine in a while.

Adriel had said she was Lani's teacher, but it felt like there was more to it than that. She just couldn't quite put her finger on it. Finally, she grabbed the brown bottle and downed one of the little purple pills. Her body would not have an immediate response, but it would stave off the impending brain lag if she didn't have it. And more than anything, she needed her brain right now.

She dressed and found a sling bag in the wardrobe. She needed to carry the book with her. Unfortunately, she would have to close it, but she felt relatively positive she could reopen it if it locked again. She stuffed a set of clothes in as well. Gabriel had said they would see the elders and then perhaps to the fountain, but this felt bigger. She wanted to be able to stay gone for longer if they needed to. She always liked to be prepared for whatever might come. She knew all too well that life could hit upside the head like a runaway bullet train.

When she was ready, she headed down to where Gabriel was waiting. She saw him leaning the way she had suggested, and for a moment, she was back home. Life was perfect and happy. It was Runar leaning against the pillar, waiting for her to leave their room. His easy smile was just for her. His blue eyes lit up when she entered the room. She shook her head, and the vision was gone. Gabriel stood before her.

"Alle, are you ok? You look like you might have seen a ghost."

Alle clutched a nearby chair and looked at the floor to get her baring. "Is he here?" she asked.

"The elders? No, we have to go to them, remember?"

"Not the elders." She looked up with a spark of hope. "Runar. Is Runar here?"

Gabriel stood straighter, realizing what Alle was asking, "You can't see him right now, Alle."

Alle's shoulders slumped again. "But he's here. Does he want to see me?"

Gabriel stepped closer to her. "It's complicated. You are beyond the veil, but barely. We can't go to where he is right now."

She held up a hand to reassure the angel. "I'm fine, Gabriel. I'm not going to try to escape to see him. I just... You just reminded me of him just now. I remembered he would be here." She put her hand on Gabriel's forearm as he reached to comfort her. "No, let's just go see these elders."

Gabriel dropped his arm, and his face returned to its normal furrowed state. He stepped toward the door. "Of course, let's go."

Alle nodded, rested her hand lightly on his elbow, and followed him through the door and into the Hall.

At first, nothing happened. "Is the door broken?"

"I don't know. I've never had this happen before." His eyebrows scrunched together.

"That is not at all comforting," she said under her breath.

"The only ones who can override the doors are the elders and the Most High. Let's hope it's the elders this time."

"What about the library? Maybe it doesn't want us to leave."

"That could also be the case. Let's try starting over."

Alle shrugged. "It works for almost everything else."

Just as Gabriel reached for the handle, everything around them started swirling. A loud ringing sounded in her ears, and it felt like they were falling. Gabriel grabbed her around the waist and held her close to his chest. Protecting her, she realized. Pulling her tighter, he whipped out his wings. He whispered, "Did you take anything from the warehouse?"

She nodded slightly, unable to focus on anything but the ringing in her ears.

Finally, the swirling stopped, and they landed hard on a marble surface. "Give me the book. I'll see if I can fix this." Gabriel released her, folded his wings away, and held out his hand.

Although she was sad to see it go, Alle pulled the blue book out of the messenger bag and handed it over. As she did, the room came into focus.

Twelve men sat on thrones around her. The room was stark white again. No sparkles this time. Fog and mist swirled about the thrones, and they seemed to be walking on a cloud. *We are certainly not in Kansas anymore,* Alle thought.

The men wore white robes. She guessed they were not angels. They seemed to vary in age, while all the angels appeared to be the same age. Some of the men appeared older with long white beards and balding heads. Some were much younger, maybe in their early twenties. They all looked regal and wise. None of them smiled. She felt exposed under their intense stares. Alle wanted to hide behind Gabriel, but she stood her ground and held her head high.

"Alle Venega, we've been waiting for your visit." The oldest-looking man spoke.

"I wish I could say the same, but I don't know who you are," Alle said irreverently. She never did well in tense situations. She tended to lose her manners and her filter.

"Alle... do not offend the elders; we need their help," Gabriel growled under his breath.

"No offense has been made, Gabriel," the elder with the long white beard said. "We have never met, but you do know us. We are the elders mentioned in revelation."

"Oh," Alle gasped, surprised. No one knew who the elders were. Many theological debates on the internet did not settle the question either. She would be willing to bet that at least a few were the apostles, leaders of the early church. And she was standing before them.

Gabriel cleared his throat as Alle looked at each of their faces, trying to guess who was who. "We have the book. Alle didn't know she shouldn't take it from the warehouse. No harm was done." He reached forward to offer it to them.

One of the elders smiled wisely and waved his hand. "We both know that this book is hers. We did not bring you here for a library fine," he said.

Alle let out a breath of relief. She almost wiped imaginary sweat off her brow but managed to restrain herself. *Who knew elders had jokes?* Alle's inner monologue was running full tilt.

"We wanted to meet Alle in person and encourage her on her journey. We've been waiting for you to emerge from the warehouse."

Gabriel handed the book back to Alle, and she carefully placed it back in her bag. She felt encouraged to speak then. "We emerged to come and visit with you." She felt Gabriel tense beside her. She had no idea what had him on edge. The elders didn't seem to be a threat to either of them. "We would like information on the fountain of Siloam."

They looked between themselves, nodding and grunting in agreement. "We will help you in any way we can." The oldest of the men voiced their consensus.

Gabriel spoke up then. "We were hoping to visit the fountain to gain guidance in the journey you spoke of."

Another elder spoke up. One that had remained quiet until this point. He did not appear old or young. All the elders looked smudged like someone had taken an eraser and smoothed out their wrinkles. It gave them a dreamy, glowing quality. "The fountain is here. Beyond the veil. You can use the doors to navigate to it, but it would be best if an elder who has seen the fountain went with you."

"Yes, of course, we would love to have the wisdom of the elders as our guide." Gabriel was so proper and knew exactly what to say in this situation.

"I will tend to young Alle and Gabriel," an older elder with a short beard and balding head said. He stood from his throne and walked toward them.

"Please let us know if we can help you in any other way. Gabriel knows how to contact us," the middle-aged elder said.

"Thank you," Gabriel and Alle spoke in tandem.

The three of them walked back toward a door. "Have you ever been to the fountain of Siloam?" Gabriel asked.

"Oh yes, once. But it was long ago. This door should take us directly to the fountain."

Alle wrapped an arm around her suddenly aching stomach. She grimaced, but thankfully, neither the angel nor the elder seemed to notice. With answers so close, anxiety threatened to cripple her.

Alle grabbed Gabriel's hand, needing more than just an elbow touch. She wanted to make sure she wasn't going to get lost. His warm hand helped to steady her nerves. As the three of them stepped through the door, she noticed the elder was not touching either of them. He had a sweet smile on his face. She thought she saw him give a little wave.

They emerged into another beautiful white room. The middle of the floor was padded with a wooden path around the edge. There was equipment in the middle similar to what Alle used to pass on her walks in the park. The walls were lined with weapons and armor.

"Gabriel, this doesn't look like a fountain, and where did the elder go?"

Gabriel turned quickly to try to go back through the door, but the door had disappeared. "No, no, no, no." He slammed his fist on the wall.

"Gabriel? What's wrong."

He turned toward her and glared. "This isn't the fountain. I don't know where the fountain is. I have never been to the fountain, which is why we need an elder who has been there."

"Right, so we would be in the right place when we went through the doors."

"Except the elder did not touch me as we went through the door. I didn't think about it then because I don't usually need to touch someone else to get to where I'm going."

"The elder is at the fountain, and we wound up here?"

"Yes. I must have been thinking of training."

"Gabriel, where are we?"

"The Gauntlet."

"Like in King Arthur?"

"Much, much worse than that."

Gabriel's defeated look was scaring Alle. He had never looked concerned for one second they had been together. But now he looked scared. "Ok? Can't we find another door?"

"There is no other door. The only way out is through."

Chapter Fourteen

Alle looked around at the equipment. Weapons and armor hung from the wall. Every space was utilized. An obstacle course stood in the middle of the room. She shrugged, "On the other hand. This looks kind of fun. I've always wanted to use that equipment at the park where I take Lani."

"Fun? I hope you can make it through because we could be stuck here for eternity if you can't."

"It seems like you are overreacting a little." She pointed to the equipment in the middle. "This doesn't look that hard."

Gabriel pursed his lips and tucked his chin to his chest. Alle watched him clench and relax his biceps and pectorals. He waved his arms toward the center of the room. "This is just training equipment. The Gauntlet will be the hardest obstacle course you can imagine."

Her face went slack. Gabriel's worried tone sobered her up. "Is there a human setting? I could maybe make it through then," she said with a slight quiver in her voice.

"I hope the Gauntlet will tone it down a little for you. Much like the library meets your expectations, the Gauntlet knows what you need. I'll have to teach as we go." He grabbed her shoulders and hunched down a bit to meet her eyes. "Ready?"

Alle nodded and gave him a weak smile. "As I'll ever be." She shook off the discouragement and started jogging in place to warm up.

Gabriel explained the task ahead as Alle stretched her arms across her chest. "Ok. The Gauntlet is made up of three parts. Physical, which is running, climbing, and weaponry." He took a breath to continue, but Alle interrupted by raising her hand.

He dismissed her gesture. "This isn't a schoolyard. Just ask your questions."

"I'm just wondering why angels have to climb and run when they have wings." She balanced on one foot while she pulled the other behind her, stretching her quads.

Gabriel watched her incredulously with arms crossed over his chest. "Not all angels have wings, and we can't always use our wings. We use them when we can, but we don't want to rely solely on them. It could be a liability."

Happy with that explanation, Alle nodded for him to continue.

"After the physical training, the room will shift to the mental portion. We will have to solve a riddle or puzzle. It will be at least as difficult as opening the book."

Alle rolled her eyes. It took her hours to open the book. Well, what felt like hours.

"Don't worry. We're a team. We can help each other." He waited until he thought she was prepared to explain the last part. "The last part will be the trickiest. You will have to use spirit. I'll do my best to teach you what you need to know, but it will be difficult if you can't even see the veil."

"I'm here, though. Shouldn't I be able to see beyond the veil now?"

"You've been doing great with direct interaction. But the veil is in the peripheral." He shook his head and waved a hand. "We'll worry about that when we get there. The good thing is, if we fail in one room, we go back to the beginning of that room, not back to the beginning of the Gauntlet, and there is no time limit."

"True, that would suck to have to start all over. But I know how that feels. Have you ever typed a twelve-page paper for a hard-headed college professor only to have it mysteriously deleted the day before it was due?" Alle rambled nervously.

Gabriel crossed his arms and glowered.

"I know it doesn't seem like the same thing, but it is. It is." She patted his arm and added, "So, where do we start?"

"We start with a lesson in weaponry." He called the sword from his arm by flicking his wrist. It lit up in a blaze, but the flames quickly died down. "You are human, so you won't be able to call the weapons. You will fight the same as fledgling angels do. Everyone has to earn their weapons. No one awards them. They appear when they are needed. Fledglings have no weapons, so they must carry them. We have a few to choose from and armor to make it easier. You won't use weapons at first, but you will need them at the end of the first room, so you must make it through the obstacles with weapons intact. Pick something maneuverable and lightweight, like a sword, daggers, or maybe an ax."

She perused the weapons adorning the walls. Laughing at the fact that Gabriel said a few. *A few hundred more like,* she thought. She didn't see anything that particularly called to her. She never wanted a weapon, nor did she need one until recently. She had some experience with pistols and bows, but blades weren't something she had considered needing to learn to use in the 21st century. She picked up a small, sharp sword that looked like she could stab someone from a distance with it. Gabriel picked a lightweight suit for her. It was black leather, corsetted, and made to fit an adult female. The leather was soft and supple. She ran her hand over it as Gabriel fastened the gold rivets up her torso over her t-shirt. "What is this made of?" she asked.

"Lamb's skin. Of course," he said as if that was the dumbest question she could ask.

"Oh, of course," she mimicked.

"If we make it through this in one round. I'll let you keep it." He didn't make eye contact, and she wasn't even sure if that had been a joke or if he would let her have it.

"I'm not sure why I need leather armor after this, but it is nice."

Gabriel grimaced and didn't argue with her claim that she would need it.

"This fits like it was made for me," she mused. Gabriel remained silent as he tightened the armor around her.

He handed her the two forearm guards. She pulled them up and held her hand out for him to tighten them. A sense of deja vu hit Alle hard. She remembered doing this exact thing before.

"Gabriel, have we done this before?"

"This exactly? No."

"But you said there are many times I've come in contact with the spiritual? Are you sure I've never attempted to complete this Gauntlet before?

"You've never accidentally ended up in the Gauntlet room," He said while he pulled the laces tight and tucked in the knot.

Alle noticed how careful Gabriel was with his words. She decided to let it go and add that to her list to worry about another time.

The armor had a flexible built-in compartment for the sword in the back. Gabriel explained that if it were rigid, her arm would need to be much longer to get the sword out of the sheath.

"Move around and see how it feels."

Alle bent to the left and right and made a circle with her upper body. She gave Gabriel a thumbs up. "Fits like an old glove."

He nodded in reply.

As soon as she was suited up, the room changed. It went from the unassuming training room they had entered to an episode of Ninja Warrior she had seen on late-night television. A very daunting obstacle course was before her.

Alle backed up to the wall. "I cannot do this. What happened to the easy exercise equipment? No wonder you were freaking out."

Gabriel was by her side. "You have to do this. You can. You will."

After a few seconds, she looked him in the eye. His intensity and his belief in her gave her courage, and she nodded.

She examined the course. The first obstacle seemed easy. Just slanted plywood spaced apart, she had to jump quickly from one to another to make it through. She yelled and jumped through the path before she could talk herself out of it further. She made it to the landing with relative ease. Gabriel was right behind her, practically floating over the obstacles. The landing was marginally big enough for the two of them, and his chest pressed up against her back. She barely had time to think about the contact as she assessed the next obstacle. Gabriel had said there was no time limit, but she felt pressure all the same. She did not want to be stuck here when she could get answers and wake Lani.

A track was attached to the top of the next obstacle. There was an upside-down bicycle attached. Alle would have to leap and then hand-crank her way across. "Seriously, do y'all watch American television or something? And is every obstacle better suited to male upper body strength?"

"Stop complaining, or you're out. Also, if you fall, we start over." Worry tinged his words, but he sounded as if he was starting to have a bit of fun.

"No pressure," she grumbled.

Gabriel grabbed her around the waist, and she yelped. "Sorry. I can help you remember. I just can't do the obstacles for you." He didn't even grunt when he lifted her.

Alle relaxed. "Ok. Thanks for the lift." Once she grabbed the handrails, she got in a rhythm of turning the pedals. She made it across easily, but her arms felt like jello by the time she reached the other side. She wasn't sure she could make it through if other obstacles required upper body strength.

She watched Gabriel make it across in the two seconds, then put her hand on her hip and glared. He didn't even smirk. Alle bumped him with her hip. "Show off." She huffed, trying to keep the mood light. Inwardly, she was worried, which was typical when she didn't know what was coming. She turned to see what she had to do next.

Alle groaned. It wasn't that she couldn't do it. She probably could have, with fresh arms and four or five years of training. "This… is too much," she said, trembling with fatigue and shaking her head. She backed away and almost fell off the platform. Gabriel placed his hand on her back and leaned close to her ear.

"You can do this, and you must if you want to get to the fountain and find a way to save Lani," he whispered.

Alle nodded her head as she peered up at the glass tower. The tower had holes in the walls. The holes were randomly spaced so that pegs could be inserted, and the climber could use them to maneuver to the top. Two pegs lay on the floor at the bottom. To make it an even lovelier time, water streamed down all sides. Without the water, she could have braced herself with her feet as she moved the pegs. The water would make it too slippery to use her feet at all. And would make it even harder to hold on to the pegs with her hands.

"Ok. I think I have an idea. Any rules for this one?"

"Just make it to the top. Harness in and zip line to the next platform. No rules on how to get to the top, except no wings. If you fall, we go all the way back to the beginning, making this even harder. So don't fall." Gabriel coached with an emphasis on the last two words.

"Right. That's one good thing. I don't have wings, so there is no temptation to cheat on this one. Let's get started." She stood at the bottom and immediately let the water soak through her clothes. She placed one peg in the first set of holes and placed the second peg just slightly higher. Using the slippery wall as leverage, she pulled herself up and put her knee on the first peg. She moved one peg up and then pulled the lower peg and moved it up. It was slow. Painfully slow. Her knees and shins were smattered with bruises.

The water ran faster and harder as she reached the top of the tower. She could feel the cool air from the top of the tower. She was just a few feet from her goal. She pulled the lower peg to move it up one more time. As she did, the rushing water pushed the peg out of her hand, and she dropped it. She could hear the tink, tink, tink as it hit the bottom. She knelt on one peg with the end in sight.

Minutes ticked by as she weighed her options. She could jump for it, but it seemed too far. She decided the space was small enough to brace her backside against one side and walk her feet the rest of the way up. She used her remaining peg as a backup so that if she slipped, she wouldn't fall all the way down. Inch by inch, she made her way to the top of the tower. Her triceps burned as she pulled one arm over the edge. Then a leg. Finally, she hauled her body over. She felt the victory of the moment. Making it to the top was a feat.

She looked down at her sopping clothes. Her leather armor was utterly ruined. She hadn't even needed it yet, which caused dread to form a ball in the pit of her stomach. She didn't think Gabriel would give her armor she didn't need. *What could possibly be after this?*

Her arms and legs shook with fatigue and hypothermia. After stepping through the harness, she pulled it to her waist. She barely had enough strength in her fingers to tighten the straps of the zip line. The shivering made it even worse. But as she launched herself over the edge, she felt freedom and accomplishment. She could do anything if she could reach the top of that tower.

She landed and had barely stepped out of the harness before Gabriel barged his way to her. She rolled her eyes. He had done this a million times, or it was easy for him because they had played it down for the human. Either way, it was annoying.

As he landed, he said, "I'm going first on the next one. That was torturous."

"Hey, I made it to the top and didn't fall."

"Well, let's just be glad you aren't competing in that television show. Your time would never win."

"Let's just be glad that time stands still here. Be my guest if you want to do the next obstacle first." She gestured for him to go around her.

He gave a little bow. "Thank you."

Gabriel surveyed the next obstacle, "This will work great. I'm going to help you with this one." Alle looked where he was pointing. A wall stood before her. Just a wall. She almost breathed a sigh of relief until she realized it was fifteen feet tall, more than twice the height of the angel, curved inward and smooth as glass. "As soon as I make it up, you run and jump as high as possible. I'll grab your hand and pull you up."

Alle nodded, hoping that would work.

"Don't worry. You get as many attempts at this as you need. If you fall, you don't have to return to the beginning."

"Great! I've reached the Mario halfway mark. Do I grow bigger?"

Gabriel gave her a questioning look.

She squinted back at him. "You know the obstacle course show, but not the greatest video game in history?" She shook her head at him and patted his upper arm. "Go ahead, I'll bubble." With a smirk, she stepped aside.

Gabriel took off running, jumped, and grabbed the top with the tip of his fingers. There was no way Alle would be able to pull that off. She shook her head. But he pulled himself up easily. Ugh. She didn't know if he had supernatural Angel strength or what, but it was so annoying he was amazingly good at everything. Her competitive streak was rearing its ugly head.

As soon as he was up and ready, she launched herself as fast as she could. She ran and jumped and missed his hands. She crashed to the ground and lay there for a few seconds before jogging back to the platform. Alle's fatigue was evident on her second attempt. She barely made it off the ground.

"Alle, we cannot be stuck at this one obstacle forever. We are almost done. Dig deep and find the energy to make it through. You can do this!"

Alle had made it back to the platform. She was tired. She wanted to curl up and sleep for days. She almost did. Then Lani's sweet baby face popped into her head, and she resolved to make it through this Gauntlet if only to see her daughter again. She took deep, steadying breaths and focused on putting every ounce of energy into reaching Gabriel's hand. She stepped off the platform and pumped her arms and legs harder than ever. She used the wall as a bounding wall and jumped higher with her arms outstretched. Gabriel finally grabbed hold of her wrist and pulled her up. She giggled with relief and took a minute to catch her breath at the top of the wall.

But they weren't finished yet. There was a reason she needed a weapon, and it stood before them. Black outstretched wings raised above them. A sharp talon at the apex of each. The wingspan was easily twenty feet. Thin lips curled back from razor-sharp teeth dripping with saliva. When the saliva hit the ground, a hissing smoke rose. Corded muscle bunched under charcoal grey skin and covered every appendage. There were six. Each appendage ended with claws the size of a human finger.

Alle froze, and Gabriel started yelling directions. Take out the appendages, don't let the saliva touch you (duh), and cut off its head to succeed. Leave the wings. They were a liability for the monster in the small space. It cut down on how well the beast could maneuver.

"But how am I supposed to get to the head? It's forty feet tall?"

"You aren't. I will take the head. You take the feet." With that, Gabriel unfurled his wings.

"I thought we couldn't use wings."

"If the monster has wings, we can use wings."

"Show off," Alle muttered again.

"Think positive, Alle. I can't fight you and the beast."

"I think you have the wrong human. I was born a Debbie Downer, you know."

The monster roared in front of them, impatient with their conversation. He took a swipe at Alle. She rolled away like she had done this a hundred times before. Alle grinned at herself.

Gabriel called his sword from his arm while Alle pulled hers from its sheath on her back. Her arms quivered, but she gave it her best. There was no time to worry about the pain in her body. Gabriel flew to the top of the monster while Alle ran toward the feet. It was more about her avoiding the monster's giant claws and dripping saliva, but she did manage to slice the monster a couple of times. It was probably like a paper cut, but the monster screamed in agony each time bright green goo poured out of the cut. A high-pitched freeze-your-blood scream. It reminded her of when babies hurt themselves. They freak out like it's the end of the world, but it's barely a scratch.

"Gabriel, is this a baby monster?" she asked.

"Little busy right now to worry about the age of this thing," He grunted. "But yah. Usually, these are twice this size full grown."

The beast screamed again. Alle covered her ears, lost her balance, and slipped in the green goo. One good thing was that it seemed to neutralize the acidic saliva. The beast froze as she thought about rolling around in the stuff. It fell to its knees and then to the ground with a loud *oomph*. The head of the beast landed next to it.

Alle's chest rapidly rose and fell as Gabriel landed beside her. After a few seconds, the monster flickered and disappeared. Even the green goo disappeared from Alle's clothes. Confusion clouded Alle's face before she collapsed into Gabriel's arms.

Chapter Fifteen

Alle's eyes fluttered open with a groan. She was so tired. More tired than she had ever felt before. She tried to move her pinky finger just a smidge to see how bearable the pain might be. It wasn't sustainable at all. Every single muscle she had was sore. It hurt to move anything. Gabriel, who had been pacing, was by her side instantly. "Alle, I'm so sorry. Are you ok?" He took her hand and kissed her knuckles.

The butterflies that were pretty much constant swarmed to hurricane levels in Alle's stomach. She sat up slowly. "I think so. Did we pass the gauntlet?"

Gabriel shook his head. Alle looked up quickly. "You mean we have to do all that again?"

"No, no. We still have two more rooms. That room is over. But the door to the hall has not appeared, so we have to keep going. Fortunately, this room, the puzzle room, had a cot, food, and water. I've just been waiting for you to wake up."

"How long was I out?"

"Long enough for me to start worrying. You were exhausted. I'm so sorry. I should have seen the signs, but we had to make it through without stopping, or we would have had to start all over. Going through the Gauntlet on fresh arms is difficult. Doing it fatigued is nearly impossible. We can begin the next round after you've eaten."

"Good. I can't think when I'm tired," she announced.

He pulled her up, and she hobbled to the table. It took a few steps before she could stand fully upright. To her surprise, the armor was still soft and supple. Not at all stiffened by the freezing water. She shrugged. *It must be magic.* She decided this was an excellent way to explain anything she didn't have the energy to try to understand.

She guzzled half a bottle of water before sitting it down. Gabriel watched her intently as she grazed on the nuts, fruits, and cheeses. Alle began to pepper him with questions to relieve the attention on her. "So I see you are not wearing a shirt again." She smiled. "Is that so you can pop out those beautiful golden wings."

"You think my wings are beautiful?" The angel blushed, actually blushed, and Alle thought she would die there.

"They are. I wish I knew how that worked," she replied instead.

"I will show you," he said as he moved closer so she could see the designs. "Angels are not created with wings but aren't earned either. They are bestowed after a time of trial and testing. It requires a great deal of trust in the Most High. And when that trust is given freely, we receive our wings." He showed Alle his bronzed muscular forearms. "It's the same with our weapons, although we have to earn those more with training. The light of the spirit creates them within us and sets the ink. The ink is infused with the spirit and linked with our soul. It is part of our being and cannot be taken away. Our wings and our weapons can only be given up freely. But it would be excruciating to cleave the spirit."

Gabriel turned to let her inspect the lines that covered his skin. Alle traced the wings with her eyes and reached up to trace them with her fingers. Gabriel tensed just as she was about to touch, and she froze. Her hand hung in the air. "Can I touch them?" He waited so long to answer that she was just about to drop her hand when he nodded, allowing her this intimacy.

Tracing the wings brought the intricate golden designs to life. The lines sparkled and moved under her touch as if they were a part of her as much as him. She had never seen anything like it. Gabriel clenched and relaxed his fist until she took her hand away. He rolled his shoulders and walked away without a word.

That was intense, she thought as she watched him pace on the other side of the room. She was sure he would have bolted if he could have left the room.

If she was honest, it stung a little bit. The butterflies always appeared when he smiled at her or during the momentary touches. But Gabriel walking away reminded her to protect her heart a little more. There would be no dating her guardian angel. This wasn't a TV show; it was real life. Human and angel courtships were definitely frowned upon in the bible. She thought for a second. *I'll have to look that up when we get out of here just to make sure.*

"You'll have to look what up?"

Alle's face instantly reddened. She hadn't realized Gabriel had returned. "Did I say that out loud?"

"I'm pretty sure. I can't read human minds," he said gruffly.

"Oh, whew." Alle swiped the imaginary sweat from her brow. "I was worried for a bit." Her hand landed on Gabriel's forearm, but she yanked it away quickly. "I was just having a conversation in my head, and it must have accidentally come out of my mouth." Alle shrugged. "It happens sometimes."

Gabriel nodded like it was common for people to have internal conversations. "You should eat."

"I thought that I wouldn't need to eat here." She grazed absently.

"Sometimes the human body doesn't fully accept that it doesn't have to eat to survive here. The veil adjusts to meet your needs and your expectations."

Silence fell between them as she ate and could finally think past her pain and her hunger. When she was satisfied, she clapped once loudly. "Alright, let's go solve a mystery!"

* * *

Alle found herself bouncing on the balls of her feet, ready for the next round.

"What is wrong? You seem nervous. I can't read you right now." The tough archangel Gabriel had returned and was back to his brooding. Apparently, Alle almost dying of exhaustion wasn't enough for happy Gabriel to stick around.

"I'm actually excited. And nervous. And happy." She could see why Gabriel wasn't getting a good gauge of her emotions. She was all over the place. "This is actually kind of like an escape room. And I love a good mystery."

She rubbed her hands together in giddiness.

"Escape room? That's a recent thing in the natural world. I don't understand why people purposely trap themselves in a room and have to solve riddles to get out." When Gabriel looked at Alle's pursed lips, he added, "For fun."

Alle sobered. "It's fun if it's not real, life and death on the line."

"Don't worry. This isn't life or death, just eternity."

"Ok. Rules?" Alle asked, refusing to let Gabriel's pervasive bad mood affect her.

"Solve the riddle and make it to the next room."

Alle cocked a hip and crossed her arms. "Those are instructions. What are the rules?"

"There are no rules."

"Ok, great." She said, rolling her eyes. She didn't like it when there were no rules. Chaos usually ensued. "How do we start?"

Gabriel raised an eyebrow. And by George, if Alle's knees didn't weaken slightly. "Now you want instructions?" he asked.

"Sarcasm is not becoming," Alle retorted.

He smiled back in response. Now that was becoming. "We start with the golden envelope." He pointed to the round table in the middle of the room. She went to retrieve the envelope. What she thought had been gold-colored paper was instead actual metal gold. Alle simultaneously wondered what was with all the gold in this place and wished she had envelopes like these for her wedding. A tinge of sadness forced its way into her heart at the thought of Runar. She carefully opened the riddle. There was one sentence on the linen paper inside.

"Until I am measured, I am not known. Yet, how you will miss me when I have flown."

"Seriously?" Alle huffed. "That's it?"

"You were expecting different?"

"Well, I was expecting something harder," she whined.

"Surely you realize the Gauntlet is very difficult."

She hung her thumb back. "Oh yeah, that was difficult." She jabbed her finger in the other direction. "I'm sure that will be difficult. But the difficulty level on this portion is lacking."

"Well, then, what is your answer?"

"Before I answer, how many tries do I get?"

"We can guess until we answer correctly."

"See, where is the fun in that?"

"Perhaps you are getting a pass here because you don't need the challenge? Let's not press our blessings."

"I think you have the idiom incorrect there. But it doesn't matter. I see your point." She lifted her chin and tapped her finger to her head to think about the riddle. "Any guesses?"

"I would like to hear what you have to say first."

"Oh? I get to go first?" she said with genuine excitement. "This is really simple. What is something that is both measured and flies?"

"Birds fly, insects, angels."

"Yes, yes. But although those things can be measured, the measurement does not reveal them to the world." She had begun pacing and paused to think aloud, "Gabriel, do you have clocks in the Hall?"

"Clocks? No. The Gauntlet is not timed."

"But I haven't seen a clock anywhere?"

"It would be impossible to use clocks here."

Alle smiled, as did Gabriel. "And why is that?"

"Because clocks measure time, and time does not exist here."

"But it would exist if you measured it."

"There is simply nothing to measure time by. No day or night. This place exists outside the realm of time. Which is great, but time does not have wings; it cannot fly."

"Have you heard the phrase, 'Time flies when you're having fun?'"

"Yes, it is said quite often in the natural..." Gabriel formed his lips into a silent O. He smirked and nodded. He pointed to her to answer.

"The answer is Time."

The room began to rotate as soon as the answer spilled from her mouth. All the furniture disappeared. When the spinning stopped, they stood in the middle of the round room. There was nothing but concave white walls, a white floor, and a ceiling. She had somehow ended up under Gabriel's protective arm. Again.

"Well done." His eyes lit up, but the lines on his face were all business. Alle smiled back at him. She loved the praises he showered on her and found herself wanting to make him proud just to hear them.

"On to the next and final challenge. Possibly the hardest."

"Hardest. You were there when I literally almost died from exhaustion, right?"

"This is different. This is the last room. And this is the spirit room."

"Ok. How do we get out of the spirit room?"

"We have to pull back the veil."

"Super easy. You do that all the time."

"Not this time. We must do this together, or you must do it yourself."

"How do you know?"

"Because this is not my Gauntlet. It is yours. If I do it, we fail. Or I get to move on and leave you behind. Neither option is acceptable."

Alle sunk to the floor in defeat. "That will be difficult, considering I can't see the veil or beyond the veil. I can't see demons or angels or any of that. If I could see, I wouldn't be here in the first place because I would have prevented a demon from attacking Lani."

Gabriel knelt beside her. "I know." He didn't point out that she could see some of those things. He wanted Alle to discover for herself just what she could do.

"That doesn't help."

"I know that also."

"Then why say it?"

"Well, you were stating the obvious. So, I thought I would join you."

Alle buried her hand in her face. "We are going to be stuck here forever."

Gabriel sat and lounged back on his elbows. "Yep."

Alle whipped her head up. Gabriel just shrugged. "We will be stuck here if you can't pull back the veil. You are good at stating the obvious."

Alle took a deep breath, willing herself to try. "Ok. What do I have to do?"

"Nothing."

"Nothing? I mean, don't I have to hold my hands like this." She formed her hand like she was getting ready to karate chop a board.

"That's my method. It doesn't have to be yours. It helps me focus, though. There is usually chaos when the veil is being opened, and I have to be able to block out the chaos." Gabriel leaned forward and gently touched her temple. His piercing eyes met hers and probed. "You must find a way to settle the chaos here."

"The chaos in there is not my doing."

"It usually isn't." Gabriel moved away then and laid on his back, letting Alle figure out what to do next. He napped while Alle sat in silence. He slept while she meditated. He cracked an eye open when she started doing yoga poses, then quickly adjusted his arm behind his head and returned to napping.

Alle nudged him in the ribs with her toe. Suddenly, she was on her back with the angel leaning over her. Murder on his face.

"Ticklish, are you?" Alle chanced a smile.

It didn't do much to ease the seething anger etched on Gabriel's face, but he took two more breaths and moved away from her. "Sorry, sometimes I wake up, and I'm unsure where I am. You startled me," he said with his head bowed.

Alle sat up. "No worries. My dad is the same. I didn't realize you were really asleep or that angels could be traumatized."

"I've seen much in my long years. I've fought many battles. My trauma is innate."

They sat silently for a little while, Alle staring at the white wall and Gabriel staring at his feet. "I think I'm ready," she said.

Gabriel's lips lifted at the corners. That was all he needed. She didn't have to do all of it herself. He just needed her to be ready to try.

"Ok. Stand up," he commanded. "We don't have to open it fully. We will be exposed to the natural world, and opening for even a fraction of a second will allow humans and demons to see you."

"Right, that could be bad."

"Don't worry about that now. We're just opening a sliver. It won't hurt anything."

Alle blew out a breath. Gabriel took her hand and guided her in front of him. "Close your eyes and block everything else out."

She did as he said.

He guided her arm up and rotated it into position. "Keep your eyes closed and imagine a curtain in front of you."

Gabriel's smoky Christmas aroma swirled around her, and she inhaled deeply. The hair on her arm stuck up in response to his touch. She found herself leaning into his warmth and his scent. She noticed that Gabriel didn't move away and may have even inclined a tiny fraction toward her.

"Concentrate," he grumbled.

Alle shook her head and focused back on the task at hand. She cleared her mind of everything. Gabriel was near her, touching her arm and a place on her back. But that faded away as she focused on the space around her. "You cannot see the veil by looking straight at it. It will always be in your peripheral vision." Gabriel continued murmuring instructions and directions. "If you can feel the veil, it is even better." After a few seconds, he whispered, "You have the power to pull back the veil. You just have to believe the veil is there, and you can move it. Infuse belief with power, and the veil will part. What is unseen will be seen." His breath tickled her ear. As he said the words, she could feel the magic at her fingertips like a sheer silk curtain floating over them. Her breath hitched.

"Good, you've found it." Gabriel's words were a gentle caress. "Now, just push your energy through your fingertips. This will cut the veil." When she tensed, he added, "Don't worry. It will heal itself when you pull back your energy."

Alle tried for several minutes. Gabriel patiently held her arm and waited for her to find her way. He was practically wrapped around her now. Giving his support and guiding her with small movements. When Alle was about to give up, he whispered to her again, "It's okay. Just keep your hand in the veil. We'll do this together."

Alle could feel the warm pulse of his energy. It crawled down her arm to her wrist, then to her fingers. When it reached the tip of her finger, Gabriel wrapped his fingers around her wrist. Gently, he guided her hand down through the air. Not as far as he had when he brought them all through the first time.

"Open your eyes."

His words caressed her cheek, and she did as she was told. She could see through the opening they had created. It wasn't fully open. It looked as if she was looking through a screen door. She could see her house in the far distance. Everything looked normal except that it was completely dark. She breathed a sigh of relief it hadn't been totally ransacked or burned to the ground. Gabriel pulled back his energy. Alle immediately felt its loss. As the veil began to seal itself back, movement caught her eye. A shadow on her front porch. The veil fully closed before she could tell who or what it was.

Gabriel rested his chin on her shoulder. "You did it." She twisted in his arms. To her surprise, he let her.

"We did it!" She smiled. "I couldn't have done that without you." Before either of them could change their minds, she closed the gap between their lips. He pulled her close and groaned as her lips parted. Their tongues met in a soft caress. Her fingers wound their way through his perfect hair.

Alle's stomach shot to her throat. Everything around them fell away. She was no longer kissing Gabriel, the archangel and her guardian. She was kissing Runar. He felt and tasted just the same. Joy sparked through her. She broke the kiss and opened her eyes. The illusion ended. It wasn't Runar wrapped in her arms.

She pushed away then. "I'm sorry. I shouldn't have done that."

"Alle, I need to tell you…." His words were cut off when the room shook and changed. The door appeared before them. Alle grabbed his hand and rushed to their freedom. Neither wanted to be trapped in the Gauntlet room for another second. They stepped through the door together.

Chapter Sixteen

Alle and Gabriel ended up in the cafeteria she had seen on the way to the library when they first arrived. This was better than the fountain. There wasn't anyone else around. It was like they were closed for the night or something. She knew that couldn't be right since there wasn't day and night. But she guessed there had to be some sort of schedule.

On each side of the cafeteria, there were glass cases. The cases would light up as she walked past each one, like the grocery store freezer section.

She looked longingly at the ready-to-eat salads and full platters of what looked like a brisket barbecue plate. She had thought earlier that meat wasn't served here, but she might have been wrong.

"Alle, we don't have time to eat. We need to get to the fountain."

"You said time doesn't exist here."

"You said you wanted to get this show on the road."

"You're right. I did say that, but we're here. I'm famished and exhausted. I know I'm not supposed to need to eat. But my body hasn't gotten the message. We should eat. Right? You never know when we might have another chance."

Gabriel paused at her logic, then gave in to her demands. She jumped and giggled like a little girl as he walked back toward her. The euphoria from completing the almost impossible task clung to her. Then, she started choosing foods to eat. Surprisingly, they had all her favorites. Gabriel didn't select anything. They found a table and sat across from each other. Alle spoke between bites of food. She did everything she could to avoid the topic

128

of their kiss. That was done and over with. It was out of her system, and she could move on. She wasn't sure what he was about to say before the door opened. She didn't know if she wanted to know. She knew that when Lani woke up, things would return to normal, and she wouldn't see Gabriel again unless she was in trouble. She knew from the past year and a half that even though she could get through the loss, she didn't want to go through it again.

Alle ate all her favorites and didn't even feel guilty about it. Surely, the once on the lips, forever on the hips rule didn't apply here beyond the veil. Where humans didn't age and time stood still. No weight gain and tight pants here. After she finished her main course, she even had some of the most delicious cherry cobblers ever created. She cleared her plate and signaled for Gabriel to commence down the hall.

They quickly found a door. Alle grabbed Gabriel's little finger and stepped through with him. When the flash of light that always accompanied the transition faded, she opened her eyes to a beautiful garden. She dropped Gabriel's hand immediately and looked around in awe.

Enormous willow trees stood around the green space. The wispy branches gave the area an ethereal quality. Flowers of every color imaginable and some unimaginable lined the paths. Small bushes crowded behind comfy benches and gave the feeling of privacy to whoever might be sitting. In the background, she could hear the babbling of water. The air was cool on her skin. It was the perfect place of peace. She wanted to roll in the carefully maintained grass or sit and read on one of those benches. This was quickly her second favorite place she had visited so far.

Gabriel led her deeper into the Garden, where the sound of water was louder. It sounded more like rushing water. It thundered around her and drowned out all the sounds of birds and scurrying animals.

"If there were a garden of Eden, it would look like this!" she said. Gabriel raised his eyebrows. Alle almost swallowed her tongue. "Wait, this is the Garden of Eden!"

"Yes, though all the problem trees have been moved to safer locations. They are guarded by the type of angels you never want to meet."

"Well, that explains why I, a human and descendant of Adam and Eve, have been allowed to enter." She still looked around in awe of the colors. She heard a roar in the distance, which sent her scurrying to Gabriel's side.

His lips pulled back into a warm smile. "No need to worry. The animals here don't eat humans," Gabriel whispered down to her.

Alle stood up straight and put her worries aside. Strutting like she hadn't been scared at all and bobbing her head, "Ok, ok," she added. "Is the fountain here in the garden?"

Gabriel closed his eyes. "I don't remember seeing the fountain before. I just thought this would be a good place to start looking. The Garden has many fountains since it's surrounded by rivers."

"I don't think rivers supply the fountain of Siloam, though. The book said it was created with tears of suffering. Is there a river here named Suffering?"

Gabriel shook his head, "It could be figurative."

"I don't know. It talked about the Spirit collecting the tears."

"We'll just take a look around and see what we can find. If we don't find it here, we'll go back to the library and try to get more information."

"That sounds like a great plan. Lead the way." She motioned for him to go forward.

Gabriel smirked and began walking again. Alle kept close by his side in case any unfriendly lions lurked around the corner. As a human, she didn't trust that they wouldn't eat her, even if Gabriel assured her they didn't.

The trail became more rugged and eventually turned to sand and gravel. This part of the Garden was less maintained and a bit wilder. The undergrowth filled in spaces between trees. The ground couldn't be seen for all the bright green vegetation. Except for the path they were walking on, Alle wouldn't have known there was soil at all.

Alle noticed there was no death here. Leaves didn't litter the ground. There were no dead branches or tree trunks. In the natural world, everything was a cycle. Death supplied life. She didn't understand how it worked here. There must be another mechanism.

They walked a bit further through the Garden's forest. Gabriel cleared a branch and held it back for her to walk through ahead of him. If he wanted to see her face when she saw what was ahead, he was not disappointed. The castle ruins were barely noticeable, but Alle's face lifted, and her eyes filled with wonder. Gabriel grinned, but Alle was too busy running to the ruins to notice.

Moss covered the gray stones. The turrets had caved in, leaving gaping holes in the roof. Ivy had overgrown the high walls. It was a large castle, and most of it had fallen. Stones piled on top of each other as evidence of age. It seemed that living things didn't die, but they would reclaim the unnatural. Alle longed to climb the tower. "Is it safe?" she asked, inching closer to the opening she found where a door leaned off its hinges.

Gabriel nodded and showed his back slightly. "Wings, remember? If you fall, I'll catch you. Always."

Alle caught her breath, but she nodded and started climbing the spiral stone steps.

At the top, she looked out through a crumbling window. The tower was above the canopy, and she could see the four corners of the Garden. Rivers surrounded the Garden, but it was impossible to see beyond that. Mists blocked the view. She didn't know if anything was living in the mists, but exploring would be spooky and exciting. Maybe Gabriel would bring her back when this was over. If she ever saw him again. She didn't want to allow herself to hope.

Looking over the Garden, she felt Gabriel's warmth behind her. His Christmas pine scent wrapped her in peace and comfort. The tension in her shoulders loosened, and she rolled her neck. Somehow, it was comforting to know he always had her back. Being here with him in this Garden, she felt peace over her. She even felt muscles in her forehead relax. *This place would make a great spa,* she thought absently. *I could get rid of that little wrinkle between my eyebrows.* She smiled at her own private joke.

If she could stay here forever, she would. But she had to get home. She wanted to have a normal life without demons or angels. She wanted to watch Lani grow up and see who she would become.

"Who built this place?" she asked, leaning against the window frame.

Gabriel placed his hand high up on the other side of the window frame.

"A king for his queen."

"That's rather vague."

"I cannot tell you more because I don't know the history."

"But I thought humans didn't live here."

"They did once."

"Adam and Eve?"

Gabriel nodded. "And their children." He paused at the confusion on Alle's face. "Their children before they made their bad choices," he explained further.

"Before the fall."

"Yes." Sadness momentarily shrouded his face.

"I knew it!" She pumped the air with her fist in triumph. "I knew there were more than just Adam and Eve in the garden."

"Well, their sin affected all of them. Everyone was required to leave. That part is not written." Gabriel looked out over the Garden and leaned easily against the opening. This was the most relaxed she had seen him.

"You love the height!" Alle realized.

Gabriel hooked his thumb over his shoulder. "Angel," he said like she wasn't the sharpest tool in the shed.

Alle sighed and smiled softly. "Runar loved heights. He said it was freedom. He would have been a great pilot or astronaut even. But he said it would take him too far away from his family." Her eyes pricked at the memory. Gabriel didn't move. He just continued to stare over the landscape. "I wish he could see this. He would love it... or would have."

Gabriel looked at her then. He came closer and put his arm around her. She turned and buried her head into his chest. She was embarrassed by her tears but couldn't hold them back any longer. With her guard down, the tears had a mind of their own.

"It's ok to cry. Your tears don't scare me," he whispered. Gabriel held her and let her weep. The same way Runar had when he was alive. The way no one had since he died.

When her sobs finally subsided, Gabriel released her just a little, giving her the freedom to pull away. She looked up at him through damp eyelashes.

"Sorry," she said sheepishly, swiping at his chest.

"Alle, you are one of the strongest, fiercest women I know. You do not have to apologize for having emotions or how they are expressed. The Most High saw fit to create you. Don't apologize for it. "

Alle dismissed him with a flip of her hand. She hated crying in front of others, not because of her own emotions but because she didn't want to deal with their pity.

"Alle. There's so much I need to tell you…" A loud growl sounded behind them, cutting Gabriel off.

He grabbed Alle and stepped in front of her as he turned to face the threat. Gabriel's sword instantly appeared. Peeking around him, she was met with big golden eyes and four-inch canines slipping over thin black lips. Corded muscles stretched under gold and brown striped fur. Four muscular limbs narrowed into paws tipped with long black claws. Fur stood on end to give the appearance that the animal was larger. "I thought you said lions wouldn't attack us," Alle whispered.

"*Ssshh.*"

The big cat sniffed the air, sensing her prey. "You brought a human into my den, Strong Man?" the lion spoke. It was different than humans. There was a lisp because of the sharp, giant teeth. Teeth Alle knew could rip her to shreds in seconds. She was trembling. This lethal giant had just spoken.

"You know, she wouldn't have made it this far if that were true, Tugev."

The lion's nostrils opened and closed, using her heightened senses to assess the threat. "She smells… wrong. But I know the smell of human."

"We were just leaving." Gabriel held up his free hand. "Let us pass peacefully."

"Yes, you were." The lion crouched, preparing for her attack. She filled the entirety of the opening to the stairs, blocking their escape. There was no intention to forgive their trespass.

Alle assessed her options. She could tuck and roll under the cat's attack, landing near the door. But that would have had Tugev chasing them down the stairs. They could fight the beast. She didn't want to hurt the magnificent animal if she could help it. Fortunately, Alle didn't have to make any of those decisions.

Gabriel doused the flames of his sword. In one graceful movement, the sword disappeared. Gabriel turned, wrapped Alle in a bear hug, and leaped from the tower. The second they cleared the structure, his glorious golden wings swept out with a pop. Tugev pounced. The saber stopped short of jumping out of the window after them.

As they flew away from the magnificent, dangerous animal, Alle shifted in Gabriel's arms. It had been a narrow escape, but having lived through it, she wanted to see what other dangers might lurk in the reticent gardens. She watched the canopy of the wild forest transition back into a manicured garden but couldn't see any other threats.

The pair circled around. Gabriel fluttered his wings as he landed softly. Then gently swiped the dark hair from her forehead. "Are you ok?"

"Never better." She smiled sadly. "I thought the animals here were tame?"

"I never said they were tame. I said they wouldn't eat you. I believe the saber was protecting her young. I hadn't realized she made her den there."

"A saber? As in saber-tooth tiger?

Gabriel nodded.

"A saber tooth tiger that can talk?" Alle stood slack-jawed.

"All the animals in the Garden can speak. Most choose not to."

Alle took a deep breath and grabbed her temples. "This is too much. We need to find the fountain."

"Agreed. I didn't see any signs of the fountain during our flight, but I thought you might like to see one more thing."

"Ok. Just as long as I don't get eaten by talking animals."

Gabriel walked past her. "This way."

She followed him along the path. "Don't think I didn't notice that you didn't make any commitments that we wouldn't get eaten." Here, the stones were inset into the grass. "Who made this Garden? And all these structures."

"When the Most High placed man in this Garden, he tasked them with maintaining it. Adam did most of the initial work. Prepping and designing. He made aqueducts and fountains to redirect water from the rivers to nourish the plants. He was a great engineer."

"The Romans invented those things. How did Adam know how to make them thousands of years before they were used?"

"Everything old becomes new again. Adam had divine wisdom. He conversed with the Most High daily. The knowledge was lost when he left the Garden. But man is creative and inventive. The spark of intelligence was gifted by the Most High. It just took longer when they didn't consult with Him."

They continued walking along the path in silence as Alle took in the beauty of the Garden. She kept her hands clasped behind her back. They strode past rose bush after rose bush. Some grew by themselves and had tiny, mostly pink buds. Other bushes climbed up carefully placed trellises. The path became wider. Arches covered the path, equally spaced apart. Alle realized these were the aqueducts Gabriel had just mentioned. Vines covered the arches, and at the top, on each side, a small space had been created. They looked like the flower boxes her neighbor hung on the windows. In each of the boxes, flowers popped up and hung over. Green grasses flowed out the top and spilled over. She had heard of the thriller, filler, and spiller container gardening methods. Whoever had created this was a master. It occurred to her that these plants were hanging from the arches.

"Are these the... Hanging gardens?"

"Mmm hmmm," Gabriel responded. Alle thought she might have seen the corners of his mouth turn upward.

She squealed, "You brought me to see the hanging gardens? One of the seven ancient wonders of the world?"

Gabriel raised his eyebrows at her. "Of course. I know how you love plants and nature in general. This place is slightly different since the Most High supplies life and energy." He spoke softly to keep from disturbing the peace of the moment.

Alle continued to look up in awe as they passed under each of the seven arches. "You know they say these gardens never actually existed. There is no evidence, written or archaeological," she explained.

Gabriel tilted his head in agreement. "There's no evidence because they are here. If this were in the natural world, it would be a pale comparison of its current state."

"So nothing dies, but the Most High supplies the energy needed."

"Yes, there is no cycle of death here. The organisms that feed on death simply do not exist or get energy in another way."

"Surely this place would be overrun if nothing ever died."

Gabriel shrugged, "The Most High keeps the balance. Besides, he could just create more space if he needed."

"Ah. Yes, of course." Even though she was full of questions, she didn't really need all the details of how that worked. She was fine enjoying the Garden. "What's beyond the Garden? In the mists?"

Gabriel turned sober immediately and grabbed her by the shoulders. "You must never go to the mists. It is too dangerous for a human. And I could not protect you there." He held her like that until she nodded her affirmation that she understood. He didn't seem angry, just overly protective as usual.

"Alle," he growled.

She gently pushed his hands away from her upper arms. "I promise not to go the mists unless it is necessary to save someone I love."

Gabriel scoffed and turned away. He seemed to conclude that he wouldn't get much better from her. "Fine. I accept your vow."

His behavior only caused her to become more curious, though. She would heed his warning. For now.

They came to the end of the path. The door appeared in front of them. It was time to leave the peace and beauty behind.

"Where should we go next? Any ideas?" Gabriel asked quietly as he grasped her hand.

Alle answered thoughtfully. Her vow reminded her of who she was fighting for. The emptiness of her arms was evident again. "I want to find the fountain. But right now, I really need to see Lani again."

"Of course. We'll head to the healing rooms." Gabriel began to walk through as Alle continued.

"And then maybe we should consult the journal again. Maybe there's a clue I missed."

Gabriel pulled her in and put his finger on her lips. His face was close enough to kiss her. The fresh Christmas pine scent filled the air around them. His chest rose and fell rapidly as he leaned his forehead against hers.

Alle wasn't sure what was happening but knew if their lips met, there would be no coming back. She didn't know how much more breaking her heart could do or if it would ever be able to heal again. So she stepped away and changed the subject.

"Do you control your smell?"

He scrunched up one side of his face in confusion. "What?"

"Well, sometimes you smell like Christmas. Like pine and snow and a hint of cinnamon. And sometimes you smell like a campfire." She shrugged. "I was just wondering."

He pulled away from her completely. "I don't control it, nor do I even know that it is happening. Sometimes certain scents might accompany certain emotions," he shrugged and walked away. He seemed offended by her question.

"That went well," Alle said under her breath. *Maybe it's rude to ask about an angel's scent.* She thought. She hurried after him down the hall to the stasis room.

Everything appeared the same. The white pods with orange translucent lids were neatly aligned in a grid pattern. Equal and even space surrounded each pod. She quickly made her way to where she had last seen Lani.

She looked down at the pod. Horror struck. She couldn't catch a breath and stumbled backward, nearly bumping another pod to catch herself. She clutched her chest. When she could finally speak, she screamed.

"Gabriel?!" She couldn't be bothered to worry about waking the patients in stasis. He rushed to her side as she pointed to the pod. "Where is she?!"

Chapter Seventeen

The pod contained an angel who looked like his wing might be healing. "She was here last time."

"It's ok. They may have just moved her to make room for other pods." Gabriel searched for one of the strange healer angels and called her over. She hovered over with her blank expression. "Can you tell us where Lani was moved? The human girl."

"Oh yes, this way." She turned and walked toward the center. "We felt moving her to the center was best. She could be more protected."

"Why were not informed she would be moved?" Gabriel demanded, his tone harsh.

"We sent a messenger to the library. Lex. He was unable to find you."

Gabriel didn't respond. He continued his angry glare as he followed the healer through the pods.

"Why didn't he mind speak with you," Alle asked, confused as to why Lex wouldn't communicate with his commanding officer.

"The Gauntlet cuts off all communication, but he should have informed me as soon as he could feel my presence again. I should have checked in, but I was distracted." He seemed to be angry with himself rather than Lex or the healers.

The healer pointed to a pod. "Here she is."

"You will supply Alle with a monitor," he ordered. His tone was not at all friendly, but he added, "Please," out of respect.

The angel bowed and floated away, still not phased or showing any emotional reaction to Gabriel's gruff proclamation.

Alle breathed a sigh of relief. Lani was there. Still and peaceful. She hadn't moved or grown or anything since she had left her there. The monitors on the side of the pod showed she was alive, but that was the only clue. Another tear slipped from the corner of Alle's eye. Partly from relief and partly from the fact that she wasn't much closer to getting out of there. They still hadn't found the fountain or many answers at all.

Gabriel squeezed her shoulder. "It's ok. We'll get her out of there. And get you both back to your lives." He kissed the top of her head.

"Is that what you want? For us to go back to our lives?"

"Yes, Alle, I want you and Lani to live normal human lives."

Alle let him keep his hand on her shoulder. She should have shrugged it off, but it felt good to have support right now. The healer returned with Alle's wrist monitor and placed it in her hand.

"This will show her location within the veil and her status. The monitor is connected to her pod. The pod will give you updates on her health. You can monitor her remotely. We can also communicate with you if there is a problem."

"It would have been great to have this when we first arrived," Alle said.

"We assumed you would not be here long enough to need one."

Alle shrugged off Gabriel's hand and placed hers on her hip. "Well, everyone knows what you get when you assume." She was tired, and the moment of fear turned to anger. She was having trouble regulating her emotions.

Gabriel glared at her. His shoulder bumped her a little off-balance, probably on purpose. "It's time for us to go so we can get Lani out of here." He turned back to the healer. "Thank you for your time."

"Of course," the healer replied as she floated off.

He turned to her. "Alle, try not to make the healers angry."

She scoffed. "I'd like to see just one emotion from them."

"They have emotions. They are very good at hiding them."

Unable to direct her anger at the healers, she turned on her guardian. "What would happen if I made them angry, Gabriel? What would happen if I made the elders angry? Would they imprison me in this place? Would

139

they take Lani from me? Would they keep taking care of her or let her wake up with a demon inside her?" Alle took a few calming breaths. The truth was that she was angry. Angry that any of this had happened at all. Life was not supposed to be this way. Bad things were things that happened to other people. She read about them in the online newsfeed. They weren't supposed to happen to her or her family. The anger at these circumstances threatened to overwhelm her.

Gabriel gently placed his hand on her shoulder again. "Alle, your anger is draining."

She glared at him.

He continued anyway, "Not just for me. It drains you and everyone around you. You can continue to be angry. Or you can channel it into something useful and do something about it."

She glared. *He doesn't care if I cry, but anger is his downfall?* The thought made her angrier. Anger was justified sometimes, even if she didn't want to hurt those around her. There was no way to turn it off or "channel" it. She didn't know how.

Heat rose up from her belly. Her face and neck turned red from the emotion as she turned away and focused on her baby girl. She renewed her promises and said goodbye to Lani again, longing for the day there wouldn't need to be goodbyes.

She backed away from Lani's pod and walked toward the closest door. Watching her daughter rest peacefully allowed the anger to diminish for now. It was still simmering below the surface, waiting to be called up. "Let's go." was all she said to Gabriel as she walked away.

* * *

"Do we have to return to the Gauntlet to retrieve my bag? It has very important items in there," she asked curtly. She wasn't trying to be rude.

"No, the hall will return your things to the library."

"Oh? Nifty... and convenient." She was exhausted, and Gabriel's words in the infirmary and the news about her bag did nothing for her bad mood.

140

They stepped through the doorway but walked directly into the library instead of entering the hallway as expected. Alle chose not to question it, plopped on the green couches, and looked around. It almost seemed like the library had rearranged itself.

"Does the library look different to you?" she asked.

"The alcove is in the same place. The stairs are the same. As I said, the library will give you what you need when you need it. It is probably working out what you need next."

"Is the library sentient?"

Gabriel moved his eyes up and to the right, thinking. Then he shrugged. "That's as good an explanation as any."

Alle shook her head. "This place gets weirder and weirder."

"The place is the same as it always is."

Alle rolled her eyes. "Never mind."

A new voice echoed through the library. "Hello, Alle, Gabe." Lex half bowed to them in succession. He delivered Alle's forgotten bag to her.

"Lex, it's so great to see you! It's too bad you couldn't have found us sooner and told us about Lani being moved." Alle was a little put out with the angel. Well, angels. Gabriel included. Lex was at least humble enough to look embarrassed.

"Alle, it wasn't Lex." Gabriel sat on the couch beside her but kept his distance this time. "I had told him we had a lead. I didn't tell him where we were going. Then, we ended up with the elders. The Gauntlet was a complete surprise, then the garden. When we were in a place where he could communicate with me, we were already in the stasis room."

Lex sat in the armchair adjacent to the sofa and grabbed her hand. A sharp look from Gabriel had him quickly dropping it. "Alle, I'm sorry. I would have told you, but as Gabe said, I couldn't reach him mentally or find either of you."

Alle paused for a moment and finally accepted his explanation. She sighed and rested her head on her hand. "I apologize for snapping at you." A thought hit her then, and she sat up. "I'm so sorry. I must be affecting both of you with my emotions." Gabriel had said as much in the infirmary.

The angels looked at each other. Neither wanted to make her feel worse. "It's not that big of a deal. We are used to dealing with humans' emotions." Lex said graciously.

She leaned her head against the back of the sofa. "I'm so tired. I'm heading up to my room. That will probably help." She looked at Gabriel. "I need a fresh head, but can you wake me in thirty minutes… I mean, what would typically be thirty minutes."

He nodded. As she walked up the spiral staircase, she overhead Lex. "There's been some activity at her house." Alle froze to listen in, but their voices lowered. She couldn't bring herself to care at that moment, letting Gabriel do the worrying for a few minutes. Hopefully, he would fill her in later. Doubting he would volunteer the information, she made a mental note to ask him about it.

After a quick shower, she wished she had told Gabriel longer on the nap. She could have spent her entire thirty minutes in there. But when she got to bed, she collapsed, exhausted from the disaster of a day. *No, it wasn't a disaster. It was actually a good day*, she thought as she drifted into a dreamless sleep.

* * *

She woke when she heard the door slam. She bolted out of bed and onto the floor opposite the door. She waited and listened. The towel she had wrapped around her after her shower was the only thing she had on. It would be unfortunate if she had to fight for her life right now. She continued to wait until Adriel poked her head into the room. Alle breathed a sigh of relief and stood. She stared at the angel, still contemplating how she knew her.

"Hey girl, Gabe sent me in to wake you."

"I'm glad it's you, actually. I was so tired I fell asleep in my towel."

"Yes, I see. Get dressed, and I'll wait for you in the living area. Gabe thought I might be more helpful to you with locating the fountain."

Alle gave her a smile and a thumbs up. As soon as Adriel left, Alle mimicked her use of Gabriel's nickname. "Gabe this and Gabe that. Everyone around here calls him Gabe? Well, it's a dumb nickname," she continued to mutter under her breath as she pulled on a new t-shirt and jeans. She pulled her shoes back on, ready to move at a moment's notice if they found something. Her movements were jerky as her annoyance grew.

"Alle, is everything all right?"

Alle sighed, feeling silly about being jealous. She took a few deep breaths to clear her head and her heart. "Yes, coming." She hated that the angels could pick up on emotions.

She sat down next to Adriel on the stiff white sofa. She pulled her bag up and took out one of her pills. She took it without water. The constant exhaustion was a sign she hadn't been taking them regularly enough.

She laid the book on the table. She had no idea if it would open, but when she tugged on the edge, it opened right up. *It must recognize me now,* she thought.

Adriel leaned forward and flipped her long blond hair over her shoulder. The light shone on it in a way that practically glowed. Recognition hit Alle at that moment. Alle sat up straighter. "I know you now." She pointed. "You're the one Gabriel spoke to when we went to pick up Lani one day. I can't quite remember what happened or why Gabriel was with me."

Adriel blushed. "I am. I'm sorry I couldn't tell you sooner. Gabriel swore us to secrecy."

"And you said you're Lani's guardian?"

"I am."

"But Lani always talks about her daddy guardian."

Adriel sat stiffly. "He, um. Comes around sometimes. Children are more sensitive to the spirit."

Alle closed her eyes in confusion. "I'm sorry, what? You're saying Lani can see my dead husband; she thinks he's her guardian angel." Now, Alle was undoubtedly jealous. Why hadn't Runar come to see her? She gave it a second thought. Maybe he had, and she wasn't in tune with the spiritual realm. She wondered if she would be able to see him now she had been here.

Adriel didn't make eye contact but looked at the book on the table. It was

143

turned to the page of the fountain. "You should talk to Gabriel more about that."

Alle made another mental note to make him tell her later. This would be a long conversation with everything she would have to drag out of her guardian angel.

They both looked at the page with the fountain. "Have you seen this before?" Alle asked.

"The fountain? No. The book, yes."

"Ooo kay? Any ideas about how to find it?"

"Other than another trip to the elders, not yet. Let's read through this again."

Alle reread it. The spirit created the fountain to store the tears of anyone who was oppressed. This typically meant humans, but she guessed there might also be angel tears. The fountain itself was nothing special, but it would reveal their past when a person looked into the water. It was a fountain of remembrance. Almost nobody went there because everyone could remember their past. It was the future people wanted to know.

"Oh, this is interesting." Alle looked closer at the drawing of the fountain. "This symbol etched in the stone base; it looks like my birthmark." Alle raised her forearm for Adriel to see the faint outline on her forearm. "My mom always said it looked like a dove. I never could tell, honestly. But seeing the exact shape on that fountain has me wondering."

"Alle, that isn't a dove. That's an angel crest. This shape also appears on one of the doors in the hall."

Alle thought for a moment. "Wait, I've seen a few symbols on the doors?"

"They let us know what is beyond."

"Well, I've just been following Gabriel and making sure I'm touching him, so we go to the same place. I haven't looked for the symbols."

"Well, that is one way to navigate, but not all of us have his power level. Most of us go through the hall using the symbols."

"That makes sense. I wondered how I could get around if Gabriel weren't here."

Concern contorted Adriel's beautiful features. "Alle, it could be dangerous

144

to go anywhere alone. It's best if an angel escorts you."

"Oh, I know. I've been to the Gauntlet and almost got eaten by a saber-tooth tiger. Well, not eaten. Gabriel said she wouldn't eat me. But regardless, I don't plan to go anywhere by myself."

"I think we have a good lead. I'll let Gabriel know. Why don't you get something to eat before heading back to find this place."

Alle did as Adriel suggested. The kitchenette was fully stocked. She browsed through cabinets and finally settled on something sweet. She leaned against the counter and popped a strawberry pastry in her mouth. She almost moaned as the flavors swirled over her tongue. She was certainly going to miss the food in this place.

As she snacked, she closed her eyes and let her mind wander to Gabriel. If nothing else, he had become her friend while they were here in this place. More than just her protector and guardian, he was someone who had brought her comfort and support. She thought of his smile. They didn't come easily, but when he did smile, he was jaw-droppingly gorgeous. He didn't need the smile for that, but she would rather see it than not. She was a sucker for dimples. While Runar had been her best friend, he never seemed to brood. He was always trying to make her smile. Gabriel was strong and broody. He was always serious but didn't care if she cried. She closed her eyes and thought of his smell and how it changed his moods. She could smell it now. The smoky campfire mixed with the clean pine scent and the cinnamon.

Gabriel cleared his throat. Alle jumped, and her eyes shot open.

"Umm, hi. I was just enjoying this pastry." She pulled apart a cinnamon roll she had picked up and forgotten about. "Did we ever find you a bell? You really need a bell."

Gabriel gave a smug look. "I rather like being able to startle you, actually."

Alle glared. "I'm guessing Adriel let you know what we found?"

"Yes, we will head there now, but I must tell you something first."

"Look, I know what you are going to say."

"You do?"

"Yeah, and it's cool. I'm cool. I mean, I know I kissed you in the Gauntlet.

Then there was that other time in the hall and all those moments in the gardens where you know I wanted to throw you against a tree and make out with you. And honestly… you are magnificently gorgeous… I don't know why anyone would not want to… you know, make out with you. But I don't know what has gotten into me. Other than it's been a while since Runar. And I can't. I can't start something I won't be able to finish." She waved between the two of them. "And so this is strictly a guardian-human relationship. I will control myself from this moment forward. Strictly platonic."

Gabriel furrowed his brows and sat on the couch. "I see."

"Good. Wait, you don't seem like you see. Isn't that what you've been trying to tell me?"

"Not even close."

"Great. Ok. Well, I'm glad that's out there now. I don't have to worry about it anymore, and we can just keep moving forward with missions figure-out-how-to-get-the-demon-out-of-Lani and why-are-the-demons-attacking-us."

Alle put everything back in the bag and slung it around her. She turned her back on him and left the room. Gabriel followed her and tried to stop her. "Alle, wait, I need…."

She turned and held up her hand. "Is what you're going to say going to keep Lani or me alive?

He shook his head.

"Is it going to kill Lani or me?"

He shook his head again.

"Good, then you can tell me another time, Gabe, Gabriel. Ugh." She squeezed her eyes shut at the slip. "Let's just complete this so we can move on."

Gabriel replaced his mask of stoicism and nodded. He led Alle out of the library and into the hall, barely touching her when they passed through the door. He immediately distanced himself when they made it to the other side. Now Alle knew more about the doors. She wondered why he bothered bringing her to the hall at all. He didn't slow his long strides as he usually did, and she had to run to keep up with him now.

146

They walked the seemingly endless hall again. She noticed the doors did indeed have symbols. Some were obvious, like a fork for the cafeteria and a plus sign for the medical ward. One door had an X with a P through the middle. She had no idea what that meant.

They finally reached the door with the symbol they had seen this morning. Away at the end of the hall, it was no wonder no one knew where it was. Seeing the image more closely now, she realized it wasn't a dove at all. It was a sword with wings on either side. She looked at the birthmark on her arm. She couldn't unsee the new shape. The book, this door, the fountain, Alle. They were all connected by this symbol.

Gabriel finally spoke then. "Alle, there is no other time to tell you this. I don't know what you will find on the other side of this door. But one thing you must know before we enter is that…."

"You are not fully human, Alle." An old man spoke behind them.

Gabriel turned to assess the threat and pushed Alle behind him again.

The elder from earlier glided around the corner. He had a twinkle in his eye that warned of mischief.

Alle pressed him further. "Why should I believe you? You've already tricked us once." She waited a second and added, "It wasn't a very nice trick either."

"It was necessary for you to enter the Gauntlet, Alle. Gabriel is a wonderful guardian angel. We had decided he would not have allowed it any other way. Now you both know what you are capable of in human form." He gestured to both of them. "To your question, you don't have to believe me. Gabriel was about to reveal this very thing. I just saved him from having to explain it."

She looked at Gabriel for confirmation. He nodded. Looking between the two, she sighed. She didn't believe either of them. How could she be an angel?

Gabriel turned toward her again and spoke quietly. "Do you remember I've told you once, but it might have been a slippery memory since it dealt with the spiritual?"

Alle tried to recall being told she was an angel. "On the porch the day we met. Yes, I remember now. You told me I was an angel and that you were my guardian." Alle recalled the memory slowly. It had been shrouded by many other things that had happened since then.

"Humans aren't able to enter this place at all, Alle." Gabriel gestured to the hall.

"But you said I could come here because I was beginning to gain my sight."

"That is partially true. You are partially human. But the angelic part allows you to enter, and it allows you to see the veil. If you were fully human, you would have to die to come here. And even if you didn't, humans aren't allowed in the gardens, the library, or anywhere except for paradise." Gabriel explained.

"Oh, you took her to the gardens? Interesting."

"I respect you, Elder, but keep your scheming to yourself." Gabriel's voice echoed along the hall.

"Wouldn't we want the opposite so at least we know what he was scheming?" she whispered so only Gabriel could hear. She hoped. Gabriel didn't respond. He pretended not to hear her. He was on edge with the elder nearby. Obviously, they had been leaving Gabriel out of their plans.

"Yes, yes, of course. We only carry out the will of the Most High. We have no plans of our own." The elder, fortunately, didn't hear her, and he pointed to the door. "Before we enter, what do you know about the fountain?"

Their discourse distracted her from the bombshell that had just been dropped. Alle shared what she had learned. She left off the little tidbit about the etching on the fountain matching her birthmark.

"Good, I don't have much to add. Other than Gabriel, I think you shouldn't stand too near Alle when she looks in the pool. It might disrupt what she sees. However, I would like to see how this works. Do you mind if I accompany you inside?"

Alle looked at Gabriel for guidance. He didn't move, allowing her to make the decision. She didn't understand heavenly politics, but she also didn't see the harm in it unless he tried to trick them again. Deciding she would rather have him close by if that was the case. She nodded and allowed him to follow them inside.

Chapter Eighteen

The trio pushed through the door with the winged sword symbol. She would've thought that a door leading to a fountain would have a symbol of water. Maybe even the tears the fountain was said to have held. This was obviously not something the Most High or maybe the elders wanted just anyone to find.

They continued to walk. This was another garden but not as beautiful or cultivated as the Garden of Eden. There were not any trees. Head tall grass lined the path. The area was wild and overgrown. It wasn't neatly manicured. Alle realized the wildness carried a beauty of its own. Though most of the garden continued in controlled chaos, their path allowed them safe passage. Someone had cleared it and placed cobbled stones together to form a walkway. Moss and shorter grasses filled in the spaces between the stones. Dew covered the ground, and droplets of water covered the tall blades of grass to either side of her.

The sky here was the color of the dawn as the sun lifted into the heavens. It never changed. There was more than enough light to see, but it seemed dim, as if the absent sun was paying its respect to the fallen. She felt instinctively this was a place of mourning and loss. The sadness weighed heavy on her soul. Even still, there was a certain peace residing within the sadness.

With that feeling, Alle finally let the idea of being an angel sink in. "If I'm an angel, why would I choose to be a human? Why would anyone choose to leave heaven? All of the places I've visited bring calm and peace. Why would anyone enter the chaos of humanity willingly?"

"You chose to be human because you loved The Most High with everything you had. But you still didn't feel like it was enough. You looked down in the natural world and saw humans choosing to love Him even though they had never seen Him. Their only experience with Him is in spirit. You wanted to be able to choose him that way, too. So he allowed it. He said he would guide you only in spirit, the same as any other human. You would be treated and loved just as they were. You wanted the human experience to live and be loved by other humans in community. But to experience the joy, you also had to experience the pain. I'm not sure you knew what that meant, but it was still your choice," the elder explained.

"Is that why the Most High hasn't graced us with his presence while I've been here?"

Gabriel and the elder shared a look. "You are still currently human, Alle. You are welcome into the throne room any time... through prayer."

The elder interrupted, "We thought it best if you didn't visit him physically just yet. You may still be able to fulfill your mission. If you visited the Most High, you would likely choose to stay. Almost everyone does. "

"I believe this is a unique circumstance. Alle has been in His presence before and chosen to leave." Gabriel and the elder discussed her as if she wasn't standing right there. She didn't mind, and she didn't interrupt. They would likely reveal something they didn't mean to if they forgot she was there.

"Yes, but she chose to leave as an angel. She would be making the choice now as a human, and she has seen much suffering. The Most High is allowing her to make the decision. She wanted this experience. He will not end it abruptly because the demons have taken an interest in her."

"Isn't he all-knowing? Why not just give us the information?" Alle inserted herself back into the conversation.

"Alle. The ways of the Most High are often mysterious. He could stop everything, save all of the humans, and reset humanity. But he allows them to make their own choices. We learn better that way. Do you think Lani would learn better by you telling her not to touch a hot stove or by touching a hot stove herself?" the elder asked.

"Although I would never purposely let Lani touch a hot stove just to learn the lesson, she would definitely learn the lesson better with experience."

The elder nodded. "I don't speak for the Most High, except to say he loves us. Each of us, as his own children. He has placed us in his royal court as sons and daughters. He simply desires to be with us. He hates the suffering humans endure, but it is a part of the human experience. He offers his spirit as guidance, comfort, and peace. It just takes faith to trust that he is there even when your humanity is mudding up the waters."

Alle shrugged. She didn't remember her time as an angel, but she remembered her time as a human. She sighed. "Well, I understand it now in a way no nonhuman ever could. But I also understand love, trust, and loyalty like no other being ever could."

"I believe modern humans have a saying. It's not the destination that counts. It's the journey," the elder countered.

"Yes, that is a saying people usually use when they can't reach the goal they want to achieve."

"They are partially correct. The destination is important, but the journey helps us grow and gives us the skills we will need to use once we reach our destination."

"That is very wise, Elder," Alle complimented, stepping over a hole in the path where the cobblestones had separated and sunk into the soil. It made her sad no one had been here to maintain this area. It seemed forgotten. "Gabriel, you are very quiet."

He grunted in affirmation. "I don't want my opinions to confuse the matter further. It probably wouldn't be helpful."

Alle tilted her head. "I value your opinions and insight. I wish I heard them more often, actually."

They continued walking in silence. Other than their footfalls and the swishing of the grass, quiet reverence surrounded them. The tall grass gave way to a hidden meadow. This was not something anyone made or a fountain at all. This was a natural spring that flowed into a series of pools. The water was crystal clear, and so deep there was a blue-green hue. Trickles of water poured over several clefts in the rock. Moss and hyacinth hung over the edges. She saw the large stone with the winged sword symbol on one of the ledges.

The book she had found explained that the water in the pool wasn't water at all. They were the tears of those who had suffered on Earth. The tears the spirit bottled up. She was sure she had supplied plenty herself. Spirit didn't let these tears go to waste. They were brought here to the fountain of Siloam. The fountain of remembrance.

Alle hadn't begun to look in the pool. She was still afraid to face her memories and those of so many others. "So why do the demons care about an angel-turned-human?"

"That's why we're here, Alle. To find out what they might want. Why the attacks? How they found out about you," Gabriel said.

The elder finally spoke again. "We don't need to look in the pool for those answers. Demons are drawn to hope, love, and faith because they have none. They long for it. But because they can't have it, they want to see it destroyed." He shrugged his shoulders. "Beyond that, maybe they don't have a good reason. Maybe they just like destroying things that bring light to the world. They like darkness because it hides their hideousness. The guilt that eats away at their soul isn't as painful in the dark. And you are currently the brightest light. They would have recognized it when you shared your energy. It's tough to disguise that light."

He gestured to the pool. "We can look to the pool for answers and restoration of sorts. But it can be a blessing to not remember in some ways."

"I want to remember. I need to remember so I can keep Lani safe. I think more knowledge is better than less in this case."

The elder nodded. "Then let's begin?"

Alle took a deep breath and stepped a little closer to the pool. Gabriel nodded his head in support. He wasn't allowed to touch her, so he didn't interfere with her memories. He stepped back a few paces. His proximity was still supportive, and he was close enough to swoop in if there was a problem.

She finally looked at the water at the bottom of the pool. Tiny ripples traveled around from the waterfalls above.

Alle placed her hands on the stones beside the largest pool and leaned over the edge. Finally, making eye contact with the water. Tension and anticipation built in her chest, but nothing happened as the seconds continued.

"Umm, guys? Am I supposed to be seeing something," she yelled.

"Maybe it's not working because she isn't fully human?" Gabriel offered.

"No, no. She's exactly who it is supposed to work for," the elder chastised.

"Maybe because I haven't died, and I'm here because Gabriel needed to hide me somewhere?" Alle countered.

The elder stroked his long beard.

"I honestly have no good reason why this shouldn't..."

While he was explaining, Alle was distracted by something moving out of the corner of her eye. Everything dropped away. Gabriel and the elder were no longer there with her. It was just her and the pool. As she leaned back over the water, her palms contacted the edge. There were no words.

Memories of her life flashed before her, human and angel, but it was from someone else's perspective. From the outside looking in. She tried to pull away, but the pool had frozen her body in place. *I'm stuck,* she thought, unable to look away until the pool was ready to release her. A little ember of panic started in her chest.

The scenes sped by, filling her with dread and grief. The fountain showed her the demon attacks and scenes of moments that had slipped away while she slept. Memories of helping the Most High avenge his people with plagues flashed by. When she was sent to punish a man who loved the Most High but let his pride get in the way. When the Most High's chosen people disobeyed him and brought retribution down upon themselves. The fountain also showed her all the times she wanted to bring vengeance, but the Most High held her back. There were more times of mercy than vengeance, even before his sacrifice.

But the fountain wasn't finished yet. It showed her the memories of the others as well. The pain and suffering of humans on Earth passed before her in seconds. She could faintly hear Gabriel yelling behind her. She could feel the heat rising in her core. Everything burned. She had no time to question what was happening to her as she took in all the suffering. Wars, famines, mass murders, raping and pillaging, unspeakable atrocities, demons inciting humans to do awful things to each other, and humans doing terrible acts without demonic influence at all. The images flashed before her at high speed.

Finally, Gabriel grabbed her around the waist and flung her away from the fountain. She crashed to the other side of the meadow and quickly righted herself like she had been practicing it her entire life. Gabriel was in front of her in a flash. She seethed, wanting vengeance for all the pains endured by humanity. The human suffering that needed to be avenged. Her hair burned bright. Fire pulsed from her eyes. She glowered at Gabriel, who stood between her and the pool.

"You dare keep me from my right to avenge?" she growled. Alle's humanity had retreated deep inside. The fire that always simmered below the surface took over. After seeing the images of the horrible acts, the urgency to meet justice for the world engulfed her body, mind, and soul.

Gabriel met her with a fire of his own. "You are human, Alle. You aren't equipped."

"Then I will shed my humanity." She moved to do just that. Fire erupted along her arms.

"No!" Gabriel screamed. "If you do, Lani will be alone. She will lose you." Alle paused, trying to understand why she should care. Lani was a vague memory in the back of her mind. Buried deep beneath a mountain of every hurt humanity had faced for the millennia of its existence. Fury burned in and around her. "Remember how you love Lani. Remember how you love...me."

Gabriel turned his voice into a soft whisper and moved slowly. Like he was talking a jumper off the ledge. Inch by inch, he reached out to her. Never taking her intense gaze off him, she allowed him to approach. He cupped her cheek and made gentle circles with his thumb.

It took ages for Alle to remember Lani, her human daughter. Everything within her longed to rage and burn. In the core of her being, she knew it was time to burn the world and avenge those whose tears filled the fountain.

Her chest rose and fell rapidly as the fire inside her threatened to consume her and everything around her.

She heard the voice of the Most High like a balm on a wound, "Not yet, Alle. Not yet."

Combined with Gabriel's soothing words, the fire inside Alle slowly dimmed.

"Remember Lani's chubby baby cheeks," Gabriel cooed. "Her hugs and kisses and baby giggles." With each memory of Lani, the fire finally reduced to a glowing ember. The flame was still there, ready to be ignited. She could erupt at any time. Now that she knew, it was not going to be easy to control the need to avenge every evil thing done to those the Most High loved.

Alle slumped to the ground. Gabriel fell to his knees beside her, wrapped his arms around her, and squeezed. She didn't return the embrace but rested against him. "I'm sorry I brought you here. I thought it would help," he whispered.

After many long minutes, Alle sighed. "It did help. I know why I asked to be human."

Gabriel loosened his hold and backed away. "Care to share? If you can handle it? I do not want you to lose your humanity just yet."

She patted his muscular arm. "I think I'm good now." Alle smiled. "The anger is still there but on a low setting, ready to be reignited any time."

"That's what I'm worried about. You can choose to step away from this life anytime you want, but…" he trailed off clearly, thinking about Lani.

"I know. I don't want to leave Lani alone in that cruel world. I would never do that to her. She is my number one priority now. Humanity can wait to be avenged. But I don't know what to do if something happens to her." Alle continued to look at her hands until the last second. She finally looked into Gabriel's deep eyes. He searched her face, and Alle wanted to close the space between them to kiss him, even if she had promised not to. Instead, she leaned away and stood. "Guess you knew I'm an avenging angel."

"I knew. But I didn't know the pool would trigger your angel abilities."

"I wonder if the elder knew?" She looked around, but the elder was nowhere to be found.

"He seemed to know a lot of facts about it, but I don't think he even knew the pool was made of tears until you found it in that book. They are elders, but they aren't all-knowing either."

Alle shrugged. "Yeah, well... I'm an avenging angel. I wanted to know why I should avenge the suffering of humans. I loved—love," she corrected herself, "the Most High, as you said, but I was just so tired of fighting the same battles over and over. So, instead of wondering, I decided to experience it firsthand. To get a better perspective. Experience is the best teacher, after all." She smiled at the fact that the elder had just said that.

Gabriel crossed the distance she had placed between them and wrapped her in another hug. He seemed emotionally softer now. "I'm sorry, Alle. I should have told you, but I knew you wouldn't believe any other way."

"It's fine. It's a lot, though." As she tried to pull away. This time, Gabriel held her close. She snapped her head up to his face. He held her tight with one hand, and with the other, he brushed his hand along her cheek. His familiar scent threatened to take her under where she could not control the need to kiss him and hold him like the world was ending. She put her hand on his muscular chest. She wanted to get lost in his eyes. She wanted to kiss him and never come up for air. Instead, she pushed herself away from him again. A broken heart was not going to help this situation.

He had just mentioned the fact she couldn't leave Lani alone. Dating her guardian angel would just be a no-go, even if the angel-human pairing had been somewhat resolved.

I've done long-distance relationships before. They don't work. This would be beyond a long-distance relationship. She thought. She pushed away from Gabriel. "I can't do this. I have to stay human for Lani, and this couldn't go anywhere. It's just not possible."

Gabriel sighed. "There's something you should know."

"What else could I need to know? What other earth-shattering, life-changing information could you pile on me right now?" She didn't know why she suddenly felt angry. Then, she remembered she had just been an amped-up avenging angel ready to shed her human vessel to avenge all of mankind. She could probably give herself a pass for being a little edgy.

Gabriel took the massive emotional blow-up in stride. "You're right. I shouldn't pile anything else on you right now. It could trigger your less agreeable side. I will take you back to your room and let you rest."

"No, no, no, no." She waggled her finger in the air. "You don't get to do that. I would rather get this all out in the open instead of waiting for the other shoe to drop."

"I don't know if you are ready for this." He stepped back but allowed her to make the decision to leave.

"Well, for one," she looked at the pool and said, "it would help if I weren't by the fountain of terror." She hooked her thumb toward the pool.

"You're right. Let's go back to your room and talk. I think that would be more relaxing for you."

"You don't have to baby me. I'm adjusting. But you're right. The room would be more relaxing."

They turned their backs on the pool and walked back down the path. The peace of the space was in direct contrast to the rage Alle felt just below the surface. As they reached the door, she paused momentarily and took a deep breath, trying to fill herself with some of the calm that permeated the air. When she was ready, she grabbed Gabriel's arm and passed back through the door.

Chapter Nineteen

He opened the door directly into the library this time. The library would protect the books if Alle went nuclear.

Back in her temporary room, she sat on the stiff white sofa. Gabriel didn't sit. He looked uncharacteristically nervous. He paced back and forth. Alle tracked him with her eyes. He would stop, look at her, open his mouth to speak, shake his head and return to pacing.

After about the fourth time, she raised her eyebrows at him. "I know time isn't really an issue since we are outside the realm of time. But maybe we should move this along a little," she said, twirling her fingers around each other.

"You're right. I apologize. This is just more difficult to explain than I thought it would be," he said as he finally sat. He sighed and bowed his head. "You've known me before."

"Well, of course. We were angels together before I became human."

"Yes, but when you were human, you knew me."

Alle cocked her head and tried to remember when she knew Gabriel. "Had you tried to rescue me or something? I know my memories are 'slippery.' The fountain didn't solve all those memory problems." She tried to remember something that would have Gabriel so nervous.

"No, what I mean is. I was also human at the same time you were. The fountain wouldn't have shown you that. It wasn't part of your memories."

Alle raised her eyebrows and batted her eyelashes in confusion. She didn't know what he was trying to say. "So you chose to become human also? Why would you be here if that were the case?"

He sighed and stood again. He started pacing. The floor was going to have a groove at this rate. "It's a long story. You were an angel soul that became a human." He paused to make sure she understood. Alle nodded. He placed his hand on his chest. "I had a little different experience. I decided to become human because you did. I was never as noble as you, but I never wanted to be parted from you… so I possessed a human boy." He winced and turned away from her.

Alle closed her eyes. There was so much for her to process in that statement. So many questions bombarded her thoughts. She chose to voice the one that wouldn't break her heart.

"So, how can angels possess humans?"

Gabriel released his breath, returned to the sofa, and sat back beside Alle. "The same way demons can, but that's not the point." Gabriel felt he needed to explain and justify his actions. To himself for the thousandth time, but also to Alle, who would never have approved this action.

"The boy was born without breath. He had passed away before birth, and his mother prayed for him to live again. I was his guardian and had already escorted his soul to the Most High. She was fervent in her prayers. You had already decided to be born to a human mother. I received permission from the Most High to accompany you this way."

"Without my knowledge."

"You would never have allowed me to follow or protect you. In fact, you made me promise not to interfere…"

His words triggered a memory. Alle gripped the couch as the memory distracted her from what Gabriel was saying. His voice faded away as the memory took hold.

* * *

"You don't have to do this." Gabriel's whispered words had wrapped around Alle's heart.

She'd sighed, "Gabriel, you know that I do. This need for vengeance inside of me is tearing me apart. I see what happens every day in the natural world, and I want to put an end to it all. Plus, I love the Most High with all my heart. But humans love him more, all without seeing him. I want to see how they do it. How can they love him through all that suffering." Alle had already explained this to Gabriel. Even though angels didn't marry in the human sense, Alle and Gabriel were bonded. They lived their lives together and carried out their duties and purposes together. It was a rare pairing. Alle always wanting to destroy, and Gabriel wanting to protect.

Fear of Alle succumbing to her true nature constantly haunted Gabriel. It was something they discussed regularly. "That is not your call, Alle," were his only words.

"Exactly. I know it's not Gabriel. The Most High makes that decision, but I sometimes have trouble obeying his will. The time is drawing near for vengeance. I want to fulfill my purpose and my destiny. But even though I think it's time, the Most High wants mercy. To give every soul a chance at eternity. But you've seen what happens when angels disobey."

Gabriel hung his head. He had seen. He had been on the front lines of the war that followed the Morning Star's rebellion. It had been brutal. Many angels were vanquished. Finally, the Most High cast the rebellious out of heaven to prevent more loss. The Morning Star took his rebellion to humans. In many ways, the battles continued, not in heaven but in the natural world. The Morning Star and his hordes caused most of the atrocities Alle wanted to stop. The humans brought a good bit on themselves, though.

"The Most High created you for this purpose. You are his avenging angel. Of course, you want to avenge Him and his people."

"It's been a while since I've carried out the Most High's vengeance on his enemies. I sit, watch, and wait." Alle's eyes burned with the need to dispense justice. Flames rippled along her arms. "It's not like the days before the Most High made his sacrifice. There were more opportunities to carry out his vengeance. Now, his grace and mercy rule. But fewer humans care at all. When the innocent cry out, I yearn to answer the pleas."

"Have you thought about what happens when you've avenged all?"

She nodded. "I'm hoping that I will have a new purpose after this."

Gabriel wrapped his arms around Alle and pressed his forehead to hers.

160

Her fire never burned him. "I don't want to be in this world without you."

"Gabe, I love you. But I love the Most High with all of my being. He's offered me this opportunity to live as a human so I can experience all they experience. I want to understand the need for mercy and grace. I need to know their struggles and suffering and love Him as they do. If I do, I can possibly empathize instead of wanting to destroy them for their insolence. If I get the experience firsthand, I won't want to burn the world down every second. I can understand their choices better. I don't want to defy him, but I'm struggling to control my nature. This is his plan, but I want to do this. It is my choice. We need to see it through. It will be nothing more than a moment," she reassured him, stroking soft circles on his lower back.

"I know," he said. He lifted her chin with the crook of his finger and kissed her. "I can't bring myself to talk you out of it. Not when it could help you and protect the natural world. If you defied the Most High, the natural world could be destroyed in seconds."

Alle nodded sadly in agreement. She didn't ask to be made this way but had to deal with it.

"Gabriel? I need you to make a promise," she said into his chest. She pulled back a little to look into his eyes.

"Anything, Love," he replied.

"I need you to promise not to interfere." Alle held Gabriel's gaze. She waited patiently for his reply, trying to convey her need for him to follow this plan.

"You know I can't promise that. I'm a guardian. It is my nature to interfere."

"I mean, I want to do this as a human. The Most High has promised only to guide me as he guides humans. I need the same from you."

"I'm not sure what you mean." He stepped away from her then, trying not to be hurt by her need to do things without him.

"Don't reveal yourself to me. And if you have to, you will need to take my memories. I have to be able to gain spiritual sight on my own. Otherwise, this is pointless."

"What if something happens, and you need your memories." Gabriel couldn't stay away. He was back by her side in an instant. He pushed Alle's hair away from her eyes.

"Then let me discover everything on my own. I'll leave some clues for myself to make it easier for you. Just promise you'll let me do this the right way."

"I'll do my best," he mumbled.

"Gabriel," she growled

"Fine," he sighed. "I promise."

* * *

Gabriel was at her side. "Alle, are you ok?"

Alle released the couch and looked up at Gabriel, nodding that she was fine. "I think visiting the fountain might have affected the memory block."

He took her hand. "You had another memory?"

"Yes, but we can talk about it later. You were explaining why you possessed a human boy." Her voice was flat.

Gabriel gave her a wary glance but continued cautiously.

"...We might have been forever separated if we had both been born humans. But a possession posed minimal risk."

Alle tilted her head and crossed her arms. "This is a little far-fetched."

It was Gabriel's turn to cock his head. "Even with everything you've seen, you don't believe this?"

"I'm a natural skeptic." She uncrossed her arms, thinking of the time she and Runar spent looking for ghosts. "It's not that I don't believe you, but it's just... You just happened to find a baby that needed a soul, ask the Most High, and then possess the body? At the same time, I was being born."

"Remember the time thing? How we can go back to precise moments in time? I went back a couple of years before you were born."

"Gabriel." Alle paused, knowing there was more. Knowing who had been born two years before she was. She didn't want to ask the question but knew she had to. She closed her eyes and put her hand on her forehead. "Who were you to me in the natural world?"

Gabriel took a long time to answer. He took her hand, "My name on Earth was Runar."

Alle pushed him away and started pacing the room herself. She gnawed her thumbnail in her teeth. Her nervous habit. Gabriel tracked her with his eyes, making sure the fire was in check. "You possessed Runar the whole time?" she asked.

Gabriel shook his head. "I was Runar. I lived a normal human life."

"But you possessed the human I knew as my husband, Runar?" She grabbed her stomach, thinking she might be sick. She wasn't angry; she was embarrassed. She was in love with Runar, and the whole time, he was Gabriel. Then, when she was here with Gabriel, she didn't even know he was Runar. She even asked to see Runar. Feeling stupid, she squeezed her eyes closed at the thought of being so naive.

"Yes. But it wasn't like I took over his personality. We weren't separate people. I'm Runar." Gabriel bowed his head, unable to face Alle's reaction to this knowledge any longer.

Her silence was deafening. She could feel the fire course through her veins. Her embarrassment turned to anger. She couldn't say anything without screaming. She had so many questions. "Is this a joke? Do you think my time as a human is funny or something to laugh about?"

Gabriel stood, facing her anger. "No."

"Why are you doing this? Why would you make up a story about being Runar?" Alle fumed.

"This is truth." He stood and shoved his finger toward the floor to accentuate his point.

"Why would you do this?" she asked again. "I loved Runar with all of my being. When he died, it broke me." She was still talking about them as separate people. She didn't believe he was Runar.

"I couldn't let you live life as a human alone. I did as you asked. I kept my promise. I didn't interfere as I watched your human life unfold. There was nothing I could do. It was painful to watch your suffering as a child. Lex suggested I possess a human.

"Lex? Lex knew this whole time?" Anger flared in her eyes again. Gabriel stepped closer to help soothe her anger. She held up a hand and stepped back.

"He knew I disappeared. I'm unsure how much he knows about our relationship on Earth."

"But he and Adriel have known who I am this whole time."

"You were part of this team. Of course, they had to know who you were on Earth."

Alle didn't respond. They were silent for a long time as Alle continued processing this news. Her flames continued to simmer below the surface.

"Alle, I had to be with you and not just look on as a guardian, unable to speak to you, unable to hold you and comfort you. Unable to laugh with you and make you smile. I'm an angel, but I'm not perfect, and I just wanted to be with you. I remembered the human child that died at birth and asked the Most High to answer his mother's prayer by sending me in his place."

That confession would have most girls swooning, but Alle had just discovered she was a former avenging angel with a rage issue. She was still seething. "So, what I had with Runar was completely fake?"

Pain coursed through Gabriel's face. "What you had with Runar was what you had with me, so if it was fake with him, it's fake with me. I am Runar. We are not different people. I was human, and now I'm not."

He had practically doused her with ice water. His hurt was genuine. Alle sat, her shoulders slumped as the fight went out of her. "I'm sorry. That was unfair. I went to Earth to experience real human life. I'm not sure that's what happened if I married you, an angel. The fountain didn't show me everything. Obviously, I don't remember most things as an angel, or we wouldn't be in this mess to begin with." She was slumped back in her chair, exhausted. Time wasn't relevant here, but she felt she had been up for days. She was still human and still needed rest.

She had loved Runar with all her being. His death almost broke her. If it hadn't been for Lani, she would have been lost to her despair. Closing her eyes, she wanted to ask about his death but was afraid to hear the answers. Still, she needed to hear the whole truth.

"When Runar... you," she corrected herself. "...died. John was trying to explain something to me at the funeral. Something I didn't understand at the time."

Gabriel bowed his head and rubbed his temples. "Alle, it was for your own safety. And for Lani's safety."

"Why did you leave?" she asked softly. She opened her eyes and silently pleaded with him for the answers.

He sighed and returned to his place on the couch. "I didn't want to. It was stupid to go on the ghost-hunting tour. As a human, I had become complacent about your safety. Of course, I remembered everything as an angel, but it was like a dream. I knew ghosts are demons in disguise, but I never thought those humans would have found a gateway." He paused to explain, "a thinning of the barrier. Demons use it to get out of the underside.

"Fortunately, there are very few of these places. They get a lot of ghost activity, though. I thought the ghost tour was like a fake haunted house. I didn't expect an encounter. So when they started attacking you that night, I thought it was because of me. An angel possessing a human body can be more easily detected than an angel soul born to a human. But then you let them use your energy. I knew that they would sense your angel soul. They would target you, and they did. We lost our child just a few days later. I thought if I died, they might leave you alone. I needed to return to my angelic form to protect you and Lani better.

"When John asked me to help on his ranch, I saw my opportunity. I left early to help, luring the demons to his farm away from you and Lani. I engaged the demons in a battle as Runar. I allowed a mortal wound to his body so that he would die and I could return to my angelic form. John saw the battle with the demons. He saw when I allowed a demon to wound my leg. I swore him to secrecy with my dying breath. Afterward, I visited him in the hospital. I placed a spiritual gag of sorts on him. Even though he wants to tell people the truth, he can't."

"That seems like torture. Why didn't you wipe his memories as you did mine?"

Gabriel held up his pointer finger. "First, you asked for your memories to be wiped. You wanted to do this as a human. Second, it's his journey. He had been dabbling in the occult and needed to see it for what it was. I really can't say more than that."

Alle accepted Gabriel's explanation. Tears began to spill over at the thought of the loss of Runar. It would take some getting used to the idea that Gabriel was Runar.

Recalling her memory from earlier, Alle held up a finger. "One more thing. I remembered our conversation when I was an angel. Where I asked you not to interfere, you made a promise not to, and I asked you to wipe my memories so and so forth... So, how did we end up here? With you becoming my guardian angel and interfering?"

"I did promise and kept that promise for two long natural years. I would have never interfered if I had continued as a guardian angel. I take my vows seriously. Possessing the human was a loophole. I wasn't technically breaking my vow because I wasn't interfering as a guardian. I was interfering as a human. Marriage vows supersede all others. I promised to love you and protect you. The previous vow was null."

Alle squinted her eyes. "That seems sneaky. And after... You were a guardian angel again?"

"My marriage vow to you stands, and it overrides all other promises. Even though I'm doing my best to honor your requests, death cannot nullify a marriage. Also, I didn't really die. I just left my body."

"So you decide which vows you want to follow and when? What does a vow mean to you at all?" The fire threatened to overwhelm her again. Now that she could remember both promises, they were equally important to her.

Gabriel reached out to calm her. She leaned away with a glare. His hand lingered in the air until he let it fall to the couch beside her. Not touching but close enough that she could feel his energy.

"I am trying to honor as much of both vows as possible. You wanted to do this as a human. I'm allowing that as much as possible. But I'm also trying to keep you safe. It's a difficult one to get right."

Alle didn't say anything for a long time. Gabriel let her process the information. He rose to his feet and turned to leave when Alle asked her the next question. "What about Lani? What does this make her?"

Gabriel paused at the door without looking back. He couldn't face her for the answer. "She is Nephilim." Sadness and disdain laced his words as he walked out of the room, quietly shutting the door behind him.

Chapter Twenty

Alle didn't know what Nephilim meant, just what she had heard at some point in a church service. They were the reason the Most High flooded the Earth. A race of giants. But Lani was not a giant, although she was tall for her age.

Even though Lani was apparently his daughter, it didn't seem that Gabriel was too happy about the term. Gabriel practically spat the word and then left. Surely, to angels, Nephilim were outcasts akin to demons.

Alle paced the floor in front of the coffee table. Chewing her thumb, she glanced at the book. It lay open to the Nephilim prophecy she had read about days ago.

"I trust Gabriel, but he's been lying to me this whole time. Withholding information is the same as lying, right? Right." She was thinking aloud and talking to a book. "Would Gabriel hurt Lani or me? No. I don't see that happening. But he loves us. That doesn't mean there's not someone here that…"

Alle started panicking. Perhaps Lani was in danger from the angels as much as she might be from the demons. According to Gabriel and Asa, she was in stasis and safe, but what if it was just another half-truth to separate her from her daughter? *Gabriel has already proven he would deceive me.*

That thought had Alle moving through the corridors to the medical wing of the compound where Lani was being watched. She went without Gabriel and made it just fine. The hall must be used to her by now. Or maybe it had known all along who she was, and she hadn't needed Gabriel to go through the doors.

She walked through the quiet halls, trying not to appear panicked. There weren't many angels here since not much needed to be done to those in stasis, and those she did see paid no attention to her. Their eyes didn't even flick her way as she passed.

Alle whooshed into the room where Lani lay. She returned to the pod where she had put Lani what felt like ages ago. She was there, safe and sound. The most peaceful look on her face as she slept. Stasis would prevent her from aging and keep her safe while Alle figured out their path. She breathed a sigh of relief as the tears that never seemed far away pricked the corner of her eyes again.

"She is safe." A soft whisper caused Alle to jump out of her skin. She grabbed her chest and took a deep breath when she realized it was just the stasis nurse who looked over the occupants.

"Yes. I just wanted to check on her," Alle said louder than she intended. She wasn't sure why this woman had whispered like she could wake those lying here. It would take a bit more than loud talking. Maybe it was just her way.

"I assure you. She is safe here. No one has broken into the portals in a long while. We have refortified them, so that will not happen again," she said matter of factly.

"Well, that's great. Now I can add my daughter being kidnapped to my list of worries." The anger that bubbled just under the surface started to overflow.

"What I said was meant to calm you," the golden healer said quietly. Alle's anger didn't seem to phase her.

"Well, it did the opposite, actually. But I'm not worried about demons. Now I'm worried about other angels," Alle admitted. She could not hide her fears even from those who might be her enemy.

"Why would angels hurt this precious one?"

An angel possessed her dad, and her mom was an angel turned human. She might be a...

"Nephilim," the nurse said pointedly like it didn't matter.

Alle's shoulders drooped. "Yeah, that's the label being thrown around."

169

"First, you might want to keep studying in the library. The Nephilim are not what most of your Earthly stories claim. I don't even know if she would be considered so since both of her parents were technically angels at the time of conception," she said all of this with a straight face. Not a hint of emotion per usual. Alle wasn't sure how these angels were so great at being emotionless.

The nurse *tsked*. "Go on. You have work to do. She is in no danger from angels, I assure you. I will alert you if anything is amiss." She paused and pointed her Alle's hand. "If your wrist monitor does not."

"No offense, but if you wanted to hurt her, I doubt you would tell me."

"You are at a crossroads, then. You can continue to trust us and this process, or take her home and see what happens."

"If I take her home, there will probably just be more demon attacks, and I'll lose my humanity and leave her alone."

"Seems you know the best path forward, then."

Alle reluctantly nodded and backed away. She didn't want to leave Lani again. She hated being separated and constantly worrying but didn't see a way to take her with her. Deciding that Lani was the safest she was going to be here, she pressed her fingers to her lips and pressed them against the pod.

Tears sprang back up. The ridiculous tears. It was better than fire and anger. She hated saying goodbye, and she missed Lani so much. Her arms felt empty, and she longed to hold and snuggle her. She looked up for the nurse, but she hovered now a few pods over. Clearly having been dismissed, Alle walked from the room to find all the information she could on Nephilim. Everything she did now was to save her daughter, and she would burn down heaven and hell if it meant doing so. She just needed some information first.

* * *

She walked into the library, intent on finding information. No angels were hovering around, thankfully. Honestly, she welcomed the quietness. She had gotten used to being by herself most of the time. And now she had had her fill of overbearing males.

She did not return to her room, nor did she even have to ask the library to give her information on the Nephilim. A stack of books was waiting for her on the coffee table by the green couch by a cup of milky white coffee. The coffee table had not been there previously.

Gabriel had not returned to the library. She hadn't seen him, and for now, she was glad about it. Maybe he knew she needed space. Sometimes, it felt like he knew her better than she knew herself. Or perhaps he just needed his own space. She knew Runar loved Lani. If Gabriel were actually Runar, she would trust that until she had reason not to.

Alle picked up the books to learn all she needed about the Nephilim. The first couple of books on the stack didn't give her much more than she already knew. One only had the standard definition. Had the library just pulled all the books that referenced Nephilim? It was like a Google search without the internet. In another book, the Nephilim were briefly mentioned in connection with Noah's flood and David and Goliath. She needed the refresher, so she read them anyway.

In the early history of humankind, angels left heaven unsanctioned after Adam and Eve left the garden. They left because they had fallen in love with human women or their beauty. The angels created a race of men with superpowers, essentially. The Most High flooded the Earth because of the evil that angels and humans had unleashed. It was an excellent way to get rid of this super race.

After reading this story, Alle was surprised that the Most High had agreed to let her become human. He must have had a good reason, though.

Alle gathered that these people were bigger than average humans and always seemed to be men. Even though everyone on Earth was supposed to be wiped out in the flood except for Noah and his family, there were mentions of giants afterward. Most famously, when David killed the giant Goliath. It would be interesting to find out how the giants escaped the flood. Perhaps the genetics had been passed down through Noah's family.

She finally made it through the stack to the final book. She opened the book to the title page. The Narrative of the Nephilim. "I probably could

171

have just started with this," she whispered. The book gave a detailed account of the genealogy of the Nephilim. Usually, this would make her fall asleep. Her own mother had created a book on their genealogical background. She would drone on and on about how they were related to Ghengis Kahn. That didn't make them unique. Half the world was related to the murdering, conquering rapist. Black hair was the only physical trait her mother had that even remotely resembled a Mongolian. Alle had taken more after her father. But this book promised to answer the questions that Alle had.

The book traced the lineage of the Nephilim back to Ham's wife. Ham was the youngest son of Noah. He and his wife were saved from the flood. Alle looked closely at a handwritten note in the margin. It was old and barely legible. It was written in a calligraphic style, probably with a quill and inkwell. It noted that all the children born to the original angels and human pairings were male. The giant babies tended to kill the mothers during childbirth before the medical miracle of cesarean, Alle assumed. The male babies were not infertile and went on to have children. Male children received the dominant traits and became superhumans. Female children were only carriers of the genes. Ham's wife was the daughter of a Nephilim male. Alle wondered if Noah had known that. Noah cursed his youngest son for embarrassing him, so maybe he found out later. Having been excommunicated from his family, Ham and his wife went on to create the tribe of Canaan.

It seemed the Nephilim genes were passed on through the generations, and some sects of Canaan got more than others. There was one group of very powerful humans called the Anak, or the sons of Anakim. The narrative talked about the Anak in reverence, calling them men of renown. It listed all of the abilities and accomplishments. Impossible feats. It certainly sounded like a race of superhumans. When the Jewish people came to take back their land after a four-hundred-year absence, the Anak frightened all their spies except for two.

According to the author, Goliath, the infamous giant killed by David, was Anak. Goliath had four brothers. Each of them was giant as well. After Goliath's demise, the brothers escaped East. These brothers mingled with

Asian women and founded the original Mongol tribes. They continued to pass their super angel genes, which resulted in a warrior race and one of the most feared conquerors in ancient Asian history, Genghis Kahn.

Chapter Twenty-One

Gabriel left Alle's room and went to the viewing room. Here, he could see any moment in time. He worried that it hadn't been the best decision to tell Alle who he was, but remembered what it was like when Alle left. Needing reassurance that his decision was the best he had at the time, he searched for the moment he decided to become Runar. Finding it quickly, he watched the scene unfold on the screen.

Lex had lounged on the couches in the warehouse. It had been a comfortable place for everyone to meet, but tension had hung thick in the air. Everyone had avoided the leader of their squadron if they could. Adriel had been on assignment. She only entered the hall when it was absolutely necessary. Lex was required to endure the melancholy as Gabriel's second.

Alle had left them more than two years prior in the natural world. The veil moved on without her. Besides being bonded to Gabriel, she wasn't vital to any of their missions or the guarded. It was more of an effort to keep her from destroying the world than it was beneficial to have her around. He would never say that to Gabriel, though. She was a leader, though. When it was time to shine, she was the best at organizing, planning, and carrying out her vengeance.

As if Lex had summoned him with his thoughts, Gabe walked in. Lex gave a casual wave and waited for him to speak. He didn't want to get his head bit off. There had been more than a few arguments lately.

"We have a new assignment," Gabe said grimly.

"Is it life or death?" Lex asked.

"It's always life or death," Gabe replied, leaning on the conference table in front of the couches.

"Of course. What do you need?"

Gabe didn't respond immediately. He perused the map that lay in front of him. Lex knew what he was looking for. He had been looking for it for two years. He stood by his friend and put a hand on his shoulder. "She's going to be fine."

Gabe pumped the muscle in his jaw. "She's weak and vulnerable. A human toddler."

"But she has a mother and father that love her and will protect her." Lex had made this argument many times. It never changed.

"I can protect her. I wish she would have trusted me."

"It's not that she didn't trust you. She knew your nature. Maybe she was sparing you from fighting your true self for her sake."

"We're bonded. That's the point. We always overcome our true selves for the sake of the other."

Lex moved away. "Not this time."

Gabe clenched his fist. In a flash, the chair to his right flew across the library. The lights flickered in response. The warehouse did not appreciate his show of aggression. He regained his composure with a heave of his chest.

"I know you miss her. Maybe there's a way you can protect her without breaking your promise."

Gabe shook his head. "I've been through this a million times."

"Perhaps the Most High has some ideas," Lex offered.

"He knows all, but I'm afraid to approach his throne."

"Maybe you could also become human." Lex hadn't tried this approach. He hated seeing his best friend like this. He wouldn't have suggested it earlier, but they couldn't go on like this for eighty natural years.

"It was a miracle that the Most High allowed Alle this opportunity. The bloodline had been all but eradicated. Finding another human isn't likely."

"Maybe you don't have to be born human."

Gabriel scrunched his nose like he had smelled something rotten. "Possession? That's revolting."

Lex shrugged. "It might be the only way." He looked at the map on the table. "I hate to see you this way."

"I'll consider it," he said noncommittally, looking over the map as if the conversation had never happened.

Lex nodded and said no more about it. He waited patiently until Gabriel was ready to continue.

After a few minutes, Gabriel broke his silence. "Your assignment is a pastor in Indiana."

"Indiana?"Lex scoffed.

"Is there a problem, Lex?" Gabriel growled.

"Indiana doesn't seem like a place where people would need guardians."

"There's been activity. The humans have organized a big sporting event in the capital city. It's similar to the games in Rome. We're sending several squads. You will lead this one."

"Where are you going to be?"

Gabriel raised his eyebrow and gave him a look that spoke volumes. He didn't answer to Lex.

* * *

Gabriel found another moment four years earlier...

Gabriel stood at the bedside in the hospital.

The due date was just a few days away. The doctor rolled in an ultrasound machine. He squeezed the cold gel on her belly and slid the wand around, pressing in here and there. After a moment, he closed his eyes and shook his head.

They moved the couple upstairs to the maternity ward. Instead of waiting for the due date, the doctor encouraged her to induce labor.

In the darkened room, the couple held each other and prayed for a miracle. Tears soaked the hospital gown and the sheets behind her head.

"Please, Father. I pray that they are wrong. Give this child a heartbeat and full life," the mother pleaded with the Most High. "Please, I beg you. I know you can heal all things. You have overcome death. Death is nothing compared to you."

176

But the Most High did not give her what she wanted. Gabriel had been the baby's guardian. He did not interfere with providence. His purpose was to protect humans from the Morning Star and his legions.

Guardians also guarded the soul until it entered the veil and heaven. He was here to escort the baby's soul and make sure he made it. The mother was right. The Most High had overcome death. Spiritual death. She would meet her son in heaven. It was rare for the Most High to interfere with physical death. He required an extraordinary amount of faith before it was done.

Gabriel could feel this woman's faith. The weapons and wings etched into his skin glowed brighter with her prayers and petitions to the Most High. She had the faith.

Hours later, she pushed with all her might. The baby boy was born at 3:15 AM. Gabriel had already escorted his soul to heaven, having died hours earlier. The mother rocked his lifeless body and continued to pray for her son to live.

* * *

Gabriel bowed before the throne of the Most High. "I'm asking that you answer her prayer. Allow her son to live." Intercession was not Gabriel's place. Intercession was for the one that sat next to the Most High on his throne. But he wasn't just here on the young mother's behalf.

A voice boomed in his head. It was not audible. Just an impression of words in his head. It was the Most High's way of speaking. His words could create worlds, so he rarely used them audibly. "He doesn't want to return to his body. It was his choice."

"Humbly, I have another request." Gabriel knelt frozen in place until the voice of the Most High filled his mind again.

"Rise and speak your mind."

Gabriel stood but still kept his eyes on the golden floor. It was challenging to look at the Most High. Not because he required angels to look down; the Most High was the source of light in heaven. It was like looking at the sun, but brighter. "I'm having difficulty. Alle has been gone. I'm concerned for her safety, and I miss her."

"It is your nature to concern yourself with the safety of others. I created you with this purpose."

"Yes. My duty is to serve you. I will bear this pain if I must, but I'm asking for the opportunity to protect."

"You want to be her guardian?"

"She asked me not to interfere as her guardian. I gave my word that I wouldn't."

"Gabriel, do not be afraid to ask for extraordinary things." The Most High spoke with patience and encouragement.

"I want to become human. Not as Alle did. I understand the difficulty that went into her transition. But I could possess this human child. He is in close proximity to Alle, and I believe that we would eventually cross paths. I could be a part of her life without interfering as a guardian."

"It would be many human years before you would meet. You would have to live as a human without your angel capabilities."

Gabriel nodded, "I would only ask to keep my knowledge and memories."

"This is a difficult thing, you ask."

"You are capable of all things. This would allow the human mother to have her miracle, and I would be able to be with Alle."

"Just because I can do all things doesn't mean all things are beneficial. Your time with her will be short."

"It is worth it." Gabriel didn't care if it was a minute. He needed to be with her again.

The Most High contemplated this idea. "I will grant your request. You may possess the human child's body with your memories and knowledge. You may not use that knowledge for anything other than finding and protecting Alle. She will need your love and guidance as a reprieve from her suffering. You may not eliminate her suffering. You may only help her endure it."

"Yes, Most High," Gabriel responded and knelt again.

"You may go now." The Most High stood. He walked down the six steps of the dais. Gabriel felt small in his presence but felt a hand on his shoulder.

CHAPTER TWENTY-ONE

"I will see you soon, faithful one. Go in peace."

* * *

Gabriel gave a loud cry... The sound filled the hospital room. The doctors and nurses clapped and cheered at the sound. Tears continued to dampen the hospital gown and pillow beneath Mom's head. She sagged in relief, holding her baby boy. "Thank you, Father. Thank you for answering this prayer and returning my boy."

Gabriel knew and understood every word. He was content for now. Being a guardian angel in a vulnerable human body would be the biggest challenge of his existence. He hadn't thought this all the way through. A tiny human brain could barely contain Gabriel's spirit. It was indeed a miracle.

Alle was worth every second. He would find his way to her. He had realized over these long years without her that he didn't need to guard her because she was weak. He needed to protect her because she was important.

Gabriel turned off the memory in the viewing room and headed back to the warehouse. He could always trust that it would give him what he needed.

Chapter Twenty-Two

Alle slammed the book closed. A puff of dust rose. She coughed. She placed the book on the coffee table and started chewing her nails. She needed to talk to Gabriel. No, she needed to talk to her mom. Had she known about this?

Gabriel walked to the alcove as if thinking about him brought him to her. He noticed the titles of the stack of books sitting on her table.

Alle raised a finger. "Gabriel, before you say anything, we need to talk about Lani."

He didn't respond at all. He crossed his arms over his incredible pecs, shirtless again, and waited for her to continue.

She began pacing. "I know you said she is Nephilim. I have been doing some research, and I do not see how she can be. First-" She held up one finger as she paced. Gabriel just tracked her with his eyes. "-all of the Nephilim were male. Lani is not. Second, neither of us was actually human when she was conceived. Or we both were, I'm not sure. And in reading these dreadfully boring books...

I took one for the team, there, I really did...

I haven't found one instance of a Nephilim being born from a human possessed by Angels or to humans with angel souls. Everything says they are the products of a human and an angel. Third, when the Nephilim are born, they kill their moms because they are ginormous. At least by ancient child-birthing standards. Modern times, I'm not so sure." She finished the word vomit without a single interruption from Gabriel.

He sat then and leaned forward with his elbows on his knees and his forehead resting against his thumbs but didn't say anything. She added, "I just don't want you to hate her or yourself because of what you think she is."

Gabriel's head popped up at that. "You think I don't love Lani? That I wouldn't do everything in my power to keep her safe? She talks about her angel daddy because I go to see her every day. She happened to be able to see me, and we would play like I always did with her. She... the both of you are my heart, and I would never do anything to endanger her. Frankly, it hurts that you would think so."

Her eyes widened in surprise. Words wouldn't form sentences. She fell beside Gabriel on the couch as the fight drained out of her. She was prepared to defend Lani against her own father, but her efforts were apparently misdirected.

"Alle, none of what you figured out here matters. If she is Nephilim, it makes it harder to protect her. If she is not, it doesn't matter. Right now, they are focused on you. Already, the demons are amassing for something big. It's not like we can just jump out and tell them to call the whole thing off because you are not Nephilim. They assume you have the ability all Nephilim possess. Even if neither of you are technically Nephilim, you are different than other humans. "

Alle had started pacing again but stopped with this new information. "What ability?"

"To open the veil and barrier." He paused at the look on her face. "Don't worry. Lani is safe here." Gabriel paused, trying to think of how much to tell her. "Alle, there is a prophecy."

"The Nephilim prophecy. I know. It says the Nephilim can bring down the gates of hell. I assume that means the veil or whatever it's called to hell."

"You read about it in the diary?"

"Yes," she snapped. "It would have been nice if you had told me about it. But how did you know it was in the diary?"

"The diary is yours. It has your symbol on the cover. It's hard to see."

"I noticed it when I opened it." She held up her arm and traced her birthmark. "It's the same shape."

Gabriel nodded his head, "Everything written in that book was your words and your accounts. Because I spent a lot of time with you and we are soul bonded, you trusted me. You allowed me to read most of what was in there."

Alle held up a finger. "There is so much in those statements. Let's take them one at a time, starting with soul bonded. I remembered that from before, but I have no idea what that means. Go." She pointed at him to explain.

"Before you chose to leave and become human, we bound our souls together. Our angel souls. It's like angels getting married, kind of. Angels don't marry, not in the human sense. It's similar to the concept of soul mates. We have a bond, unlike other beings. It was by choice. It wasn't created with our creation. But because we are bonded, it was very difficult for me when you became human. The Most High thought making me your guardian would be enough, but I had made a vow to you. It was painful for me, even if it wasn't for you. We devised another solution, and the Most High allowed it."

Alle rubbed her chest. She had always felt a special bond with Runar. Something that transcended ordinary human love. It wasn't painful, but something had been missing before he came into her life. "I'm sorry." She didn't know why she was apologizing, but she felt guilty for hurting him, even if she couldn't remember. "Runar." She squeezed her eyes shut at the slip. "Gabriel. I'm sorry I hurt you by choosing this path if it's worth anything at all. Thank you for following me. I always told you I wouldn't know what to do without you. I'm honestly not doing all that great."

Gabriel stood and crossed over to her. She allowed him to wrap his arms around her. "I know. I'm sorry I left you, especially without saying goodbye."

Gabriel pulled her back to the couch and sat. Alle put her hand in his and leaned her head on his shoulder. She was tired of being mad at him. He kissed the top of her head and breathed in her scent. Suddenly, his hand was cupping her cheek and pulling her lips to his. She turned to allow him access. She parted them and let his tongue to sweep against hers. She was in his lap in the next instant, straddling his waist as he caressed her back. Still kissing him, she pressed herself into him. She felt him beneath her, and her body lost control. He found restraint and pushed her back just a little.

"Alle, we can't do this now. We really might have a Nephilim on our hands. You are still human, and now I'm one hundred percent angel."

She sucked in a breath to steady her now raging hormones. She leaned her head against his neck and allowed for his embrace. Even though he started this little tryst, she allowed him to stop it and moved out of his lap.

Gabriel grabbed her hand. "I'm sorry I kissed you just now. It's been tough not to."

She squeezed his fingers and smiled. "It's ok. But we'll have to figure this out. Where do we go from here? We can't be on the fence forever. My human heart can't take it."

Stepping away to give herself some space and clear her head, she changed the subject back to the task at hand. "Can we talk about how the diary is mine?"

"It is."

"I believe you, but why didn't you tell me sooner?" She sat on the other side of the couch. No temptation with five feet of space between them.

"This is still your journey. And you made me promise to let you figure it out. You said it would be better for you to learn the truth on your own if you needed to. You knew you would never believe anyone otherwise. And as we discussed before, your human brain might have exploded if we didn't do it slowly and let you adjust."

"So in the Gauntlet, you knew I could do all those things because I have done them before."

"I suspected. I would never have let you get hurt, but apparently, the elders thought we needed that little exercise. Maybe they've seen something where human Alle might need a little angel training. I hope not, but you never know. I know you are mighty. Although I would love to have you back as an angel beside me, I don't want you to lose your humanity and leave Lani alone."

Alle raked her hands down her face. "Ok. What are we going to do about Lani? As you said, it probably doesn't matter if she is Nephilim. If the demons think she is, they might take her to open the barrier and the veil. She might even have the ability they want."

"Demons aren't the smartest. Evil and darkness have corrupted their minds. But right now, I think they are focused on you being the Nephilim of the prophecy. I don't think they knew I was Runar or have considered Lani to be significant."

"She is literally possessed by a demon right now."

"I think that was an accident to get to you. They might suspect you could produce Nephilim heirs, but I think they are focused on you being the Nephilim of the prophecy. You allowed them to use your energy at the ghost tour, so they know you are some part angel."

"I'm not Nephilim, though." She paused. "At least, I don't think I am. I definitely can't open the veil."

"You need practice with the veil, but you have that ability."

"Do you think I should practice, though? Given the prophecy."

"I think you put yourself at risk if you don't practice. You could open the veil to escape if you or Lani were attacked."

Alle thought for a minute. "I need to talk to my mom. Is there a way we can see her?"

"I don't think it's a good idea to talk to her directly yet, but I have an idea. Let's go back to the moment you were conceived."

Horror and disgust shrouded Alle's face. "Ew. No, absolutely not. No one wants to see their parents at the moment of their own conception."

"Not exactly that moment. Your birth is going to be a special case. The Most High was putting an angel soul into a human body. Maybe something that happened before or after that will give us a clue without having to go all the way through the veil and alert the demons where you are. Or having to visit the throne room and risk your choice to stay."

Alle held up a finger. "One more thing before we go anywhere. Why did you lie to me about being able to see Runar?"

"I didn't lie. The baby who died is in heaven, beyond where we can go right now and still return to earth. You can't see him. I know that's not what you asked, but I didn't lie. And you weren't ready to know I was actually Runar."

Alle thought about his words. She didn't think angels were allowed to lie.

It was a sin, after all. If they lied, they were equating themselves to the Father of Lies. The head honcho of hell. There was no way any self-respecting angel would stoop that low. And Gabriel definitely would not do that. They could worm their way around the truth, though, as he had done when she asked about Runar. *But I told him to let me figure it out*, she thought.

When it all came down to it, she trusted Gabriel with her and Lani's lives. A love like they had couldn't form without the deepest trust. She knew whatever he did was to protect them. He was a guardian, after all.

"Can we agree moving forward, you will tell me the whole truth? No more half-truths or precise wording needed?"

He scooted forward to the edge of the couch. "Alle, I have always told you the truth. I will never lie to you. But I will always do what I need to do to protect you. Even if that means withholding information from you. So no, I do not agree to this."

"How can I trust you then?"

"The same way you always have. Trust that I have your best interest in mind; I will tell you if you need to know something. I'm only doing now what you asked me to do before you left."

Alle leaned back and closed her eyes. She knew Gabriel was right. She didn't even know everything that could trigger her to shrug off her human self and start avenging everyone. But she really hated being in the dark and not having all the information. She sighed deeply. "Can you at least tell me if there is any more life-changing information I don't know?"

"If there is, I don't know about it. Again, I'm not all-knowing," he said.

Alle returned his smile. That would have to do for now. She really didn't have much of a choice. She leaned forward, ready to find some answers.

"Alright. My mom always said she prayed for me. Like prayed to become pregnant with me because she didn't think she could have kids. She and my father had tried forever."

"Ok, let's go see about those prayers. Maybe you were the answer," he winked.

"Wait, why can't I just go see the Most High and ask him instead?"

"As the elder discussed at the fountain. You would probably decide to give up the mission. He promised only to guide you the way he would a human. Seeing him directly, you might decide to give up your humanity. We're walking a fine line already. I would prefer Lani still have her mom when this is done," Gabriel patiently explained again.

"Right. So much has happened since I went to the fountain. I forgot that part. Ok. We'll go see Mom first."

They both stood. As they reached the door, Gabriel grabbed Alle's hand and entwined their fingers. Broody Gabriel had disappeared for now, and happiness filtered through Alle. But as they walked through the door, Alle remembered this would only last until it was time to go back to her life.

Chapter Twenty-Three

Alle and Gabriel stepped into the viewing room. It was yet another place in the hall she couldn't remember. It reminded her of a police interrogation room she had seen on television.

Here, they could see any point and moment in time. So they could return to when Alle's mom asked for a baby. It wasn't difficult to find. They could eliminate every moment after Alle's conception, which was roughly ten months. They could eliminate the moment of conception because no one really wanted to see that. They scoured her mom's life previous to that and finally found her on her knees beside her bed about a month before the conception.

The room was dark except for a lamp on a small table beside the bed. The clock read 9 pm. The gaudy floral bedspread was neatly tucked under the pillows and into the side of the bed. The matching dresser stood in the corner of the room, but there was no other furniture in the sparsely decorated room. Her parents had lived frugally for the first few years of their marriage.

Alle barely recognized her mom as the young woman before her. So much had changed. There were no worry lines or fine wrinkles. Her skin was smooth and plump. She didn't even have a hint of gray hair. She clasped her hands tightly and squeezed her eyes shut as if that would allow the Most High to hear her prayers better. Her white sleeveless nightgown hung loosely to her knees on the floor.

Alle could whisper the prayer with her. She heard the story so many times she had it memorized. "Please, Lord, I just want a child. A child to love. Please just let me have this one blessing." The next part was a surprise, though.

After the prayer, the room lit up. Alle recognized the man who appeared beside her mom as an angel only because of the wings tattooed on his back and the intricate designs on his arms. Also, he was shirtless because that's how angels rolled, apparently.

"I recognize this angel. He was a guardian," Gabriel said.

"Was? As in, he's retired, right," Alle asked hopefully.

"No. Angels don't retire. Unfortunately, he was vanquished, not long after this moment actually. He must have been your mother's guardian."

That made Alle sad for some reason. She had thought of angels as eternal. She didn't want them to be vanquished and gone forever. Human souls returned to the Most High, would Angel souls also? She wanted to ask Gabriel, but it didn't seem like the appropriate time.

The angel revealed himself and spoke to her mom. "Are you willing to do anything to have a child?"

"Yes." Her mom's voice trembled as she bowed before the angel. She shielded her eyes from the bright light. She didn't dare look at the magnificent being.

"Laila, you have been chosen to bear an angel soul. Because you carry Nephilim blood. You are a descendant of an ancient race of angel-human hybrids. Although your ancestry is somewhat diluted, we believe you can carry a healthy baby."

Alle leaned toward Gabriel and whispered, "Mom must have begun researching after that little speech.".

Laila was shocked but finally recovered enough to look up and ask, "What must I do?"

"Your part is already done. You must accept the role of mother to the Nephilim. I will take care of the rest. But you must know the Nephilim can only be born from an angel and human conception."

Laila's mouth opened and closed like a fish. "I love my husband very much. I don't think I can betray him."

The angel smiled. "Do not worry. Lay with your husband. I will take care of everything. You will be with child in a few weeks."

He turned to leave but paused. "One more thing… this is the only child you will have. There will be no others. This child will likely be barren as well. Your line will die with her." The angel disappeared. The scene went dark, and the dim lights of the room came up.

Alle was frozen with shock. After a few moments, Gabriel grabbed her hand and pulled her out of the room. Alle walked on stiff legs, unable to process what she had just seen.

She decided to focus on the biggest question. "So, is my dad not really my dad?"

"I think your dad is an angel," Gabriel confirmed.

"But… he said, 'lay with your husband.' Surely, Mom didn't cheat on my dad."

"No, I think Pileal possessed your dad for at least one night. Maybe he convinced him to allow it. We don't have time to look for that moment, though. I think we know enough to assume that you are indeed Nephilim."

"Still one thing. I'm not male."

"I think the book was wrong. Nephilim can be female as well. At least they can now," Gabriel said quietly. "Your angel soul is female. You were born female. You wanted a human life. Perhaps the gene for giants and superpowers is on the Y chromosome? Female Nephilim are just carriers of those traits? Pileal also assumed you would be barren. Maybe human males cannot conceive with Nephilim females. The Most High had not sent me to be your guardian or Runar, so I don't have all the answers."

Alle crossed her arms and tapped her chin. "That could make sense." They began walking back to the library.

"So wait, wouldn't the Most High know I was Nephilim?"

Gabriel nodded, "It sounds like a Nephilim descendant is the only one who can birth an angel soul."

"But what about the prophecy? Surely, he knew a Nephilim would open the veil."

"Well, if you think about it, the prophecy has already come true. You opened the veil in the Gauntlet."

The elephant that had been sitting on her chest since she read the prophecy lifted. She took a deep breath. Maybe this wasn't going to be so bad after all. She felt better, but she knew this wasn't over. The demons knew what she was, and they had plans for her. If their plans for her didn't work out, they could use Lani even though she might not be considered Nephilim. She already knew the demons wouldn't care. They would use her anyway. She was glad they hadn't had more children.

A memory clicked in Alle's head and filled her with dread. "Gabriel, you left me a gift before you died. In case I wanted to try for more children without you."

Recognition showed on Gabriel's face. He hung his head. "I just hated to see you so sad, Alle. I was trying to give you the option."

"Lani is enough. She is obviously a miracle. You heard him say that I was supposed to be barren. But if the demons got their hands on your DNA. They could make millions of Nephilim."

Gabriel looked up in thought. "They would have to find a Nephilim descendant."

"Even though Pileal said my mom's line would die with her, she can't be the only Nephilim descendant. There are tens of thousands of Ghengis Kahn offspring."

Gabriel sighed. "I'll send Lex back to prevent me from doing that. It's the easiest way."

Alle nodded. Knowing it was the right decision didn't make it easier. The moment she realized she wouldn't have any more children, she was filled with sadness and loss.

Alle's wrist monitor began to vibrate as they walked down the hall toward the library. She held it up. A bright red light blinked on and off. Then, a notification popped up in a hologram. "Unauthorized relocation," scrolled through the image. "Demons in the veil," Gabriel yelled to the angels that appeared around him as lights started flashing. An emergency sound blared through the hall.

Alle took off, running toward the stasis room. Just as they stepped through the door, another door opened into a portal across the room. A man dressed in black stepped through with the pod Lani was lying in.

"They are using the old portal system," Gabriel snapped.

Lex, Adriel, and several other angels appeared beside them.

"I thought the portals were destroyed," Lex huffed.

"They must have figured out a way to use them. No time to worry about that. We must follow," Gabriel replied.

They all ran through the medical ward, not caring if they disturbed the pods. As they ran past the area Lani had been in earlier, Alle noticed a pile of black goo beside one of the healers. The healer was either dead or unconscious. She had taken out one of the kidnapper's friends, though.

"I can track the demon's energy. We'll have to follow. Lex shut down the portals. Adriel, you're with us," Gabriel snapped orders.

A pang of jealousy flared. He had picked Adriel over Lex to go with them. There wasn't time to deal with those negative emotions. She trusted him to do what was best for Lani.

Instead of following the demon through the portal system he was using, Gabriel used his energy to cut through to the room he knew the demon would be in. They all stepped through to the cafeteria. Just as they stepped through, the demon stepped through his portal. Gabriel cut again. They all stepped through to the hall. They were closer this time but still missed him as the demon stepped through to another portal. Gabriel cut through again, and they stepped into the gauntlet room.

Dread filled Alle at the thought of being stuck in this room while the demon had Lani. The room did not function as before, with the alarm blaring, so they didn't get stuck there. Gabriel was able to cut through again. He was in a hurry. Alle just continued to hang on to his arm. She didn't want to get separated but would move away if he needed to fight. She could probably hold her own, but she had no weapons to call.

As they chased the demon through portals, it seemed like Gabriel used more effort to pull back the veil. There wasn't much Alle could do. She couldn't pull back the veil on her own. She had been trying when no one was watching her.

They were nanoseconds from catching up with the demon in the next room. The demon poured a package of powder into his palm. He lifted it to his mouth and blew the powder toward them just as he disappeared into the natural world. The sparkly powder coated Gabriel as he flicked out his sword. He tried to pull back the veil to the natural world but couldn't. He screamed in frustration, throwing all the power he had into it. The powder on his skin sparkled brighter as if it was absorbing the power he pushed out. Gabriel didn't notice. He was too focused on getting to the demon.

"I can't open the veil." He said as he turned to find his way back to the hall.

"What? What are you talking about?" Alle still held Gabriel's arm. "Try again. I'll help you."

"No, Alle. It's a safety precaution. No one goes in or out until the threat is over. If one demon figures out a way to get in, an entire horde could just as easily breach the veil. That, above everything else, cannot happen."

"What? No! We have to get to her. She's just a baby. If they discover what she is, they will wake her up and try to get her to use her power to open the veil. Gabriel, you have to get me to my daughter now!" Fiery flames in her eyes flashed through her irises.

"Working on it," he fumed. She could tell he was just as frantic as she was. He was doing a better job of controlling himself, though.

"That's not good enough!" Alle yelled. Fire engulfed her eyes and hair. Flames licked her fingertips. Adriel stepped next to Gabriel. Alle froze. She would never hurt Gabriel, but Adriel acted as if she would. Alle doused the flames before anyone could talk her down.

Adriel held her hand out as a shield. "Let him work it out. We'll get her back. Don't worry."

Alle collapsed to her knees and broke into quiet sobs. Adriel was by her side before Gabriel could reach her. Adriel communicated mentally with Gabriel that she could take this while he figured out what to do next.

Alle let them. She knew exactly what she was going to do to get her back. And she didn't need a single angel to do it. Alle shrugged off Adriel's comfort and wiped the wetness from her cheeks. She stood, allowing only fierce determination to take over.

Chapter Twenty-Four

I t turned out Alle did need the angels a little bit.

"Why did the veil lockdown right after the demon left?" Alle paced in the war room. It was a dark room with monitors she had never been in before. The angels had been keeping track of her house and Lani's school. Somehow, they had missed two demons working through the old portal system.

They had a cloaking spell where they could appear as angels. There wasn't enough for a legion of demons, or they would have already been in the veil. They wouldn't need Alle and Lani if they could cloak all the demons as angels. This had been a small op. Only when the pod moved was anyone alerted to the demon's presence. Sadly, the healing angel didn't have the skills to take on both demons and keep the pod from being taken.

An angel with blond hair and piercing golden eyes answered her, "The veil is designed to lock down in segments. I'm not sure how this demon figured that out or how they figured out how to use the old portal system.

The lockdown procedure gives us time to deal with the threat. The demon used our procedure against us. Usually, a few angels can maneuver around the lockdown by opening the veil. Since that also failed, we will learn from our mistakes and make corrections."

"Well, your mistake may have cost my daughter her life," Alle seethed. She didn't want to enrage the angels who could pulverize her with a single look, but she was having an anger management issue at the moment. This one was an archangel. She had been told his name, but she wasn't paying attention. In her head, she called him Army Guy. That's the impression he gave.

Angels moved about the room with military precision. Receiving and delivering messages. There were no glowing white robes in this room. These angels had many tattoos with weapons they could call with a single thought.

Alle continued pacing. She had begun to chew on her thumb again. Any time she stopped, she tapped her foot as she thought about what she could do to get Lani back.

"I have to go. When will the veil be back online?"

"We are working on it now. It shouldn't be too much longer," Army guy replied.

Alle didn't bother rolling her eyes or glaring. There were too many thoughts bouncing around in her head. "Where have they taken her?"

"They haven't taken her to your house or her school. We will check those places as soon as possible, but our best guess is the underside. Let's hope that's not the case."

"Why? Why are we hoping that's not the case?"

Gabriel stepped forward from the shadows. He was a protector and a fighter, but he was not the strategist here. He put his hand on the small of her back. "Angels can't go to the underside," he said lowly.

Alle stopped her pacing and slapped her hands to her face. Worry was not an emotion that made her cry. Worry moved her to action.

"Can I go to the underside?" she asked Gabriel, but Army guy answered.

"The only beings who can go to the underside are humans, demons, and Nephilim. Angels will either die or become demons," he said while never looking up from his work on the table.

"Ok. As soon as the veil opens, I'm going."

"Alle, no, we will find another way," Gabriel chastised.

"Gabriel. You just heard your friend." She gestured toward Army guy. "This is the only way."

The way Gabriel looked at Army guy made her think they weren't true friends. He pulled her away from the legion of angels in the war room.

"Gabriel, I told her I would keep her safe and couldn't do that. I have to get her back. If this is the only way, then this is what we are doing."

Gabriel growled through clenched teeth, "We will find another way. They won't hurt her. She is still safe in stasis. There is no way they can open the pod." She looked away from him, having already made up her mind. He grabbed her hands and made her look at him. "Alle, this is what they want. They took her to get to you." Desperation laced Gabriel's words.

"You promised she was safe here. There was no way they could get her here, yet she is gone. I can't take a chance they figure out how to open the pod and use her. It has to be me. If I die and she lives, it will be worth it. But I won't abandon her to that fate."

Gabriel dropped her hands and hung his head, defeated. Clearly, Alle had made up her mind. He whispered, "Michael seems to have figured out what you are. He is willing to sacrifice you to get Lani. I am not."

Alle's eyes bugged out of her head, "Army guy is THE Michael?"

Gabriel nodded. Alle cut her eyes and crossed her arms. "I should have known." She looked back up at Gabriel. "What does that mean? He doesn't care about either of us?"

"He cares, but not personally about you. His main job is protecting the veil. You could be seen as a threat, but I don't think he will do anything yet. Since the Most High sanctioned all of this." He shook his head. "I don't like it, but you are right. You are the only one that can get to Lani if she is in the underside. We won't get help from Michael or the legions. "

Alle threw up her hands, "Finally, someone is talking some sense."

Gabriel grabbed her arms and turned her back to face him. He spoke in a low voice so that only she could hear. "Alle, this is serious. If you die as a human in the underside, you stay there. If you shed your humanity and become an angel, you will become a demon. If you save Lani and make it back to the natural world, I'm not sure what will happen with Michael. He may be making plans to confiscate you both himself."

"We will deal with that when it comes. We can only worry about the troubles of today and let tomorrow worry about itself."

Gabriel sighed and returned to the war room. "Michael, I will take over this operation. Lex will coordinate things in the natural world."

If Michael objected, he didn't show it. He simply nodded and left the room, likely to plan what would happen if Alle failed or was captured.

Gabriel grabbed her hand and led her back out of the room. Adriel and Lex were waiting for them in the hall with a small team of angels.

"What is up with Army guy? You said he was all business, but he seemed to hate me."

"We don't have time to explain the nuances of all that happened before you left. You two argued a lot about this decision. He disagreed it was a good idea. Of course, he submitted to the Most High, but he has been preparing for war since that day."

Alle nodded. Unless she shed her humanity and remembered her angel life, there would be some millennia-sized gaping holes with no way to fill them. It was time to just go with it. "Isn't fighting demons Michael's thing?"

"As I said, his top priority is the veil and keeping heaven safe. He's more of a full Army battleground sort of guy. He's the one to call when you need the big guns." Gabriel motioned to his team of angels. "We're more of the black ops people. We're the ones you want when you don't want world wars and epic battles to ensue," He explained in human terms.

"Yes, let's avoid the epic battle," Alle said.

The dimmed lights finally brightened, and they all looked around. "That's our cue. We're finally back online."

"Let's get to the library, and we'll make a plan there."

* * *

The library looked pristine when they entered. Fortunately, no demons had run through here. The books on the Nephilim Alle had been reading were put away. They weren't on the table any longer. She hoped they had been locked away in a safe with a magical key. Alle ran upstairs to get her bag and her diary. As she ran her hands over the symbol on the front, she knew she couldn't take it where she was going. There was too much information in the pages. She didn't want the demons to get the information or find out anything about the veil.

196

Although she trusted Gabriel and her gang, she wasn't sure she trusted all the angels with the knowledge she had found either. She hadn't been able to read all of it yet, but she knew it was safer here.

She laid it back on the bed in her room and asked the library to look after it again. She turned to grab her bag off the floor, and the book was gone when she turned around. She smiled. The library was so quick to honor her request.

Back downstairs, their little alcove had turned into a conference room. The couches were gone, and a long table and office chairs were in their place. The planning had already begun.

A map of the little town she barely knew lay in the middle of the table. Pictures of her home, Lani's school, and surrounding areas were spread out as the angels discussed their strategy.

"I'll see if I can pull back the veil now it's online. We can't go straight from the veil to the underside, so we must go to her house first."

Alle interrupted by walking in and sitting down in one of the chairs. All the angels looked at her with wary eyes.

"It's ok, guys. I'm not going to go all avenging angel on you. And I'll get her back. I just need you to do what you can."

That seemed to satisfy them. They all nodded.

"We were just getting a few things in order before we leave," Gabriel explained.

"Carry on," she said with a little nod to the table.

Gabriel continued briefing the crew. "We need to clear the house. I know we've had some demon activity there recently. Lex, were the wards inside the house working properly?"

"Yes, there were some demons outside the property. They were probably just investigating whether she had returned yet. We killed them. We found no evidence the demons were inside." His usual laid-back manner was replaced with military preciseness. He was all business now.

"Good. We'll set up a home base at the house then and discuss the next steps there. Alle, you will need to get briefed about the underside so you know what you're getting into."

"It won't matter. I'm going either way," she said confidently.

Gabriel turned toward her. "Yes, I know. But I want you to be somewhat prepared." He looked at his team. "It's time to move out. I will pull back the veil here."

A small army traipsed into the library. "This is a small special op," Alle asked with round eyes.

He nodded. "We need to be ready for anything."

Alle took her usual spot beside him and placed her hand on his arm. Everyone behind them touched the person in front of them on the shoulder. They were a well-oiled machine, and they had done this before. Gabriel pulled back the veil, and they all stepped through.

Chapter Twenty-Five

The small angel force stood in front of Alle and Runar's house. Her old house before she moved to her small town Victorian. Alle saw the angels give each other confused looks. This was not where they were supposed to go.

"Why did we come here, Gabriel?"

He looked as confused as everyone else. "This not the place I had in mind when we stepped through."

The new owners saw Alle on their front lawn. Of course, they couldn't see anyone else. They waved, and Alle did the only thing she knew to do. She waved back. Unfortunately, that encouraged them to come outside to talk to her.

"Hi. I didn't mean to barge in. How is the house?" Alle made small talk while the angels discussed what had happened.

"Hi. We didn't see you pull up," the man looked around for her car.

"The house is great, Alle. You can't have it back," his wife joked.

She laughed politely. "You haven't noticed anything unusual around, have you?"

The new owners exchanged a look. "Like ghosts? You didn't sell us a haunted house, did you?"

Alle gave her a fake laugh again. "No... Nothing like that. Just thought I would ask. Sometimes, this neighborhood could be on the crazy side."

"It's been really quiet, actually."

"Great, that's great. Well, it was great seeing you and the old house. I love the bushes you put in. They look great!" She gave them a thumbs up.

Behind her, Gabriel growled. "They do not look great."

Alle shushed Gabriel, and the new owners gave her a wary glance. They started backing up inside. "Ok.. bye." She gave a little finger wave and trailed off as they disappeared behind their door. "Please, don't call the police," she murmured.

At just that moment, Alle's mom drove by. She rolled down her window and gave Alle a suspicious look. "Alle, why are you bothering the new neighbors?"

Alle spoke to Gabriel from the side of her mouth. She didn't want her mom to think she was crazy, too. "How does time work in the underside?"

"Similar to the veil. They cannot travel to any point in time, but it will be as if no time has passed for Lani."

"Ok, we have some time then. I want to get to Lani as quickly as possible, but maybe we can regroup at Mom's house. She already knows about y'all, so it would probably be ok. Dad probably does, too."

Gabriel nodded.

"Hi, Mom. Can we invade your house for a little bit? It's probably time we talked anyway."

"Alle, what's going on?" Laila looked concerned. Then, she noticed Lani wasn't at Alle's side, and there were no cars.

"I'll tell you at your house."

Laila trusted Alle, but she was worried. "Ok, hop in, dear."

The angels flew over the truck as they drove the few blocks to Laila's house. When they arrived, she parked the truck and looked at Alle. She expected them to talk right away. Alle's mom wasn't super patient and hated being cooped up inside. "Inside, Mom. I'll explain inside."

They walked up the front steps. There was no way the truck could be pulled into the garage. It was a store room and Laila's method to keep the house decluttered. Alle's dad opened the front door. He could see through the glass in by the black oak door, but he must have been expecting her mom. He always helped her unload the car from shopping trips. He looked surprised when he saw Alle standing on the front steps. "I didn't know you were coming by, Alle."

"Joel, hush." Laila had had enough. She had a pretty low tolerance, actually. "Alle Ginger Venega, you had better start explaining right now!"

"Ooh, pulled out the full name, dear. That's pretty serious." Joel's teasing tone received him a glare from Laila.

Alle walked over and sat at the bar that separated the kitchen from the dining room. She looked around the room at the angels. They had begun placing protective wards on every wall, floor, and ceiling. Gabriel nodded, and she began her story.

"Lani has been abducted," she said calmly and without crying.

Both her parents gasped. Laila reached for her phone. "Have you called the police? What about the FBI? I can probably find the number if you give me a second."

Alle put her hand on her mom's arm. "No, please don't think I'm crazy, but she's been abducted by demons."

It was her mom's turn to sit down in shock. Her dad moved to the kitchen. "I'll just fix us a drink then."

"Look, I saw your prayer, Mom. I know what I am." Alle pursed her lips together. Even though she knew the truth, she wanted her mom to be honest with her for once.

Laila looked shocked. "What you are?"

Alle nodded. "And what Lani is. When Runar and I went on that ghost-hunting tour, the demons found out about me. They were there, and they could sense I was part angel."

"Joel, honey, can you get some batteries out of the garage?" her voice trilled. She never took her eyes off Alle.

Alle's dad chuckled. "Laila? You don't think I know about the angel?"

Laila turned to her husband in shock. Joel went to comfort his wife. "I allowed it. It was the only way we would have children, and I wanted to make you happy."

Alle put her hands in the air to stop them. "I don't need any mental images, ok, *parents*?" Alle put her fingers in her ear. "But now that we all know we are on the same page, I'll fill you in on the rest."

Alle replayed everything that had happened to her over the past few days.

"Alle, I'm so sorry. I should have been there for you more," Laila said and hugged her daughter.

Alle tucked her head into her mom's neck. "Mom, you couldn't have prevented this from happening." She sat up. "Can you see the angels standing in this house?"

"Sometimes I see movement out of the corner of my eye, but I can't see them," she said, disappointed.

Alle felt Gabriel's warm presence behind her. "She saw Pileal. She can probably see us if she concentrates. But it might be best if they are not part of this."

"Ok, Mom, this is going to get really weird because I will be having some discussions with them. Is it ok if we make your living room a home base for now? Gabriel is having some issues with portaling at the moment. We need to regroup."

Laila patted Alle's hand. "We'll make dinner, dear. You talk with your friends. I'm glad to have you home, even if it didn't feel like you left." Joel nodded in agreement. Ever the strong, silent supporter of his family.

As Alle stood, she held up her finger. "Oh? One more thing... You will have to stay here until we fix this. They might come for you to use as leverage, too."

Laila smiled and winked. "They can try." Alle had the feeling there was still more to learn about her parents.

* * *

Alle went to the living area where the angels were waiting for her. "Anyone know why we ended up here instead of my house?"

Adriel explained, "We believe the demon used a potion or some substance on Gabriel to keep him from being able to pull back the veil and follow. They may not have known about the veil shutdown protocol after all. We'll take precautions, though, just in case."

"And when do we think this potion will wear off?"

Gabriel stood. "Hopefully soon. But unfortunately, it could last forever."

Alle grabbed his hand. "I'm so sorry." She knew all about lifelong conditions that were beyond her control. This would devastate an angel everyone counted on to open the veil.

"It's ok, Alle. It will all work out. I can still pull it back; I don't know exactly where we are going. If it doesn't wear off, I'll visit the Most High once we've saved Lani. There's no time now." He smiled to reassure her.

"Alright, but how will we get to the underside now? I pulled back the veil in the Gauntlet. Maybe I can do it again?"

Gabriel raised his eyebrow. "Not many angels have the ability, but you were one of them. It's as good a plan as any. There is the prophecy, after all."

If there had been a DJ, the record would have been scratched. All the angels looked up at once. It seemed Gabriel had been withholding information from them as well.

"What prophecy?" Lex asked.

Gabriel stood. "It's time I gave you the information. It will likely come out on this mission anyway, and it could help you do your duties." Gabriel moved in front of Alle to shield her from the angels. Alle thought he might need to be close by for protection. "Alle is the avenging angel. She is considered Nephilim because of her conception. Her mother is human, and her father... was possessed by an angel." The crew of angels all looked to the kitchen simultaneously. "Alle is an angel soul in a human body. A prophecy states that the Nephilim will bring down the barrier and the veil. The three heavens will become one."

The silence lingered on. These angels showed their emotions more often than the healers, but at this moment, Alle couldn't tell what they were thinking.

Alle was the one to break it. "Look, I chose to become human mainly so I would know what I was avenging. I know who I am and will do everything possible to get Lani back without breaking the world."

"But what if you bring down the barriers and merge the three heavens?" one of the angels she didn't know asked.

"Then we fix it," Gabriel proclaimed. "If anyone would like to be reassigned, now would be the time. It won't be held against you, and no one will blame you. I only ask you all keep this between us for now."

No one moved a muscle, not even a twitch.

"Good. Let's move on. Alle, try to pull back the veil." He swiped his hand for her to take the floor.

Oh, he says do this, and I'm just supposed to jump in and do it. I haven't been able to do this without his help. It seems a bit abrupt. She kept these thoughts to herself and did as she was told. There wasn't time to ease into this.

She closed her eyes and focused as she had done before in the Gauntlet. Almost immediately, she felt the invisible curtain. It swayed over her fingers like it wanted to be touched. Once she felt it, she poured her power into drawing back. Her arm began to shake with effort, and a trickle of sweat ran down her forehead. Finally, she dropped her arm and let out a whoosh of breath.

Gabriel stepped in as Alle's knees went weak. It would be great to trade herself for Lani. She couldn't open the veil at all. There was no danger in her destroying the barriers. "You are relying too much on your power and not Spirit," Gabriel whispered in her ear. He turned to the others. "That was the fastest method. I don't want to risk Alle trying again right now."

"It's midday, so I don't think we should fly Alle to her house," Lex said.

Gabriel sat on the couch with Alle beside him. "Do you think you could borrow your mom's truck? It will take a bit longer, but it's the best option until you get some energy back."

Alle moved to stand up and then collapsed back on the couch. "I'm not sure I can drive right now. I'll definitely need a snack. But I'll ask." She didn't try to stand back up. She yelled from the living room, "Mom, we need your help."

Laila hustled back into the living area, wiping her hands on a dish towel. "Oh dear, what happened in the five seconds I've been gone?"

"I tried opening the veil. We need to get to my house so we can get to work. Everyone thinks there is a thin place in the barrier where we can get to the underside."

Laila's mouth dropped open. "In the middle of my living room? Alle! You know better than that."

"Do I? Well, it didn't work, and I'm drained of energy. No lecture needed, Mom."

"That wasn't very smart. Who is leading this operation anyway?"

"Gabriel. And we were trying to see if I could open the veil because Gabriel's ability is acting wonky right now. Mom, I don't really have the energy to explain this."

Laila sat next to her on the couch. Gabriel had moved out of the way just before she sat on him. *I would giggle, but I'm too tired,* Alle thought.

"What do you need," Laila sighed.

"We need to borrow your truck. We can't go through the veil; even though this will take some time, it's the safest option."

Alle hadn't noticed that her dad had entered the living area. He stood at the transition between rooms. Laila looked up at him for confirmation. He already had the keys in his hand.

Chapter Twenty-Six

Afew minutes later, they were bouncing over potholes toward the interstate. Laila had insisted on driving, and Joel refused to let them go alone. Gabriel rode in the truck bed while the other angels flew ahead. Alle munched on a few snacks her mom had gathered for her.

It took more than the usual hour to get to Alle's house. Laila had to go the exact speed limit. Not a bit over or under. It was always exact. Alle reminded her mom of the urgency more than once. The first time, Laila explained, "It will be worse if we get pulled over for speeding. Might as well go the speed limit and get there alive and on time." Each time after that, Alle just got a glare. Her mom didn't even turn her head, having to keep her eyes on the road. Alle's leg continued to bounce.

The small host of angels beat the truck to the house. One of them reported to Gabriel when they arrived. "We found a dead human propped by the door. There was a note," he said as he handed the note to Gabriel.

Nephilim,
The child lives. She will continue to do so if you surrender yourself to me. Exchange a life for a life. Your angel will tell you the way.
  -The Demon Prince

Alle read over his arm. "Who calls themselves The Demon Prince?"

"A Demon Prince," Gabriel growled and crushed the paper with one hand. "Who was the human?"

Alle didn't want to see a dead human, but she needed to know. They walked to the porch.

Jed slumped against her screen door. Alle gasped and looked away. She had liked him even if he had turned out to be on the wrong side. "I thought you said he was a demon."

"He had been. Looks like they killed the host." Gabriel had reverted to his gruff alter ego when Lani had been taken. Most of the angels didn't know about their relationship. There was a silent agreement to keep their connection quiet. Angels didn't often have relationships. It could undermine the mission to get Lani back. But he hugged her now. "I know you liked him. I'm sorry this happened."

Angels removed Jed's body, and one of them shot it with fire. "To keep him from being repossessed," Gabriel explained.

That thought was horrific for Alle. She did not need dead people becoming undead. There were one too many zombie shows in her Netflix history.

She pushed her sadness for Jed aside. She had more important things to worry about than mourning for a friend she had known for less than a day. Angels had swarmed her house to make sure it was safe. As she climbed the steps, she heard an awful screeching sound.

An angel had a scrawny man by the neck. His eyes were black like the pizza delivery guy's had been. He was squirming and doing everything possible to get away. The angel's tricep flexed, but he was barely making an effort.

"We caught this one on the perimeter, spying. What would you like me to do with him?"

Gabriel didn't hesitate. "He's obviously possessed. Kill him. Keeping Alle safe is our top priority right now."

"No, no… I wasn't doing anything wrong. You can't kill me." The slight man wriggled, squirmed, and howled.

"We can, and we will," the guardian declared, stepping up to his face.

"Please, I'll give you information," he screeched, looking between the two angels.

"We can't trust your information," Gabriel said as he walked away.

"Please, my master knows about Alle."

That stopped Gabriel in his tracks. He turned and had the demon by the throat in nanoseconds. The other angel moved quickly out of the way. "What does your master know, filth?" Gabriel growled.

"He knows Alle is Nephilim," the demon choked. The angel still clenched his neck, and the veins in his face began to bulge.

"That is obvious, Rat!" Gabriel seethed.

"He knows that she can open portals," the demon croaked. Gabriel turned slightly and looked at Alle. He released his grip enough for the demon to take a breath and finish his message.

"What are his plans then?"

"He knows the prophecy. That the Nephilim will break the barriers, he wants freedom for demons."

"That sounds like a lofty goal for a lowly prince. Shouldn't he worry about his city?"

"He desires to rule everyone. Everywhere."

"There is usually no end to the power struggle," Alle thought out loud.

"Is this all? Tell me quickly, or I will draw out your death with much pain." Gabriel bared his teeth.

"The girl. The girl is important to his plan."

"The child?"

"Yes. He plans to mate her to his son when the child has come of age."

Alle's anger rose to the surface with this declaration. She jumped toward the demon over Gabriel's shoulder. But before she could reach the demon, Gabriel snapped his neck.

Lex spoke up then. "That was probably the wrong information to share if he was trying to live."

"He was a plant. The Demon Prince wants us to know that information. He probably thinks this will get Alle to come after Lani if she isn't already."

"An insurance policy," Lex replied.

"Exactly."

Alle paced. "Well, he was right. Because now I'm going to rip his filthy head from his body," she said through gritted teeth. Heat began to radiate from her body, and her eyes turned to glowing embers.

"Alle, calm down, or Lani won't have a mom to come home to."

Alle closed her eyes and began to pace. She took deep, calming breaths.

"The Demon Prince is counting on you coming alone, untrained, and angry. He thinks it will be easy to trap you. He probably is also aware you will do anything for your daughter."

"Well, he's correct on all assumptions. If you are trying to calm me down, this is not the way to do it," Alle fumed.

"You know what happens when you assume." He threw her words back at her.

"That's only if you assume incorrectly."

Gabriel grabbed her by the shoulders again and stared into her eyes. Alle didn't know whether he would kiss her or throw her across the yard. He did neither. "What he doesn't know, Angel, is you are responsible for the Most High's vengeance. He doesn't know you have been trained. He doesn't know I love you. He doesn't know you as I do, and I know you will get Lani and return safely."

Alle stared at him in shock as his chest heaved. It was as if cold water dowsed her fury. The fire simmered down back below the surface. Ready at a moment's notice but not putting her in danger anymore.

"You love me?" she asked.

Gabriel growled, released her arms, and walked away.

Lex stood beside her and crossed his arms. "That's what you chose to ask about from that little speech? How could you not have known that by now?"

She watched as Gabriel walked toward her house without looking back. "Lex, if I don't come back from this, make sure he is ok. That he moves on."

"Alle, no."

"Lex, promise me, please." She turned to look into Lex's green eyes and did her best to bare her soul without words. Even though she had some training, she wasn't sure it was enough, and even if she made it to save Lani, she didn't know if she would be herself when she returned. If she came back at all. She would take Lani's place in a heartbeat.

Lex nodded and hung his head. With that, she walked inside.

Laila and Joel were sitting on her new couch. She sat in the silver wingback chair next to them. "Mom, I need y'all to stay here or stay in your house for a few days. I have to get Lani, and we don't have much time. We got some new information, and I need to get to her sooner rather than later. But I can't worry about you being in danger, too."

"You know I don't like being cooped up in the house, dear," Laila complained. "I'm retired, not dead. I'm not afraid of whatever is going on out there."

"Mom, please. This is important. You've told me yourself all my life I had a special purpose. That special purpose is being Lani's mom, protecting her, and ensuring she grows into a well-rounded adult. And I can't do that without your help. If I'm worried about you, my attention will be divided, and I need all of it on Lani."

Joel leaned forward and put his hand on his wife's knee. "Of course, we'll stay safe, love. Anything to help you."

Alle nodded. "The wards have been set in place. You should be safe within them. But they don't go much beyond the structure of the house."

"Fine, dear. I'll do my best."

She hugged both her parents. Tears threatened to spill over, but she knew if she started now, she wouldn't stop, and she did not need to be emotional now. She needed every bit of energy for the task ahead.

* * *

The angels had set up their mission command in the formal dining room. It was spacious enough to fit six of them. The rest took up guard positions around the perimeter of the house. They combed the entire property for demons. While Gabriel and Lex looked over their plans and maps, an angel approached and whispered into Gabriel's ear. As he did, he looked up at Alle. Gabriel nodded to his lieutenant, dismissing him, and kept his eyes on Alle.

"Give us the room," Gabriel said. All the angels began to leave, except Lex. "You too, Lex." Lex, to his credit, looked like he was about to protest. His eyes flicked momentarily to Alle. She nodded slightly, and he left.

CHAPTER TWENTY-SIX

Gabriel crossed the room to Alle. "What have you done to my second?"

"I haven't done anything to your second."

"He seems very... protective of you."

Alle scoffed, "He's not protective of me. He's protective of you. I'm the one that can explode at any moment."

Gabriel sighed and looked to the ceiling. He accepted her answer and moved on. "We found the thin spot in the barrier. It is practically in your backyard."

Flames flared in Alle's eyes. She was annoyed that she was so close to the supernatural and had never known it. Gabriel put a hand on her cheek. "I know you've been trying to open the veil."

"I haven't been able to do it," she said. Her shoulders slumped in disappointment.

"It's ok. Since we found the weak spot, I can open it. There's very little risk that the powder will cause problems opening a weak spot in the veil."

Alle thought about it for a few seconds. Even though Gabriel was still recouping his power, it was better than not opening it at all. She wasn't sure how she would get back. The angels were still formulating a plan for that. Gabriel had mentioned bringing in someone else as a last resort. But Alle knew she would be on her own to work out how to leave the darkness of the underside. She could only hope that everything they said about her was true and that she could figure out how to open barriers and veils when the time came.

Gabriel put a hand on the head side of her face and tilted her head towards his. He placed a gentle kiss on her lips and then pulled her close. She didn't want to let him go again, but they had done all they could to prepare. It was time to get Lani.

Chapter Twenty-Seven

They stood at the back of her property, facing a forest full of dark oak trees. Gabriel bowed his head. His expression was stoic, but Alle could see the pain, fear, and anger in his demeanor. If she could ever deny he was her bonded mate, she couldn't now. She knew him as well as she knew herself. They didn't need mind melds and telepathy to know what was going on with each other. They were one soul living in two bodies. If she was honest, it had been that way from the moment Gabriel had stepped through the veil into her life. She hadn't wanted to admit it at the time and betray Runar. But when she found out that Gabriel was Runar, all the pieces clicked into place.

He knew hers as easily as she knew his emotions behind his blank expression. He could see in her spirit that she was afraid but determined. He had known since the beginning of time. Determination was her calling card. She would not fail. As an angel, he couldn't enter the underside of the spirit world. Even without him, though, she wouldn't fail. He had complete faith in her.

Alle could read every emotion Gabriel had at the moment with just a look, but she didn't know his thoughts. She didn't understand why he felt those things.

He wrapped his big hands around her waist and pulled her close. He leaned his forehead against hers.

"You can do this. You don't need me. You never have. All you need is to believe. All you need is that faith."

She let her eyes fall to the ground. "The one thing I don't have."

"Faith is easy when things aren't hard, but it isn't something you can create yourself. It's something that comes about when you need it most. Faith is a gift that comes when you think all hope is lost."

"Well, if there is ever a moment for it to come. Now would be that time. One thing I do know is Lani will come home. I might not make it back. I'll find enough energy to send her through or at least connect to you and push her through."

"You will find the faith to get back. I know it."

Alle gave him a weak smile. "It sounds like you have enough for both of us."

Gabriel pushed a wisp of hair away from her eyes. "I do, but you will find it, too."

"This would be so much easier if you could just go with me."

"The prince knows I can only support you in this dimension and the veil. I will do everything I can for you here. It seems the Most High wants you to do this one, just you and him. His Spirit will be with you right here." He pointed to her heart. "Look for it in the darkness."

"Great," Alle groaned.

Before Gabriel could rebut her irreverence, Lex spoke, "Ok, guys, we have an idea as to where they might be keeping Lani." Gabriel broke away from Alle. A translucent map of the underside was floating near her house. Tiny dots glowed at different points on the map. Gabriel leaned over it as Lex spoke again, "We think he is the Prince of Austin."

Gabe nodded. "Who's been down there recently? Has there been activity?"

Another angel Alle hadn't met yet stepped forward. "There's been enough to suggest a prince has taken residence. But we haven't had big battles yet. It feels like they're coming through."

"We'll see. Lex, put Michael on standby and tell him about the prince." Lex nodded and rushed away.

Gabe turned to Alle. "The spirit realm is not physical, but you will be. Their world can be whatever they make it to be, and it will seem real to you. Open yourself to the spirit, and you will be able to maneuver. It will be pitch black for the most part. You'll have to provide light for yourself, or if that fails, you will have to use other senses."

"The ability to see spirit?" she asked. He nodded. *Great! Another thing I can't do.* She didn't voice the thought out loud, but she guessed she was affecting the angels with her negative energy. She tried to perk up, but another thought hit her.

"Gabriel, Lani is terrified of the dark." Tears threatened again as Alle started shaking with the urgency to get to her daughter.

He shook his head and lifted her wrist monitor. It showed the pod was still closed. "She's still in the pod and still in stasis. They have no right to her. She is a lure. They want you. They will not terrify her to the point of death and justify your cause. That's our saving grace. They will probably create light for her in some way. Once you see any glimmer, you'll know that's where she'll be. Follow that, and you will find her."

Alle pulled away and nodded, knowing this could be the last time she saw her daughter and her bonded mate. She took off the wrist monitor and gave it to Gabriel. She didn't want to lose it to the demons.

"When you find the pod, you will hopefully need to open it. Without the wrist monitor, you can open it the same way you open the veil. It won't require as much spiritual energy as opening the actual veil. If that doesn't work…" he took her hand, "… you can cut here." He drew a line with his forefinger down her palm. "Press your palm to the lock. Your blood will release the mechanism."

Alle nodded her head solemnly. "Gabriel, take care of her. Find her a good home. Don't let anything bad…." She paused. "I mean, worse than this happen to her."

Gabriel took her by the shoulders again. "Look at me." When their eyes met, he continued. "If you go in defeated, you will be defeated. You have everything, and I mean everything, you need to make it back and live a long life with Lani. She will have the safest place because she will be with you."

Alle still wasn't sure she believed that, but it was something to hold on to. Something to fight for. Shoot for the moon; if she missed, she'd land among stars and all that.

Gabriel took her hand. "Are you ready? I'll get you as close as we can."

CHAPTER TWENTY-SEVEN

She only nodded.

He lifted her hand and closed his eyes. His body began to glow faintly, concentrating the light in his free hand. He reached up and ran his hand down the air as if unzipping space. The air parted as it had so many times before. Hopefully, this meant his power was returning. Anxiety ripped through Alle as Gabriel pulled her forward. "Use everything you have and come back to me. I love you."

"I love you, too," she said. She stepped through the curtain of the veil and disappeared into inky blackness. As Gabe's hand touched the darkness, it seemed to sizzle. She let go so he wouldn't be hurt. The veil closed, and she was alone.

At least she felt alone.

She had experienced total darkness during various cave tours as a child, but this was different. It was crushing darkness and nothing at the same time.

She didn't move from where she was, trying to get her eyes to adjust. They wouldn't. She looked around for that glimmer. There wasn't even a pinprick of light. Either Gabe didn't get her as close as he thought he would, they were completely wrong about where Lani was, or Gabriel's power still wasn't right. She hoped it returned by the time she found Lani so he could get her out if it came to that.

At this point, she closed her eyes. Vision wouldn't help her here, and it only hindered her ability to use her other senses and encouraged her to panic.

She wasn't standing. It almost felt like she was floating in space. She moved her arms and legs like she was swimming. She couldn't tell if it was working because she couldn't get her bearings.

She had to find Lani and return her to the natural world immediately. Alle was a human in the spirit realm. It was a paradigm. She was a paradigm. She existed, and she did not exist. Here, anything was possible, yet nothing was.

She took a breath, but there was no air. Gabriel did not prepare her for this. Maybe he didn't know, or maybe there wasn't time. Panic threatened to overwhelm her until she noticed she didn't need the breath. Her eyes weren't bulging out of her head. She wasn't about to explode.

When Alle had calmed down, she realized where she put her focus, her actions would follow. If she focused on her panic, her body flailed about. Despair was a genuine possibility, but it would do her no good. So, she focused on one thing: her love for Lani. She remembered Lani's smooshy little cheeks when she had been born and when she first rolled over. How she used to giggle at the little things and her first words in baby babble. Her cute songs. The hugs and kisses that showered her every day. She thought about how encouraging her daughter always was. Lani had faith even when Alle didn't have any in herself. A walking testimony of the Most High's love, even at two.

As she recalled her love for her daughter, other things ignited. Faith and hope flickered. In her mind, she now knew what the spirit realm looked like. She didn't need eyes to see, just a tiny bit of faith. The oppressive weight of the underworld lifted just a bit. She felt she could move at least.

As if attracted to the hope, she sensed movement around her. Beings slithered and skulked, encircling and moving closer. The momentary reprieve from the oppression began to wane. There was no way she would get to Lani without a fight. Suddenly, piercing pain racked her head. It started at the base of her skull and radiated to the space between her eyes. It felt as though her head was being ripped in two. A scream turned to a groan, and she realized the sound was coming from her.

Somehow, within the pain was a thought. One word, really. *Salvation.* What was her salvation? The good news was she didn't have to save herself. She didn't have the power or the ability. As a human, she had asked the Most High to live within her. He placed His spirit within her years ago. She had forgotten lately, but she still had the glowing, fiery spirit of the Most High living inside her with endless power, the power of creation and destruction. A golden light surrounded her head as she thought of this saving power. A giggle bubbled up as the swooshing light tickled her cheeks and neck. The searing pain slowly subsided, and the light enveloped her head.

The reprieve was short-lived. The flesh on her arms began to bubble and peel away as if acid had been slowly dripped and was now eating through her skin. Her attention now turned away from her head and to her arms.

The darkness whispered into her ear, telling her how she would die here. She should never have come without more training. She felt long, bony fingers wrap around her hips. The acid on her arms stopped as her hands were held firmly to her sides. Claws began to move down her abdomen toward her groin. Fear worse than any pain tore through her mind. She didn't know how to stop the onslaught of so many attacks. She was helpless. But another thought took over.

Righteousness. It had to come from the Most High. Gabriel had said His Spirit would be with her. Why else would she think about this? The armor of the Most High included the helmet of salvation and the breastplate of righteousness.

The golden light sparkling around her face extended down her torso, scorching the slimy black hands as they went. The claws retracted but did not fully retreat. They were there just beyond where the light touched.

"Enough!" she screamed. "I am a child of the Most High God, and you will not touch me again." Immediately with these words, the light extended to her hands and feet as a shield around her body.

"You dare speak that name here," a voice lisped in her ear. Much too close for comfort.

"Got you off me, didn't it? He created this place just like he created every other. He is Lord here."

A gravelly laugh sounded in the distance. More joined in. It was as if one being was in multiple locations. "We'll begin."

"No, no, we will not. Take me to my daughter."

"Not before we've had our fun as the prince promised."

"You can have all the fun you want after I've been…."

"Perhaps, little angel," the creepy voice interrupted, "we should have our fun in front of your little one? How would you like that?" Alle remained silent because she didn't know what was to come, and really, how did you respond to that creep? Instead, she focused again on the feeling of her daughter. The love and hope she felt when she thought about her. As soon as love enveloped her again, the demon spirits attacked anew. But the pain and torment barely registered. She let the demons try to do their worst while she focused on finding her daughter. The golden light shield withstood the onslaught of the attack.

She remembered Runar's face and the smile that was always so easy with him. His jokes and how he always said his sole purpose was to make her laugh. He was always so good at it, too.

The spirit world suddenly didn't seem so dark. The glow that was always with her began to illuminate the area around her, adding to the golden shimmer. It wasn't over, but it was better. The longer she stayed here, though, the worse this would be. She needed to find Lani sooner rather than later. And she needed a weapon.

"There has to be something physical. They wouldn't be able to keep Lani here otherwise," she said to herself. Abruptly, as if the thought allowed it, an entire world materialized. Just as it did when the tour guide turned on the lights in the cavern.

The attack from the creepy demon guy stopped. She opened her eyes. She could see now as if there were a tiny bit of light from somewhere. There was no telling where. Alle still didn't trust her own eyes. There were no demons around, but she could feel them. The dread that came with their presence.

She went from floating to standing on a jagged black surface, surrounded by a transparent razor-sharp black rock. It resembled obsidian in the natural world. It jutted out from every surface, forming a deadly dark maze.

She realized the demons here could simply push her into their made-up hellscape at any point. Her body would believe it had been mortally injured, and she would die. But where was the fun in that? Some predators liked to play with their prey, and she doubted any demon here saw her as dangerous. She didn't have much to fight with other than the light surrounding her. Her feet touched solid ground, and a false gravity held her to it.

Once the thought of gravity took hold, it didn't let go. She could no longer float here any more than she could in the natural world. She was ground-bound. It was fortunate because she didn't think swimming through space had made much difference.

She took another deep breath to calm her nerves. Even though she didn't need to breathe, it was a habit and helped her focus.

She looked around. The place was a gigantic tunnel. No. This was a lava tube, Alle realized. It was easily fifty stories high and just as wide. It was a perfect circle except for the jagged rocks. She hoped it was permanently dormant. She had no idea how she would make it up and around obsidian spires the size of skyscrapers.

"Well, the only way to finish is to begin," she said, picking her way through her own personal hell.

* * *

What felt like days later, she was no closer to the end of the tunnel. She had various minor scrapes and bruises from falling around the sharp obsidian multiple times. She didn't feel fatigued, the need to eat, or any of the normal human functions. The tunnel was simply never-ending. The farther she went, the farther away the end was. She was on a spiritual treadmill like a hamster plodding along. She neared a black spire that looked oddly familiar, although they all looked alike. She stopped to get her bearings for the umpteenth time. Unfortunately, there were no bearings in the place. It was just a messed-up maze of funhouse mirrors made of volcanic rock. Instead, she decided to sit. She found a relatively flat spot and used her leather boot to kick away the shards of glassy rock, only to reveal more glassy rock. There was no way she was getting out of this tunnel by walking. She had to think of a different way.

As she sat, she felt for all the people she loved. It had worked before, so she tried it again. Lani was there, tucked away in her heart. But there were others, too. Of course, Gabriel, her parents, friends, and former students. All the love that had built up over the years of people she had claimed as hers. And when she searched deep down, there was a river of deep love under all that. A river she hadn't felt for a long time. She didn't know what else to do, so she explored that river within herself.

She realized that it came from one place. The Most High. Alle walked beside this hidden river and listened to the rushing waters. As she walked farther down, it spread and slowed down. It sounded more like a babbling brook. It was different than the gardens she had visited with Gabriel. This place was created just for her. So that she could meditate and spend time with the Most High. She found a spot along the river where a giant boulder had been exposed. Lichens grew on its surface. A single red rose lay upon it. She hurried over and grabbed it up. Pressing it to her face, the soft petals tickled her nose, and she smiled.

She was reminded of His love for her. Not romantic love but intimate in a different way. He knew everything about her. He was devoted to her, not unlike a father to his daughter, but with a much deeper connection.

She remembered how devoted she was to him and how she missed him. Tears leaked from her eyes of their own volition. She couldn't stop them if she tried. All of the hurt, pain, and suffering were not his doing. He allowed those things in the natural world for a time. Suffering was a natural part of things. If he eliminated all suffering, there would be no need for faith. Hope and love would be cheapened. Like a beautifully balanced meal, bitterness enhanced the sweetness.

The faith that had been missing since she had lost her baby blossomed in her chest. Like turning up the dimmer switch on a chandelier, the light swirling about grew and brightened.

Her spirit lifted, and her faith was restored. She opened her eyes and took another deep breath. "Let's go get our girl." Refreshed and renewed, she smiled and stood.

Her right hand felt suddenly heavy. She looked to see a swirling tattoo being seared into her arm. It looked similar to Gabriel's angel wings. She was a bit worried she was getting wings on her arms. With that thought, she had the feeling the light was laughing at her. "This isn't really a laughing matter."

Trust, it replied. Not out loud. It was just an impression. Was the light talking to her? She tilted her head. Yes, yes, it was. This place had truly made her go insane. What was there to do but respond?

"Yes, I do trust. Can I get something useful though, like a..." She paused as a beautiful golden sword appeared on her hand. The hilt swooped and swirled around her wrist. The blade extended out, covering her fingers. She looked closer and examined the intricate scrollwork. She could just make out the word for Spirit written in Hebrew. It had been a while since her single foreign language class in college, but she could make out the swirling glyph that made the word. It was a beautiful sword that would make even D'Artagnan jealous. "Yep, that will do. Thank you."

With her guard down, the slow clap startled her out of her skin. It echoed around the tunnel. "Wow, impressive," the newcomer mocked. "Do you know how to use it?"

A handsome man in a black-on-black suit leaned against the obsidian spire. His pitch-black hair stood in stark contrast to his pale white skin. He wasn't even looking at her. He examined himself in the obsidian mirror. Smoothing his side part, his eyes slid down to examine his full lips. He ran a hand down his own jawline. He winked, yes winked, at himself and did a kissy face.

Alle screwed her face up in disgust and almost gagged because *ew*. She wanted to ask who he was, why he was there, and where her daughter was. Instead, she said, "Let's find out." She flicked her wrist on instinct as she had seen Gabriel do several times. The sword flamed to life in her hand and extended, so she held the hilt of an actual sword. She bowed her head and sighted in on her target.

He didn't seem worried. He gave himself one more quick smile in the mirror and, without any indication of what he would do, leaped into the air like a panther attacking his prey. His limbs splayed out with claws that hadn't been there just moments ago, ready to rip and shred his victim. His eyes were dark pools of inky black. He opened his mouth, but fortunately, no canines erupted. Alle wasn't even remotely ready for this scene. She landed flat on her back as the man-beast demon thing landed on top of her and laughed. She was surprised she hadn't severed her head.

"You are not ready, little angel. Go home and come back another day. You will not beat us today." He pounced off her just as quickly as he had appeared, returning to his handsome human face.

Alle agreed. She certainly didn't feel ready. This madness happened suddenly, and she didn't have time to prepare to fight demons. She wasn't mentally, spiritually, or physically equipped but would have to make do and learn as she went. There was no giving up on Lani. It was the only thing that kept her going.

Chapter Twenty-Eight

The best thing about having a tattoo spirit sword was you couldn't drop it or lose it. She crouched and rocked to the balls of her feet, ready to react.

"Who are you?"

"The one who just bested you in under two human seconds," the demon responded with a fully human voice.

"What is your name?"

"Oh, that is such a boring question, and the wrong one, really." He gave her a smoldering look. He didn't look bored. He looked amused.

"What is the right question?"

"Better, but still boring. Don't you want to know why I am here or who sent me?"

"I know why you are here and who sent you," Alle said.

"Ah, but you are wrong."

Alle stayed low in her crouch and swiveled, looking for danger.

"What is the right answer," she asked.

Demon Noir turned to thick black smoke and popped up right beside her. He whispered, "Many." She swung the sword and hit nothing but thick black air.

"Fine. I'll play your little game. Why are you here?" She was getting a little frustrated with this little tirade.

The demon materialized just out of the reach of the tip of her sword.

He leaned against the sharp black spire. Crossing one foot over the other, he examined his now finely manicured hands as if he were bored again. "An old... friend, shall we say, sent me. I believe you know him."

Gabriel was the only friend she had that would know any demons. She assumed he would just kill them on sight. "Gabriel would never send a demon to help me." Demon Noir grinned and looked at himself in the obsidian again.

"I'm sorry, am I boring you?" she added.

"Oh, yes, you definitely are. As I've said. But I'm just exquisite. I can't get enough of my own reflection."

"Ok, Narcisse." She rolled her eyes.

"Oh? You guessed my name! You didn't need to ask after all. Is it because of my myth? I am inspiring, I know. So many worshipers." He winked at himself in the glass obsidian again. Except to attack her, he never looked at her.

Alle cocked her head. She had let her guard down just a bit. Narcisse took the opportunity to pounce again. Alle recovered in time and was able to remain standing.

"Use your fancy sword, little angel," Narcisse hissed.

Alle pushed back against him. Her sword was still out but lowered. "How is this helping me?" She crouched a little lower, ready to take another advance from her attacker if necessary.

"I haven't killed you yet. Don't you want to know why?"

"Because the boss man wants me alive. Otherwise, why take my daughter?"

"Oh, I don't work for the prince. I'm a free agent." Narcisse moved so fast. He appeared behind her. He wrapped his arm around her shoulders and across her collarbone.

"You work for the highest bidder?" Alle grunted and shoved her elbow into Narcisse. He didn't move. For being so skinny, he was strong. "And who is the highest bidder right now?" Alle remained still, realizing she couldn't best him physically. *I need a different tactic. Maybe he will reveal something I can use if I keep him talking.*

"Your friend Gabriel, of course." Narcisse pushed her away and went back to checking his manicure.

"Where would he get the funds to purchase your services?" In an instant, his hands were around her waist, his mouth against her ear. She felt like a cat toy being shoved around and drawn back.

"I don't deal in money, precious stones, or metals. I deal in secrets and favors. Your bonded mate has plenty of them, and he is the highest bidder. Currently, he owes me a favor. If I should find something more valuable, I will cancel that contract."

"And you expect me to have something more valuable than a favor from an angel?" For Gabriel's sake, she entertained the idea.

He pushed her away again and looked her up and down with hungry eyes. "Oh yes, yes, I do."

"Fine, what is it that you want?" she said, oblivious to Narcisse's ogling

Narcisse tilted his head. It didn't seem to Alle that she was boring him at all. "You don't remember anything, do you?"

Alle shook her head. "Obviously not."

Narcisse tsked. "Unfortunately, that's not how this works. You must offer something."

"I have nothing to offer."

He strolled toward her. Alle had let her guard down. The sword was still out, but she hadn't raised it toward him. She had been lulled into thinking she wasn't capable of beating this demon. "Think, little angel. What would you give to get your little one out of here?" He ran his finger down her arm and pulled her into him. This time, his lips were a breath away from hers.

"Everything and anything. Right now, I am letting you touch me. Soon, that won't be the case."

His fingers lengthened into claws at the threat. She could feel them scrape against her skin. Otherwise, he didn't seem put out in the least. He chuckled without breaking eye contact. She noticed his irises were deep pools of onyx with flecks of stardust.

"Let's think about where you are, little angel. You are lost in the spirit realm. You don't know where your precious little girl is, much less how to rescue her, and you just received a sword you barely remember how to hold. Does any of this sound in the least bit devastating to you?"

Alle shoved her palm into his rib cage and lifted her sword in the span of a second. "First, my mother taught me never to take candy from a stranger. You can take that as gospel." She motioned between them. "This feels very similar. Second, if Gabriel made a deal with you, that's on him. But he has more faith in me than I have in myself. He would never send you. So, I will not negotiate."

Narcisse smiled and put his hand in his pocket. He posed as if he were on the red carpet with 1000 cameras clicking away. He was strikingly handsome. "Well, I'm feeling a bit of goodwill either way. I will give you this first one for free."

"No. No, you will not. That is how every junkie ever becomes addicted to their drug of choice. I'll make it out of here with...." She paused because she did not want to give away anything then, though she doubted this sly creature was unaware of who was helping her "on my own."

Narcisse just shrugged his shoulders, took one last look at himself in the obsidian, winked, and was gone.

She hoped Gabriel did not make a deal with the devil. She groaned as the ground around her started to shake. She wobbled to the left and right as the ground beneath her trembled more violently. Fear threatened to paralyze her. She crouched and looked all around her. There was no place to take cover from obsidian glass falling in shards from the one thousand-foot ceiling. The sword dimmed and folded back into her hand. All she could do at this point was duck and cover. She had no doubt she would be sliced in two by the rock guillotines landing all around her. The light of the spirit did not dim one bit. *Maybe it can protect me from falling glass towers.*

Then she heard a faint voice, "Not today, little angel." The glassy shards shattered into a million pieces. She was convinced this was how she would die. A thousand cuts. Instead of cutting her, they turned to dust and fell all around her.

She stood on the wobbling ground, trying to keep her balance. An invisible hook wrapped around her middle, rescuing her from her inevitable death. Instantly, she was flying through the dark space. She saw the first light that had not come from herself in mere seconds. She could have wept for joy. She knew Lani was where the light was.

The hook didn't take her to the light. She knew this was probably some help from Narcisse. She hated it. She didn't want it, but at that moment, she was grateful she was closer to Lani.

There was a new problem, though. The hook had dropped her just outside the entrance to the cavern where the light was coming from. She was engulfed in an inky shadow. She could see into the narrow opening of the cavern. In front of the opening, there were countless black writhing bodies. They avoided the light, but she could barely make out the movement. It looked like oily black worms guarding the entrance. They hissed and clacked their teeth at each other. The bodies were wrong. They looked like people that had been twisted all the wrong ways. Heads were turned backward. Limbs bent the wrong way. Vertebrae and ribs poked out through sallow skin. She could sense a putrid sulfur smell from her perch fifty feet away. There was no way she could fight her way through them. Now what?

She hadn't lost her sword or her light. She couldn't hide in the shadows for long. They would find her sooner rather than later if they didn't know she was already here. Could it be as simple as jumping in and swinging the sword? She saw no other way and got no confirmation otherwise. She shrugged, "No time like the present," she whispered to herself.

She stepped out from her hiding place, flicked her wrist, and started swinging her sword. Fear, oppression, and death pressed in on her. She stood in a circle of light as millions of oily demons pressed in around her. All she could do was slice and turn, slice and turn.

With each turn, she made her way closer to the cavern entrance. The goal was not to kill all the demons. Her goal was to get through the demons to Lani. She saw how they avoided the light. She would be safer in the light and closer to Lani if she could reach it.

The clicks of claws and teeth followed her every movement. The light within her never faded or faltered, but it didn't grow either. She finally made it to the cavern entrance. She spared a glance behind her, unable to go further. Her back was up against the largest crystal she had ever seen. The light filtered through it to the entrance, but there was no way around it. It had been the best plan, but she hadn't had all the information. She was trapped between a giant rock and a horde of slithering demons.

She put her sword away and held out her hands. "You win. You win. No more fighting." One of the creatures stepped forward but stayed just outside the light. Just as it opened its mouth to say something, Narcisse appeared in her peripheral vision. He was still leaning against the crystal, examining his own good looks.

"Before you give yourself up, little angel, there is another option."

She scoffed without taking her eyes off the black, writhing demons in the shadows. "I know. Give you my soul, and you zip me over to my daughter and out of the spirit realm. No deal."

"I could make it so simple for you and Lani." His voice dripped with saccharine sweetness.

"First, get my daughter's name out of your mouth. Second, what good is it to gain the whole world and lose your soul?"

He pushed off the rock and dismissed her words with a wave of his hands. "Yes. Yes, that is an excellent quote. Is your soul worth your daughter's life?"

That took Alle aback. Of course, she would give up everything for Lani, even her own soul. Narcisse was good at his job. He laid the foundation for doubt.

"I will leave you with this thought. While you are fighting a losing battle out there, what's happening to Lani on the other side of this crystal?" He patted the big crystal that must have been a two hundred-ton diamond. It was clear but glowed orange from whatever was just on the other side. He waited for just a second for his threat to sink in.

"Gabriel said they would not hurt her."

"Hurt?" He shrugged. "No, they've been given orders not to hurt her. But this is Hell, dear, and we are tormentors. I wouldn't put it past anyone to push the boundaries just a bit. Especially with one so precious as little Lani." He paused to allow his words to hit Alle's heart. "My way is the easy way… Your way is much, much harder and unnecessary."

Hearing her name again in this demon's mouth did not sit well. Anger welled up. But to save herself, Lani, and now maybe Gabriel, she needed to keep a cool head. She took a few deep breaths to center herself. The air smelled of sulfur and burning rubber.

Her way was hard, but one thing Narcisse got wrong; it was necessary. Everything depended on her doing this without his help. She would be making no deals with the devil today. "I'll take door number two, Narcisse. Go away." And he vanished. She had no doubt he would return when there was another road to cross.

She faced the other demons and stepped into the shadows. "I am yours, for now. Take me to your prince." They descended upon her. Instantly, she was pulled back into the darkness. They pulled at her clothes, biting, kicking, hitting, and clawing as they dragged her by her hair through what she hoped was mud. She couldn't be sure. The light from the cavern began to dim. She was taken further away from Lani. She had been mistaken. She had thought these demons would take her to the demon prince. Instead, they continued to drag her further from the cavern. Her light dampened, but it did not go out. She focused on her connections as she took the beatings.

This really wasn't the best idea, she thought. But what else could she have done? She could have made a deal with Narcisse or even accepted the offer he said he was making on Gabriel's behalf. There was no way that would have turned out better. She would still be imprisoned but with less pain. Still, this had to be the best way. Selling out was not the right choice.

More doubt crept in. What if she never made it to Lani and was trapped down here for just as long as she was? Would Gabriel find a way to save their daughter? She didn't know if he was able. He would destroy himself in the process. Alle balked at the thought of beautiful Gabriel transforming into a soulless demon. She couldn't give up.

* * *

After what felt like ages, the writhing mass of demons grew smaller until she was left alone in a small outcropping in a cave. Round, smooth rocks piled on top of other rocks until they formed an eight-foot square-ish room. The demons left her on the floor and rolled a stone in front of the entryway.

There was no moving the rocks without very large boulders caving in on top of her.

She lay on the floor. Her hair was tangled and matted to her head in a mess any eighties rock band would admire. She gently rolled onto her side, grunting with the effort, letting gravity work to pull her the rest of the way over. Rocks jabbed into the cuts and bruises. Blood coated and crusted down her arms, legs, and torso. Her clothes were rags. She was in a bad way.

"Well, little angel. Looks like you have it all under control." Narcisse sat in the corner, still finely groomed as ever. There were no mirrored surfaces to admire himself in. Still, he didn't give her his full attention. He seemed bored, rubbing his nails on his lapel. She could tell he didn't want to be here any more than she did.

"Go away. I'm not in the mood to deal with you."

"I do hate to see you so down and out, little angel. I want to help."

"I don't want your help. I got this," she said, spitting a mouth full of blood onto the sooty soil.

He sauntered over and crouched beside her. He ran a finger gently down the side of her face. Alle winced at his touch and the pain. "Oh yes, I see you do. I just checked on precious little Lani. Do you want to know how she is doing right now?"

"I told you to get my daughter's name out of your mouth."

"Just say the word, and this can all be over."

"Go away, Narcisse."

She was messing with his bottom line, she was sure, but couldn't find it in herself to care.

"As you wish," he said as he stood, "but understand one thing, little angel. This place may not be real at all, but when the demons return, it will feel very real. And when they take you to the prince, it will feel real. And when he makes you his mate, that will feel real. He will break the bond with the angel, which will be... unpleasant. Then, he will break you. He hopes you will be able to carry his child. Once he has his own Nephilim, he can control the three heavens."

CHAPTER TWENTY-EIGHT

Alle groaned, with pain in her abdomen. "Doesn't he already have a son?"

Narcisse looked bored. "Not one with Nephilim blood. Not one that can break barriers and veils and wards."

"I guess he's playing the long game. I thought he just wanted me to remove the barrier so he could have free rein over the natural world."

"Make no mistake. He will do that and more. Do you think he will stop with the natural world? Why force you to do it when he can create little demons in his own image with the same power and have a little fun at the same time? I could have saved you from all that. I could have saved Lani from that because you have failed. Don't think she is safe in her little pod for one second."

He was gone with the next breath.

"Well, that was inspiring. Next time, I'll have a mirror so that I can enjoy his company longer." She tried to smile, wincing at the cut on her lip. She would have sold her soul if she thought it would save Lani, but she knew it wouldn't do a bit of good. Lani was tough, resilient, and tenacious. She would hang on and give them hell if she woke before she could get there.

"Mama's coming, baby. Just hang on a little longer," she groaned.

* * *

If there were ever a time to figure out how to open the veil, it would be now. *It would have been days ago, but I must figure this out now.* She remembered how Gabriel told her to connect with Spirit to make it easier. But she was spent. She didn't have much energy, and in her pain, Spirit seemed distant.

She figured she wouldn't be here forever. If the prince wanted her, he wouldn't keep her locked away without ever having seen her. Unless the worthless demons forgot to mention it to him. She wanted to be ready when they came. She didn't know how long she had to open the veil or heal her body.

The only bone that didn't feel broken was her jaw. She really couldn't move anything else. Narcisse was right about one thing-she was down and out. So she did the only thing she could think to do. She sang. And the only song she could think of was Lani's favorite. "This little light of mine." She sang the words slowly. Tears trickled from the corners of her eyes and ran down the sides of her face. She couldn't even lift her arms to wipe them away. She could feel them pool in her ears.

"I'm going to let it shine…This little light of mine…" she slurred. "I'm going to let it shine… This little light of mine…This little light of mine… oh wait, I already said that. Where was I? Oh yeah. I'm going to let it shine, let it shine, let it shine."

She wasn't sure if she had imagined it, but the light shone brighter around her. She smiled a bit. The golden shimmer hadn't left her.

She turned her thoughts inward and imagined that beautiful river again. She ventured away from the water to explore her spirit world, where she met with the Most High. The place seemed familiar. Like she had been here in a dream. She saw a large tree in the middle of the golden field. The heads of the wheat were high enough to touch without bending over. They were soft on the palm of her hand. She just wanted to walk in the field forever.

As she had that thought, a man stood before her. He had light brown hair and kind green eyes. She knew who he was. She recognized him from her dreams and memories. The Most High in his human form. As she approached him, he said nothing. He smiled and pointed. She turned to see what he wanted her to see.

At the bottom of a hill they were standing on were three children. She instantly knew they were hers. They looked just like Lani. They held hands with each other and twirled in circles. The blond curls bounced as they played. They didn't notice her, and she couldn't speak with them. She watched for hours as they played. She basked in the joy of the moment.

Seeing these three babies brought peace. A peace she didn't know she was still searching for. She thought she had found it in the veil. Peace was such a funny thing. It could heal so many wounds. Wounds that she had let fester and refused to heal. She didn't want to let go of the pain of losing her babies. She didn't want to move on with her life after she lost Runar. She had been holding onto her grief for so long that it was a part of her.

The Most High still did not speak or touch her. His presence was always there, offering support and guidance as she watched them laugh and play and giggle. She took a deep breath and let her pain drift away on the cool breeze. Slowly, she was pulled away from the meadow. Her spirit was yanked back to her body over the golden grass across the river and back to the deep, dark pit.

Her eyes shot open. She didn't know how long she had been asleep, but now she was fully awake. Her body was no longer a tangled mess. While she slept, she healed. She felt it had to do with her golden light friend and the dream she had just had. Was it a dream? It felt real. Her spirit was there by the river, even if her body was not. At any rate, she could move her arms and legs now.

She sat up and took inventory of her situation. Her hair was still matted and tangled. It would take a couple of bottles of conditioner to fix that mess. She might have to cut it entirely and start over. Her bones didn't feel broken anymore. She felt lighter than she had in years. A weight she didn't know she was carrying was gone. The gashes all over her body were closed. She was still covered in muck, and her clothes were still rags. However, her body was as good as new, and she had more energy.

She looked at her hands. The sword glimmered on her right hand, and on her left was something new. A golden chain wrapped around her wrist and up to her forearm. She assumed she could access that the same as the sword. She grinned, thinking it might resemble Wonder Woman's golden lasso.

She stood, and another thought occurred to her. Narcisse wrapped a little truth around the lie. He had said this place wasn't real. Of course, she knew she was in a spirit realm, but everything she endured here felt real. Gabriel had said the same thing. It would feel real, but it wasn't. It was spirit. Everything here was a manifestation of spirit. If she could manipulate spirit, she could control her surroundings. And if she could do that, she could bust through anything any demon created in this place and possibly pull back the veil.

She stood and dusted herself off. It was time to kick down the gates of hell.

Chapter Twenty-Nine

"Alle! Wake up." Alle's body was shaken. "Alle! Wake up."

She cracked her eyes open. She had been trying to figure out how to manipulate these dang rocks for a long while. Exhaustion must have taken over, and she sat straight up. She winced, but only a little at the soreness. She looked around, expecting to see Narcisse. But there was no one in her little hovel.

"Hmmm, did I just have a sleep hallucination," she said aloud because if she was hallucinating, who would care if she was talking to herself? It had been a while since she had had food and water. She didn't need to breathe, but she did need some sleep for healing. Maybe the other fundamentals were just a habit too?

"If I am hallucinating due to lack of water, it's going to be a fun trip through the underside." One thing she knew for sure was that she would not eat or drink anything here anyway.

"Don't eat anything, and definitely don't drink anything." The memory of Gabriel's voice when he was preparing her for this trek filled her mind. "It won't nourish you and will be more harmful than helpful."

I'm not sure he expected me to be here this long, though. She thought.

She needed to hurry this rescue and escape along. "Gabriel thinks I can do this. I'm going to try not to prove him wrong."

Standing again, she looked around her rock-enclosed cell. *Why put me here? Why not take me to the prince directly? Maybe this was a way to break me, or they aren't answering to the prince.*

She closed her eyes and remembered what Gabriel had told her about the demon hierarchy. There wasn't one. Most of them did what they wanted, but a few had enough power to control others. She wondered if Narcisse had that much power. She quickly put that out of her mind. She didn't want to summon the distracting demon just by thinking of him. She waited for a few seconds just in case. When he didn't appear, she went on about her daydreaming.

"Alright, Gabriel, tell me how to get out of here," she whispered. Her memory flashed to his explanation of the underside. The demons were envious of the natural world and beyond the veil. They wanted what they couldn't have. So they created an illusion, a copy of the things they wanted most. The cavern had been a copy to fill the void of nothingness. That's what this place was. Nothing.

Gabriel's voice rang in her mind again. "Illusions can be manipulated by spirit. If angels could descend without burning to pieces, they could easily manipulate the paltry copies."

Alle could hear the disgust in his voice as he described this place. She didn't know how they had gotten the information if they couldn't get down here, but if he was right, she only had to see the illusion and cut through it.

The best way would be to use Spirit. She had this cool sword and chain now and wondered briefly if she had wings. She tried to look over her shoulder. If they were there, she couldn't see them, and nothing felt different. She shrugged. I guess wings aren't in the equation yet.

She flicked her right hand, and the sword appeared. She would never get used to that, and it delighted her to feel the power flow through her. She enjoyed the hum the sword made. It should be no problem cutting through the illusion with her spirit sword.

With a yell, she raised the sword over her head with both hands and hacked down at the stone. It didn't move. It didn't even spark. It certainly didn't disintegrate like she was hoping. She hacked at it a few more times before she fell to her knees, exhausted already.

"That wasn't awesome," she huffed. She pulled the energy for the sword back, and it retreated into the image on her wrist. "I'll rest, and then we'll use this nifty chain." She didn't know who she was talking to. Herself? The tattoos? Spirit?

When she had regained some of her strength, she stood again. She flicked her left wrist, and the golden chain fell from her wrist. It did not have flames but glowed a buttery yellow reminding her of the light behind the veil. It seemed to be made of light. Knowing it was a long shot, she wanted to try anyway. Just one time, rather than wearing herself out this time. She swung the chain like a whip and hit the stones. She let it drop and pulled the power of the chain back. The rocks remained just as they were. There wasn't even a scrape where it had hit.

Alle sat back down on the hard ground. She brought her knees up. Wrapping her arms tightly around her shins, she rested her head in between. These two new tools on her wrists were not meant to bring down walls, even imaginary ones.

That thought triggered another memory of when she and Gabriel pulled back the veil. She had closed her eyes. The veil was not something that could be seen. It was felt. The veil had softly whispered across her fingers.

To see Spirit, she had to close her eyes. She had to feel with her spirit. Alle looked around her at the blocks that formed the cell. If she closed her eyes, she could still see them in her mind.

She found the ember of light in the pit of her abdomen. It had been there since the fountain, but she had subdued it. Gabriel was right. She didn't want to give up her humanity yet. She had put a lid on it so tight she had almost forgotten how powerful that little fire could be. Afraid of it completely taking over, she hadn't used it at all.

Searching all this out within her and around her, it dawned on her that Spirit had been with her the whole time. Even when she was human and didn't know she was Nephilim. Even before she had become human at all.

Now all she had to do was control it without it consuming her. But that wasn't right. Maybe it wasn't about being in control. Maybe she could let it consume her without it affecting her humanity.

I'm going to trust the Most High and his Spirit.

Maybe he would allow her to become human again if she lost her humanity. Maybe Spirit would keep her from losing it altogether. That would be ideal.

236

I don't presume the mind of the Most High. We'll just go with it and see what happens.

She wasn't ready to put the idea to the test until she was sure Lani was safely back home. For now, she would try to work with a little of the power within her to give her the sight and strength she needed.

The more she practiced seeing spirit, the easier it became. The rocks that were her cell were no longer there. There was a barrier, but it wasn't the same as heavy rocks she couldn't lift. She found if she pushed hard enough, there was a give. The spirit rocks were bendy.

She could see now she was floating in a bubble, not a cave of inflexible, immovable rocks. Realizing that she had never stopped floating, she examined the barrier that surrounded her. "It's like when a car backs up beside me, and it feels like I'm moving instead of the other car." She snapped her fingers at the thought. The pop echoed as if she was in a huge cave. "That's what happened when I first got here. It felt like I was falling, but it was really the barrier lifting up around me."'

With this realization, she set to popping the bubble. She pushed all her fingers together and straightened them like her hand was a knife. Gabriel had done this a few times. Remembering him pull back the veil to rescue her pulled at her heart and reminded her how much he loved her. She pushed her hand through the barrier with her fingers at a sharp point. Alle felt the moment her hand ran through. The temperature was warmer beyond the barrier of her cell. Running her hands down the rough stones, she could simply push them aside and walk through the opening she created. It had really required no more power than a simple physical push-up.

With the barrier gone, she could see all the illusions the demons had set up for themselves and others. They really had copied many things from the natural world. The fake gravity was still in place, though. She wasn't going to be able to fly just yet.

Now, she needed a plan. She could find the nearest demon horde and yell, 'Take me to your leader.' That might be easy, but they may be just as likely to throw her back in a cell. Even though now she could break out, she didn't want to waste time or energy back where she started.

She returned to the opening where the demons had captured her before. This time, there were no demons that she could see. She guessed they had been waiting for her before. Or Narcisse had placed them there to encourage her to take his offer.

She knew Lani was in that cavern. Perhaps she could find another way in or around the giant crystal blocking the path. Of course, she could just cut through all the barriers to get there and probably make it out with Lani. That would accomplish the goal, but he would keep coming after them if she didn't take care of the demon prince. She wanted Lani safe forever, not just safe for now.

She decided she would save the barrier-cutting thing until she needed it, as long as she could work around their obstacles. That was her escape and her ace in the hole. She needed to be strategic about this. The demon prince might know she was supposed to be able to open the barriers. He didn't need to know she had finally mastered it.

She made her way through the darkness. Before she reached the cavern, she noticed another rock outcropping. It looked exactly like the little cell she had just escaped. It either hadn't been there before, or she hadn't noticed it with everything else going on. She realized someone else could be imprisoned there. She hoped it wasn't Lani, but she had to be sure.

She climbed down to investigate and peeped through a crack in the rocks.

A raspy voice croaked at her presence, "Who's there? Is that you, nasty demon? I will stab you if you don't get away from me."

"I'm not a demon," Alle replied. "Who are you?"

"This is a trick, isn't it? You aren't getting me to reveal the secrets of the Most High so easily this time."

Alle gasped. Had this been how the demons learned about who she was or how to get around the portals in the veil?

"I'm human. The demons took my daughter. I've come to rescue her."

There was a long silence. Alle wasn't sure what to do. Should she let this stranger out of his prison or let him figure it out on his own as she had to? She took a few minutes to decide. The stranger in the rock prison remained quiet. She didn't know whether it was out of fear or if he had thought she had left. In the end, she figured there was a reason she had seen this outcropping. If she had figured out how to manage the darkness, shouldn't she also help others?

"I'm going to get you out of here," she resolved.

"Don't bother. I'm already dead anyway," the raspy voice sounded fainter.

"Well, let me open the door, and we'll reassess," Alle said as she pulled Spirit in and brought down the barrier of the outcropping. Once the rocks were removed, she allowed her light to surround the stranger.

The man was skin and bones. His eyes were sunken in his skull. She could see every bone of his skeleton. His skin was covered with dirt and grime, and rags hung from his form. He hadn't seen light in so long his eyes had become cloudy with underuse. Limp grey hair hung down the sides of his face to his shoulders. He had been forgotten. This was what she would have become if she hadn't fought for her freedom.

She moved closer and reached out to put her hand under his arm to pull him up. He scurried away. She knelt down to seem less threatening as he crouched in the corner of the prison.

She held out her hand like he was a nervous puppy. "My name is Alle Venega."

"Thank you for coming, but I must stay here. I'm waiting for someone," he managed to croak out.

"Who are you waiting for?"

"A girl. A woman now, I guess. I have to warn her not to help the demons."

"What is her name?"

"I don't know her name. She is the prophesied one. I helped in her creation."

Alle sat back. She had an idea about who sat before her, although it shouldn't be possible. "What is your name?" she probed.

"I used to be known as Pileal. Though I have been forgotten. My name is lost to time now."

"You haven't been forgotten, friend. You were thought to be vanquished."

"That explains why my brothers didn't come for me. But it didn't bother me. They would have wasted away here as I have done. And I've been waiting for another."

"You've been waiting for the Nephilim?"

He put his finger to his lips. "*Ssh*. Don't let them hear you say that word. They will take everything from you."

"They already have. But I'm going to get her back."

"Who are you?" he asked, staring blankly. He moved closer, slowly, like a frightened animal. He gently reached out and put his fingers on her face. She let him rake his grimy hands over her. He had been in the dark so long his sight was gone, physical and spiritual. She let him create a mental picture. She couldn't imagine what it took to break the angel.

"I am the one you are waiting on. I am the Nephilim," she whispered.

"You?"

"I am your daughter."

"Not mine, surely?"

"Did you not possess a man named Joel twenty-two years ago?"

The man laughed a bit. It startled Alle to hear the sound in such a place, from such a man. "Oh yes, several times. That was a fun few months."

Alle cringed. Gross. She still did not want that mental picture. "Well, here I am. Technically, your daughter in the flesh."

He took her hand and started crying. "I'm so sorry. Once you were conceived, I left and didn't return. My purpose was to help you, an angel soul, enter a human body."

"I know mostly what happened. So many people went out of their way to help."

"The demons must have been watching, though I don't know why or how. They trapped me after you were conceived and brought me here."

"Maybe it was a coincidence." Alle knew the demons would have interfered long before now if they had known who she was.

Pileal seemed less frightened of her now. He relaxed at her side. "No. Your parents moved and hid you away soon after you were conceived. The demons have been asking me where they went for, I guess, decades now."

Alle wasn't aware of any moves in her childhood, but maybe they had moved before she was born. She looked him over again. Other than the state of his body, he seemed fine. He didn't look to be turning into a demon.

"How have you survived? I thought angels couldn't come to the underside."

"I'm not an angel anymore, Alle. I've been here for too long. It's a drawn-out process, and I've been fighting it with everything I have so that I can warn you. I knew they would find you eventually and bring you here. I couldn't help some of the things I told them. But soon, I will be nothing more than those filthy, wriggling little demons. Snapping and biting at anything that moves."

She tensed beside him. He noticed and patted her leg. "Don't worry. It won't be that soon."

"Can you walk? I need to find my daughter before I try to open the barrier to the natural world, but you can come with us." He stopped her before she could explain her plan.

"No, Alle. I've only stayed here for you. The demons will try to make you do terrible things. You must resist them. No matter what sacrifice you must make, you must. Everything is on the line."

"I'm not willing to sacrifice my daughter, but don't worry, Pileal. I have a plan, too." She grabbed his hand and held it for a long time. It seemed to give him comfort.

"The child is important," he agreed. "She must be saved." It sounded like something he had said to himself many times. A mantra to keep himself going. Alle didn't know if he was speaking of Lani or herself. It didn't matter, really.

He took raspy breaths. "It is time for you to go, child. When you go back through the cavern as you must, there is a small opening between that giant diamond and the wall. It is a tight squeeze, but you can definitely get through it."

Alle shook her head. "I didn't see that before. I must have been distracted by a horde of demons and Narcisse. But I can get through any obstacle now."

"Try not to manipulate the barrier until you are ready for everyone to know you have mastered your ability. Avoid Narcisse at all costs. That devil," he spat the words in disgust. "He might be worse than the prince," he said, confirming Alle's suspicions.

"He said that Gabriel made a deal with him," Alle replied.

"No angel would make a deal with the devil, but Heaven help us all if he did."

Alle remained quiet, thinking about the consequences of such a deal. She hoped she was right that Gabriel would never make such a mistake.

"You must go now, child. Time is running thin." Pileal pushed her away with what little strength he had. She barely moved.

"Pileal. Please come with me. We can help you."

"The process of becoming a demon will continue even in the natural world. This is where I belong now. I'm blessed to know that you have found your way. Now I can truly die in peace."

She nodded her head. She understood. He didn't want to endanger anyone that wasn't in the underside for a reason.

Alle stood and dusted herself off. "Thank you for all you've done."

"Don't thank me. I have put you in more danger. I can't remember all they've tortured out of me. I'm broken in so many ways."

"It doesn't matter what you've told them. What's done is done, and we'll deal with what comes. I'm going to get Lani and get her out of here. Take care."

She patted him on the shoulder.

"Peace be with you. The prince will have a throne room nearby. He likes to keep his prizes close."

Even though he couldn't see it, she smiled sadly. After saving Lani, she would come back for him. They would find a way to keep him from turning into a demon. There was an entire warehouse full of knowledge at her disposal. She had to leave him for now, though. Lani was the priority.

"Goodbye, Pileal. Until we meet again."

She could see his tears as they splashed to the ground. She couldn't bear the pain of goodbye any longer. She had to accomplish her task but promised herself that she would save this angel, too.

Anger swept over her as she took one last look back at the former guardian. Righteous anger filled her at what they had done to Pileal. She let the anger spread just enough to move her to action. She whispered to herself as she stepped back toward the cavern, "It's time to end this."

She left the prison doors open and walked away.

Chapter Thirty

I t didn't take long for her to return to the opening where she had fought the demon horde. She would get Lani out quickly and then return for the despicable prince. Once he had been taken care of, she would save Pileal, too.

The glowing crystal blocking her path was miraculously gone. There wasn't a single obstacle in her way, so much for all that planning. She slowed and crouched lower.

There was a problem. Either the demons were not expecting her to come back through this way, and they had removed the obstacles for grins and giggles, or they had expected her, and this was a trap.

As soon as she had the thought, the sound of scraping claws on metal rang in her ears. It grated on her bones as she cringed at the sound. She turned to see two giant demons behind her. They were as big as Gabriel and Lex. If these guys didn't have midnight skin, she might have mistaken them. Just by looking at them, she knew she couldn't take on either of them in hand-to-hand combat unless she shed her precious humanity. She would if needed, but that was the last resort.

So she ran. She had learned in her kickboxing classes that the best way to end a fight was to get away as fast as possible. Criminals were usually lazy. She doubted these demons would be, though.

As she ran, she looked for hiding places. She was completely exposed in the wide-open space of the cavern.

A thought occurred to her, but no one had told her it was possible. Either it wasn't, or they hadn't thought she could do it. If she could manipulate the barrier to bring it down, could she manipulate it to erect a hiding place? Did that work on demons? The ones in the cell seemed to struggle with the stone, and they were affected by the fake light. The phony reality worked on at least some of the weaker demons as it had on her at first. She hoped these two demons would fall into that category.

The demons were gaining on her, and she would need to learn on the go. To her right was a chasm, and in front of her was a waterfall of lava that turned into a river and flowed to her left. The lava gave light to this room, and it was stifling hot. Sweat began to trickle down her face. Either this was real lava, or her hypothalamus had been tricked again.

She was grateful Lani wasn't being kept in the dark, though. The pod would take care of the rest.

"First things first, can I pull off creating a hidey-hole?" she whispered as she ran. She would have to stop. Putting as much distance between herself and the demons as possible, she turned toward them and closed her eyes. She pulled the power from Spirit and built a shield around her with the barrier.

The demons skidded to a stop just before they hit her. They sniffed the air like the predators they were. Of course, they had seen her disappear and knew she was somewhere around. They couldn't see her now, though. To them, she had vanished.

She watched them through her barrier like a two-way mirror. The demons searched for a few seconds and seemed to get bored. A loud noise by the entrance distracted them from finding her. It drew her attention, too.

Pileal stood in the cavern's entrance. The two massive demons ran toward him with claws ready to slash through him. As they approached, he flicked his wrist. His sword appeared, although there was not a lick of fire to the blade. He wasn't too far gone to use his spirit sword. He leveled it at the demons. Alle watched as he fought them with every bit of strength he had left. At first, he could block a few blows and even get in a nick or two himself.

It wasn't enough. One of the demons slashed the tips of its claws across his back. Pileal dropped his sword hand. He no longer had the strength

SACRED VENGEANCE

to lift it. It gave the other demon an opening. He plunged his hand into Pileal's chest cavity and pulled out his still-beating heart. She could see that it dripped with black sludge instead of vibrant red blood.

Her hand slapped over her mouth to keep from screaming. Pileal's body slumped to the ground. His eyes cleared, and he met hers. He smiled peacefully as the life drained out of his face. The battle hadn't been long, but he fought bravely.

Alle turned from the scene and scrunched her eyes shut, trying to erase the sight from her memory as tears spilled for the angel she barely knew. Even in just a few minutes together, their connection was real. She had wanted to save him. Instead, he saved her and gave her another chance to rescue Lani.

The barrier around her was still intact, but with the sadness of Pileal's loss, it threatened to come down.

She gave herself a moment, then pushed the scene aside. There was nothing she could do now. She could only go forward. Pileal had made his choice, and his sacrifice had bought her time. She wouldn't waste his gift.

She looked back to ensure the guards hadn't returned to continue hunting her. Pileal's body had already been moved. A smear of black on the rocky floor was the only evidence he had been there. The demons returned to guarding the entrance as if nothing had happened. They had forgotten about her. She breathed a sigh of relief. *At least these guards are stupid,* she thought.

She pulled the barrier tighter around her and started searching the space. She naturally shied away from the heat of the lava.

She searched for Lani. She couldn't see the pod anywhere in the large cavern. She looked down the chasm. Nothing greeted her except inky blackness. There were no ledges, just sheer cliffs to a bottomless pit. She rolled her eyes. Of course, there was a bottomless pit.

A short ledge rose to a towering cliff on the other side of the chasm. *What was with this world and cliffs?* she wondered to herself. *Can't these demons think of anything more creative?*

As she looked up the cliff, she spotted another ledge. There was the golden pod. Her heart leaped into her throat. She had found Lani at last. In her excitement, she almost dropped her barrier cloak. She hadn't seen any new demons, but that didn't mean they weren't around. Just as she had that thought, scrawny beings moved along the bottom of the cliff on the other side of the chasm. There were probably more guarding Lani at the top of the cliff, but she couldn't be certain. The prince must know she couldn't fly.

Ok, how am I going to get across this chasm? Can I fly across since none of this is real? She hadn't had that floating problem since she first arrived. Gravity still felt real, and she didn't want to risk falling forever, nor had she figured out how to maneuver while floating. She walked along the chasm, looking for a less risky place to cross. The problem was that the ledge on the other side decreased as the chasm narrowed.

She spotted a mechanism that looked like a metal drawbridge. That must be how the demons got across. She thought that once *you feel gravity, suspending that sensation, even for demons, must be hard. Maybe they don't want to float around in their self-made hellscape.*

As she was about to give up and just jump across and hope to fly, her left arm began to warm. She had forgotten about the chain. It was a part of her now, but still new. She didn't know how to use it yet. *Can I use them while also being invisible?* She didn't want to fight more demons than necessary before she was ready.

She shrugged. This was the only way across, so she would have to handle whatever came up.

She returned to the little ledge below Lani's pod and searched for something to wrap her chain around. She found a small rock that might work as a hold. She would only have one chance at this.

She flicked her left hand, and the chain dropped down. To her surprise, the demons didn't look her way. She swung the chain like a lasso and threw it across. It grew as it whipped out and wrapped securely around the rock.

She pulled on it to test it. No, give. This just might work. "Well, here it goes," she whispered. She winced at her mistake. Fortunately, the demons still didn't hear her.

She held on to the chain with her left hand and took a running leap. As she got to the ledge, she dropped the barrier cloak and flicked out her sword on her right hand. In a single stroke, she killed the five demons guarding the ledge. She gave herself a silent pat on the back as the demons dropped from existence. All that remained were black streaks on the ruddy soil.

As she reached the face of the cliff to begin climbing, the chain and sword retracted immediately. She pulled up the barrier around her again. The cliff face was sheer, but there were plenty of hand holds and foot holds when she looked for them. She had never been a rock climber, but she imagined this would be like climbing El Capitan in Yosemite National Park. Except she didn't have a ropes system. She didn't think she would die if she fell, but it would hurt and take some time to recover. She didn't have that kind of time.

Lani was at the top. That thought got her moving. She searched for handholds and pulled herself up. *Why is everything targeted for upper body strength?* she thought. Then, mentally applauded as she pulled herself up another two feet.

She placed her foot on a tiny sliver of rock and pushed. Finally making it to the ledge holding Lani's pod, she was surprised not one demon had stopped her.

From this ledge, she could look down on the entire space. If this were a cave tour, they would call this the ballroom. Aside from the lava river, she could imagine rough riders and outlaws hiding from the sheriff's posse. Or gangsters running it as a speakeasy during prohibition. Near the lava (water)fall, she saw a black throne. Even from here, she could tell it was made from obsidian. The prince was not there. The court was not in session.

"WHERE IS SHE?"

Alle ducked at the soul-piercing sound, then jumped and moved quickly to the pod. "Time to go, baby girl."

She gave her hand a shallow cut and pressed it to the pod. She could not open the barrier wide enough for the pod yet. She hoped Lani would wake up and release the demon to make it easier to protect her.

The pod popped open with a hiss. Just as Alle lifted the lid, Lani opened her mouth. Black smoke spewed out of her little body. She didn't open her eyes, though.

The smoke flew away with incredible speed toward the throne room, and Lani's body collapsed on the satin cushions. Alle searched her face. The pod indicated that she was still alive, and her little chest rose and fell with her breath. She needed to get her to Asa and Gabriel. They would know how to wake her.

The demons spotted her just as she was about to reach in to grab Lani's limp form. She could hear the yelling. She risked popping her head up to see over the ledge. They were all pointing up at her. Alle had dropped the barrier cloak without realizing it. It was time to move.

She reached in to grab Lani's hand but dropped it when she spotted the familiar shape leaning against the cliff close to the edge. Alle flicked her wrists and prepared for a fight.

Chapter Thirty-One

"How do you keep finding me?" Alle hissed through clenched teeth. "You willingly shared your energy with me, little angel. I can find you any time in any realm. We are bonded in a way."

Alle let out a low growl and raised her sword. "I'll never be bonded to you."

Narcisse lifted his hands, palms out. "What's done is done. I'm not here to fight, little angel. Just offering you one last chance for my help." He still looked bored.

"I've told you before. I don't want to pay the price for your services. I don't want Gabriel to pay the price, and I definitely don't want Lani to pay the price."

Before she could swing the sword, he was behind her, pinning her arms down with his hands. He inhaled her scent. And whispered into her ear. "You are mine, Alle. You just don't know it yet."

She broke loose from his grip and swung her elbow to his face. He leaned away from her, barely escaping a broken nose. He grinned, turned to smoke, and reappeared at the other side of the ledge.

Alle ignored him and concentrated on pulling Spirit toward her. The space around her began to light up in a way she was starting to recognize. It didn't take much for her to see the barrier now. She heard the roars and claws of demons climbing the cliffs behind her. She needed to hurry if she was going to bore through the barrier and get Lani home.

Now that the pod was open, it was more important to get Lani out safely. If she didn't, she didn't even want to think about how the demons could use her. She would have left her in the pod if there was any other way to get her through the barrier.

She longed to hold her baby and escape, but she was safer in the pod, even opened, for now. Especially if Alle was going to have to fight their way out. Narcisse kept watching from his perch on the ledge.

She pushed the power of Spirit into her hand. It began to glow brighter until she saw a little hole forming in the barrier. The sounds of the demons below were getting closer, and she worried they would reach her before she could finish. Her worry and fear dampened her spirit and made this take longer. Alle groaned.

Narcisse spoke, "I'm all for bringing down the barrier. But the horde is almost here. You might wait a bit, little angel, unless you want the horde to burst into your home."

"I don't need to bring it down. I need a little hole to push Lani through."

That little hole wasn't happening, though. She couldn't cut through with worry and fear pushing down on her. She worried she wouldn't be able to open the barrier, making it harder to open it. Narcisse watching made her nervous, and the demons climbing the cliff to get to Lani were stressing her out. With all the pressure, she couldn't connect with Spirit and open the barrier. They were running out of time. She would need another plan. Expending all her energy before needing to fight her way out wouldn't help.

She turned back to Lani and pressed the lid to the pod back down. Looking at her sweet face renewed her strength.

The sword felt light in her hand. She stood to face the horde ascending the cliff. If they believed the pod was locked, perhaps they wouldn't bother Lani now. She readied herself to protect her daughter.

The first of the demons hopped over the edge. It had the face of a dog skeleton. Fur draped along its neck. Its gray skin hung in places and exposed ligaments and tendons in others. It hunched and hobbled, scraping the ground with its long black talons.

Assuming beheading would be the best way to kill these guys, she swiped her sword across the demon's neck. The dog's skull fell to the ground, but the body remained upright. She kicked her foot into his chest. The body flew backward off the cliff.

More popped over. Three at once. She removed head after head. There was no slowing down. There were too many of them for her.

"The demon prince doesn't want Lani. He's content to leave her here until the end of time. Maybe it's time to put away the sword and live to fight another day, hmmm?"

"You'd like that, wouldn't you?" she said with a groan.

"You in the hands of the demon prince? Hardly. But if you don't make a deal with me, I see no other option for you here."

"There's always a choice," she grunted as she continued to fight the demons popping over the ledge. For now, the climb was slowing down the number that climbed over.

"Yes, your choice here is to let me help or let the demons take you. They will not kill you. Not right away." He smiled his evil smile.

"There's always another door, Narcisse."

Alle killed the next set of demons over the top of the ledge. In the few seconds' break, she bumped open the pod and pulled Lani out. She held her close to her chest and smelled her sweet baby scent. She wrapped the barrier around both of them. She backed up to the cliff face. Looking up, she realized she couldn't climb with one hand. She was going to have to risk everything.

With her back against the wall, she did the only thing left she could do. She put all her energy into the five steps to the ledge and leaped out as far as possible. It was far enough to clear the demon horde, scaling the wall like zombies. She squeezed her eyes closed and tightened her hold on Lani. *Gravity isn't real. Gravity isn't real.* She chanted in her head.

She was high enough that she barely cleared the chasm. She turned so she wouldn't land on Lani at the last minute. She hit hard, but not as hard as she should have. She landed on her left thigh. She was still in rags, and the skin scraped off instantly without protection. Through all that, Lani still slept in her arms.

She shifted her over to her other arm and felt little arms pull closer around her neck. Alle had never felt so much relief in her life. She had wanted to get her back home before she woke, but she hoped she could explain all this away as a bad dream.

"Ok, baby girl. Let's find a safer place where I can get you home." Alle stood carefully. The chasm was inches behind her, and she didn't want to climb out of that.

She limped away from the horde. They were still invisible, but she guessed it wouldn't be long before they figured out what she had done. She thought about what Narcisse had said. *If I open the barrier, will all the demons flood through? But what choice do I have?*

She ducked again at another roar and crash as the pod sailed over the cliff's edge. "FIND THEM!"

She made her way away from the ledge where the pod had been and in the opposite direction of the throne room. There was no reason to get closer to the demon prince's court. She found a little outcropping of giant boulders, perfect for what she needed to do.

She laid Lani down behind a large boulder. She kissed her little cheek. She kept her hand on her arm as she crouched nearby, needing to regroup and get a plan. If she couldn't open the barrier, this would go south quickly.

She was filthy, and the pain from the wound on her leg was distracting. She took some cleansing breaths. Breathing the nonair was more difficult. This portion of the ballroom was closer to the lava river and stifling. She looked around for other ledges or a way out of the ballroom. Knowing this was the only place with a light source, she tried to keep Lani out of the darkness.

She built a little bigger barrier around them, calling on Spirit. It finally flared to life within her. "I can't do this on my own. I need your help."

"Ask," she heard in a whispered breath against her ear.

"I want Lani out, but if I don't put an end to these demons… We'll be right back here in dealing with this again later." She looked at Lani. She didn't want to keep going through this but was unsure if she could do what she had to do next.

"Ask," she heard again.

Alle sighed and bowed her head. "Spirit, give me strength. We are going to end this today."

The golden light wrapped around her. It restored her leg and filled her with energy. When it was over, she bent over Lani. "Sleep and rest, baby girl. Join us when you are ready," she whispered, kissing her on the cheek. She laid a barrier over her. The demons could probably still smell her, but all she needed was time.

Alle stood in her hideout. She could hear demons scouring the ballroom for her. She shut that out. She couldn't leave Lani here to be found again. She needed to get her to Gabriel, and then she could deal with the rest.

She concentrated on her daughter's face, pulling from her memories of Lani and Runar and their sweet moments together. She built up that love and faith in her core and hoped the light growing around her was still shielded by the barrier, but she couldn't worry about that now. *Just focus on that love,* she reminded herself. Finally, that pressure of power had built inside her. Reaching forward, she formed her hand to slice down the barrier.

She remembered Gabriel standing behind her, giving her his power to open the veil. She could almost feel him now, giving her his strength and support. Feeling the barrier, she ran her hand down to create the opening. Finally, she could see her house and smiled at the angel pacing on her porch.

"Gabriel!" she hissed, and his head popped up. He was at the barrier in a second. "I need you to grab Lani." She tilted her head to the sleeping girl.

"Ok, keep the barrier open. I'll reach in and get her."

Alle pushed with all her strength. Gabriel reached his hand inside the opening. Smoke started to rise from his flesh. He grabbed Lani's hand, pulling her up. Her eyes were still closed, and her head flopped back. Her blond curls were soaked with sweat. He began to pull her up and looked back at Alle, waiting for her to step through on her own. Horror contorted his beautiful features.

"Alle, look out!" A popping sound behind her accompanied his shouts. He had dropped Lani's hand to flick out his sword and protect them both. Lani fell back against the soft ground where Alle had laid her.

Gabriel was helpless to stop what happened next. In one fluid motion, Alle kicked him in the chest, let the barrier close between them, and flicked out her wrist to protect Lani. Adrenaline kicked up a notch to help Alle perform that superhuman feat. Her sword rose to meet the claws of the biggest demon she had seen.

His body towered over her by at least four feet. His muscular neck was thick enough to hold up his head. It had to be to support the giant ram horns that curled around each side. The ends filed to a sharp point. His skin was a bright shade of red. All the Halloween costumes and pictures that depicted the devil with red skin and pointy horns didn't come close to being scary enough to compare. She didn't have time to cower in fear as he swiped at her again. He smashed into the rock barrier that hid them from view.

Alle had a couple of things going for her: he was slow and didn't seem to be trying to kill her. She didn't know if he could see her or not. His eyes were entirely black. It made it difficult to tell whether he was looking at her.

With all her focus on the beast, she didn't see the other demons approach. Within seconds, she was surrounded. These creatures didn't seem to have a problem with the light from the lava. As the beast swung his arms like a big, slow lumberjack, Alle jumped out of the way.

She was successful at putting space between their current battle and Lani. But another demon, more humanoid with putrid green skin and a hunched back, grabbed Lani from where Alle had hidden her. He threw her over his shoulder and ran off toward the throne room. Lani's little head bounced with each of his steps.

"Nooo!" Alle's high-pitched scream had some of the lesser demons covering their ears. The distraction allowed the beast to swipe his giant hand against her shoulder and shove her into the wall.

Her head hit first. Her vision went blurry, and the last thing she saw was Lani's hand reaching toward her as she bobbled away over the shoulder of a demon.

Chapter Thirty-Two

The demons dragged Alle by her elbows into the throne room. Her head lolled to the side, and her toes scraped the ground. Her hands and feet were bound with rusty iron manacles that dug into her skin. She had lost everything.

The demons released her. She fell to the dusty ground and lay on her belly before the demon prince, hair over her face. His laugh ended with a vicious growl. "Bring it here," his scratchy voice commanded no one in particular. His hunched form slid across the dais. A black sword scraped the ground as he crouch-walked along the stone floor, circling and sniffing Alle. His putrid breath swept across her face and blew a piece of her hair from her nose. She almost gagged at the stench. It took all her will to remain unflinching, showing no emotion.

"You are truly beaten!" he huffed. "There is no escape. You and your ilk will remain my slaves until I tire of you." His black, soulless eyes reflected no light. "By then, you will have produced my Nephilim heir." He beat his chest with his slimy fist.

Alle rose to her knees; anger contorted her face. "I'll produce nothing for you. You're vile. Besides, Nephilim are the creation of angels and humans."

He cackled. A devastating laugh that filled Alle with dread. "Maybe." He lowered his head and smiled maniacally. His lips pulled back away from missing teeth. His tongue protruded and flicked up and down like a snake. "I think you know you are different than the Nephilim of old. You are an angel soul, yes? And human. I wonder what power we would get from an angel, human, and demon mix. I shall enjoy experimenting." He licked his lips again and rubbed his hands down his crotch. Saliva ran down his chin. Alle shivered. She gagged at the thought of his hands on her.

"Why are you doing this, demon?" Alle spat out the last word with disgust.

He jacked his eyes up and put his finger on his chin. "Let me see." He tapped his chin. He mimicked her tone. "Since you are here before me, chained like the dog that you are, perhaps I should share my plans with you. You are just the tip of the iceberg." He laughed. "The demon king didn't think I could do it. But here you are in my snare, just as I knew you would be."

"Why am I so important?"

"Haven't you discovered the prophecy? You are the Nephilim that will bring down the barrier."

"I think your interpretation of the prophecy is a little skewed. The prophecy says that the Nephilim will open the veil. I have no power to do that. I've tried. You can let me go now."

He cackled again. His gnarled claws curled under her chin. "Oh, little angel. Do you think that is the only plan I have for you? No. We are going to have such fun. Although, I think you can open the veil. I'm certain you can open the barrier. I saw your little friend earlier. I saw you kick him back through the barrier." He smiled. "That was such fun to watch you in action. To allow you to show off all your... talents."

Alle opened her mouth to curse him, but he held up a finger.

"I'm not done." He shoved her head toward his throne. "After you open the barrier, and you will because I have your precious little one. You will open the veil because...." He grabbed her by a fistful of hair and pulled her head back towards him. He put his hand to his ear, "...I can't hear you, Alle. Why are you going to open the veil?"

"Because you have my daughter," she hissed through her gritted teeth.

"Yes!" He stepped back and clapped. "This is so much more fun than I imagined." He turned and pranced back to his throne. Alle was grateful to have a reprieve from the stench of decay and rotting flesh. "Then you will be chained to my throne, where we will have our fun." Alle could see the bulge in his pants as he thought about all he would do to her. She almost vomited right there. "And after you've produced three or four heirs for me, I might let you go. If... you are good."

She tried not to let the fear of that scenario course through her veins. Fear was no good to her here. She needed to keep a clear head to get herself, and more importantly, Lani, out of this alive. Hope, faith, and love were all necessary to have the strength to do what she must.

The sound of claws scraping the rocks signaled that demons approached. A squeak and the rattle of chains filled the cavern as the grate was lowered across the chasm. Lani shivered on the ledge across the chasm. Alle did not look at her. She didn't trust herself not to break and give these evil beasts what they were hoping to get from her. They wanted her fear, her anguish, to see her break and snuff out what little light she had left. She might be beaten, but she would not give them the satisfaction.

"Strip her and tie her to my throne! I will have my heir sooner rather than later."

Alle smiled cooly as she saw the demons beside her grin and rub their greedy hands together. They would enjoy watching this scene. "You should know. I'm barren."

He held up a hand to stop the order he had just given. It was the prince's turn to smile. He grabbed her chin again and held her head to face the chasm where Lani stood. "I think not, Nephilim."

Alle finally looked at Lani. Her heart cracked, and desperation bubbled out. "Don't hurt her. I'll do as you ask. Willing. Just don't hurt her."

"Oh... where is the fun in that? Yes, you will do as I please." He poked his dirty, twisted finger in Alle's chest, then pulled it back to himself. "And I will do as I please." He looked hungrily at Lani. "I do like having this leverage, though."

The grate barely hit the ledge before the prince's voice was booming, "Come!" Lani shook her head. She cowered and covered her face. Before Alle could react, the demon prince extended his black claws, grabbed her hair, and yanked it back to expose her neck's smooth, pale skin. A sharp claw landed directly over the artery. He dragged her to the chasm. All he had to do was press, and it was all over. "Come, or your mother dies," he hissed at

Lani. Alle stilled, scarcely breathing. Partly because doing so would cause her to inhale his rancid breath and partly because any movement would cause her to die.

Lani stood. "Mommy?" The prince snickered at the nickname. Recognizing Alle, Lani started across the grate. All traces of fear were gone now that she saw her mom.

Safely across, the demons allowed her to run to Alle. The prince removed his threatening claw and threw her head toward the child. Alle wrapped her arms around Lani as much as the chains would allow. "Shh, don't cry. I've got you," she whispered. She pulled back a bit. She took Lani's head with both hands and wiped her tears with her thumbs. "I need you to be a really brave girl right now." Lani nodded and sniffed. As the demons approached to separate them, Alle bowed and touched Lani's forehead with her own. "I love you, baby girl."

Alle could now see a thick cord between her chest and Lani's. It was a dark golden color. Instinct told her that her connection to her daughter was spiritual and physical. It had always been there, but now that she could see the spirit world, she could see their connection. They would always be bound in this way. Nothing would separate them from each other. Not death, darkness, or a filthy evil demon prince.

A soft glow between them began to grow. It was a bright source of light in the dim room. Alle waved her hand and pushed Lani hard toward the chasm she had just crossed. The prince cackled, "You killed your daughter to save her?" He laughed until he saw that Alle had opened the barrier and shoved Lani through. Then, his face changed to pure rage.

Alle could see Gabriel in her front yard. An army of angels waited. They were about to bring down the barrier by some other means. In a second, she saw his relief when the barrier opened, his surprise when Lani fell through, and his fear as she closed it. Then she went to work.

The light that started from her love for her daughter grew. The golden aura filled her until the cavern's darkness was utterly overcome. Spirit infused the light to make it stronger. No longer a glow but almost as bright as the sun on a cloudless spring day.

She asked Spirit for strength to stand. She rose to one leg and then to the other. She lifted her chin and threw her shoulders back. She would not be afraid any longer. The light incinerated the metal on her wrists.

Demon lackeys shrank away, but the prince was trapped between his throne and escape. His pride added to his stupidity. And though Alle lacked daggers or claws, she had the only weapons she needed to defeat the darkness. Love and light. As she stood, she felt the brush of her golden wings lengthen down her back. Fire raced along her arms. Her hair, her eyes, and her face glowed white-hot. The rags she had been wearing were incinerated and replaced with the armor of angels. The demon prince she had long feared now cowered before her, sensing his reign was ending.

Alle wrapped her golden chain, summoned with a thought, around his neck. He clawed at the chain with those awful black claws, doing nothing but causing his hands to sizzle. Smoke began to rise from every place that the chain touched his hide. He collapsed on his side. His feet scraped the rocky floor as he tried to escape this avenging angel. It only served to tighten the chain around his neck. He gurgled and squirmed. His eyes bulged, his head separated from his body and rolled away. The rest of his body went limp and disintegrated.

Alle felt the presence of evil in the shadows where her light did not reach. The memories of every evil event in the history of humanity began to filter in through her connection with Spirit. She longed to shed the human vessel and take her vengeance on these demons who had caused so much human suffering. "Vengeance is mine." Her mantra returned to her mind. She stepped toward the cowering demons.

A tiny hand grabbed Alle's fingers. Startled, she turned and stared at the face that called her mommy.

"Come back to us, Alle. It's not time yet," she heard Gabriel's familiar voice in the distance through the opening in the barrier.

Alle struggled to reign in her need for retribution. She wanted to fulfill her purpose. She needed to. Just as she was about to tug her hand away, she heard a little voice whisper, *"You have a new purpose now. Lani needs you first."*

260

CHAPTER THIRTY-TWO

She looked back down at the little girl. Then, back to the demons.

"Come after me if you feel you must, but if any of you come within fifty feet of my daughter, this will be much worse for you." She pulled back the flames that had engulfed her. Her weapons and wings tucked away, she picked Lani up, walked through the barrier, and collapsed onto her front lawn.

Chapter Thirty-Three

Alle awoke to the smell of bacon. It was the best smell to wake up to. She sniffed the air and smiled. Her belly grumbled with hunger. She cracked an eyelid open and then rubbed the crust that poked the corner. Light filtered in through the window by her bed. Surely, she had overslept.

She sat up, and the blankets fell from her torso. She looked at both her wrists with curiosity. Had she gotten drunk and ended up at the tattoo parlor? Why had she chosen a chain and sword? Weird.

She looked at the space beside her on the bed. Panic wracked her body as she searched for Lani, patting the bed. Lani had always slept in her bed. Had she gotten up early? Her side of the bed didn't look slept in at all. What if someone had taken her? Would the kidnappers have stopped to make the bed and cook breakfast? She didn't even remember having bacon in her refrigerator. She tried to shake away the confusion.

She grabbed her head as the memories of the past few days—or was it weeks—burst through the morning haze. It felt like a waking nightmare, leaving a headache in its path.

She rushed down the stairs and burst into the kitchen. Lani sat in her usual chair, eating fruit loops. Alle's mom stood in front of the stove. Her dad sat on the couch with the newspaper folded over. He was old school. Alle had never convinced him to convert to digital.

"Oh, good morning, honey. I'm glad you're up. Want some breakfast?" Laila's singsong voice came from the kitchen.

Alle calmed her racing heart and took some deep breaths. "I... um... sure,

Mom," she stammered. She felt the rush of adrenaline drain from her body. "Is there anything I can do to help?" she managed to ask.

Her mom just glared at her. She didn't like Alle to help in the kitchen. She was more in the way than helpful. Laila had a method to her madness, and adding more bodies didn't fit into the equation. Alle would help with cleaning up when they were done.

She grabbed the aspirin bottle from one of the kitchen cabinets and sat next to Lani. While she waited for her mom to bring her a plate, she poured a couple of pills into her hand. She downed them with the coffee sitting in front of her.

"How did you sleep, dear," Laila asked.

"That's the best sleep I've had in ages. I think," she explained to her mom.

"Good, dear. I'm glad to hear it." She returned to her cooking but kept up the conversation. "We took Lani to the grocery store this morning. I hope you don't mind. She had slept with us last night. She wakes up so early."

"Don't I know it?" Alle murmured. She gave Lani a toy that had fallen on the floor. She pulled her out of her highchair. She wanted to snuggle her and hold her close. It felt like years since she had held her.

"Mommy, I miss you," Lani said, putting her hands on each side of Alle's face.

"I missed you, baby girl. I'm glad you are here safe and sound."

Without missing a beat, Laila continued, "You didn't have a single thing in the fridge. What were you feeding the poor girl?"

"We make do. I had some condiments in there. Besides, we had just moved in. I hadn't had time to stock up."

Alle received another look.

"Well, we filled your fridge with the basics. But you need to make your meal plan and keep up with it," Laila scolded.

"Yes, Mom," Alle rolled her eyes and turned to her dad. "You going to help me out here?"

He just popped his paper up and kept reading. He pretended not to hear the conversation. Alle smiled and shook her head. He knew better than to take sides.

"Mom, I know you can't see the angels, but do you know where they went?"

Laila turned to face her daughter. Sadness veiled her face. "No, honey. Lani ran into the house last night. We were so relieved to see her. She pulled us outside. You were passed out on the front lawn. You hadn't been gone long, but you were a mess of dirt and rags. We got you both cleaned up and put to bed. It was no easy feat, but we managed."

Alle sighed, wondering where her angel armor had gone. *Maybe it's like the tattoos and only appears when I need it?* She could remember most of the events of the previous days. No one had wiped her memories. She was sure that anything she didn't remember was due to trauma.

She gave her mom a shy smile. "Thank you. I'm glad y'all were here."

Laila patted her on the hand. "Me too, babe. Me too. " She turned back to her cooking, plating up Alle's breakfast. "Speaking of which, your dad has something he wants to talk to you about."

Alle groaned. "Ugh. You only have Dad talk to me when there's something I'm not going to like."

Laila remained silent. She raised her eyebrows and told Alle to sit down and listen without saying a word.

Turning back to her dad, Alle gave him an expectant look. He put the paper down and leaned forward. She was not going to like this at all.

"We like this little town, Alle," he said as her mouth dropped open. "We are putting our house on the market and moving down the street."

"Down the street? What? No!" She huffed. "That is too close. Why do you think I moved in the first place?" She hadn't moved because of her parents, but they didn't need to know that.

"We think you need some help with Lani. And when you start dating again, you will love this idea."

"I will not be dating again. Gabriel is it for me."

"Daddy angel!" Lani screamed with excitement at the mention of the guardian's name.

"Gabriel is an angel. You can't be with an angel. Besides, he essentially left you lying on the front lawn." Joel crossed his arms and squinted his eyes.

"Dad, there is probably a good explanation for that. And I'm not having this conversation with you. You are not selling your house. Being an hour away is close enough."

"I would love to hear a very good explanation from the invisible man who left you on the lawn," her dad continued.

"I'm a little hurt that you wouldn't want us to be closer." Her mom piped up from the kitchen.

Alle turned and slammed her head into her hands. At least it hadn't been a dream, and they had all been able to keep their memory of the events.

"Fine, you can move to this town, but it must be at least two neighborhoods away. And I do not want you driving by my house every day to see if my car has left the driveway."

"I think we can manage that." Her dad looked around her at her mom. Her mom waved her hand in the air and went back to cooking.

* * *

Months went by without any sign from Gabriel. Lani had stopped talking about her Daddy angel. It worried Alle she wouldn't remember him. She would grow out of her innocent baby phase and lose the ability to see him.

She sometimes wondered if she had hallucinated the whole thing, except that the evidence adorned her skin. And her parents continued to talk about the invisible men. She hadn't been able to access her wings or her weapons, but she had swirly golden tats on her back, too.

"What good are the tats if I can't use them?" she whispered to herself when she had discovered them. She considered her inability to access the wings might be the same reason she hadn't seen the angels anymore. There was evidence of her faith, but she wasn't in mortal danger. There was no need for her abilities. She worried some days that if the day came when she had to use her wings or weapons, her humanity would be lost.

She considered putting herself in danger to see if Gabriel would show up to protect her. Or to see if she could use her new arsenal, but thought better of it when she looked at Lani's face. There was no risk she would take that would further endanger that sweet little girl.

Her parent's house had sold in five hours. The buyer offered twenty thousand over the asking price. Cash. Alle would never expect them to say no to that. The house they purchased was exactly two neighborhoods away. She hadn't budged on that stipulation. She had threatened to sell her own home and move three states away. As it turned out, it was amazing having them nearby. She could run errands, and her parents loved watching Lani.

She did not start dating, much to her parent's despair. Much like restaurants, there weren't a lot of options. She was also waiting for Gabriel to return and explain how he could leave her on the front lawn and disappear. The longer she waited, the angrier she got. *How could he leave without a note of explanation? He probably thinks he is protecting Lani and me by staying away.* The thoughts swirled in her mind on a daily basis. *What if he is here, and I just can't see him?* That thought had fear clawing its way through her spirit. It threatened to suffocate her. *If I can't see angels, I won't be able to see or sense the demons either.*

Her secret was out in the spiritual world. Instinct told her the demons weren't finished with their family, even if she had destroyed the demon prince. Since her marks didn't work, she decided she needed to train and stay fit. She set up a course in her backyard with many upper-body strength-building obstacles. Every day was arm day at the Venega house. She would be ready.

Training reminded her of Gabriel, though. Everything she did was a reminder of him. When Runar died, she ran away from her life. She was a different person now. There would be no running away from the memories this time. She would embrace them, willing them to make her stronger.

* * *

Alle lay in her bed asleep. She had continued to keep Lani close by. Her little chest rose and fell next to her.

Alle startled awake as she felt a breath on her cheek.

"Hello, little angel," Narcisse whispered into her ear. He was lying beside her, separating her from Lani. Fortunately, on top of the blankets and fully clothed.

"How did you get in here?" she whisper-screamed so Lani wouldn't wake, but Alle didn't move a muscle. Narcisse examined his manicure. "I have my ways."

Alle tensed.

"Don't worry. I'm not here to hurt you."

Alle sprung out of bed to face him. She threw on her satin robe. He leered. She was trying to lure him away from Lani, but Narcisse didn't take the bait. He just continued to rest his head on his elbow with his legs crossed. He was still in the same black suit he had been wearing when she saw him the first time. He was still shockingly pretty. Too pretty.

"I just came to thank you for killing dear old dad." He winked.

Alle's jaw dropped to the floor. "You're his son? The one he was going to bond Lani to?"

He smirked. "Yes. She's a little young for me, though. I'd much rather have an experienced woman to worship me."

Alle glared, anger rising in her at his presence and the disgusting thought of him bonding with her baby.

He continued, "I couldn't allow him to create new heirs with you. I would have killed him or you before he had the chance. But fortunately, you saved me the trouble. I was rooting for you the whole time." He finally looked her in the eyes. It was one of the only times she had seen him look at anyone but himself. His eyes were an unnatural shade of lilac. The effect was alluring.

"I'm sure you were. There was never a deal with Gabriel, was there?"

He ignored the question and looked her up and down. "I do like the idea of having Nephilim heirs of my own, though."

Then he was beside her. His arm wrapped around her waist again, pulling her into him. His breath smelled of honey. He caressed her cheek with the back of one hand while he held her tight with the other. His eyes zeroed in on her lips. He leaned closer...

She didn't lean away but continued to look him right in the eyes. She flicked her wrist. Bright light filled the room. She was no longer afraid of this demon.

It didn't bother him in the least. He pulled her closer and pressed his lips to her ear. "Now, now, little angel. You wouldn't want to put sweet Lani in danger, would you?" She could feel his grin on her cheek. He released her. She stepped back and raised her sword to attack.

He flew in a puff of smoke to the other side of the bed, extending his claws over Lani's chest. His wicked smile was deathly beautiful, "Put the sword away, and I'll make you an offer you can't refuse."

THE END

The Sacred Series continues with Sacred Mercy.
Visit EvangalinePierce.com/store for more information.

As I said, not everything could fit in the story when we started this journey. If you want to read Runar's battle with the demons or what John saw at the funeral, get on the list! These scenes and more are exclusive to my email pals.

www.evangalinepierce.com/contact

Psst... It could be over right here. Or you can tell me how much you loved my book! Please leave a review on Amazon or Goodreads. It only requires twenty honest words, and it really helps to get new readers!

Acknowledgments

First, thank you, Jesus, the Most High God.

I also want to thank you, readers. Without you, I'm the only one that reads this story. That's boring. I appreciate the ability to share my writing with you.

I also want to thank my family. Randy, you are the most supportive and encouraging person I know. I love you, and I'm so glad you married me. You are the best soul mate a girl could ask for. Thanks for listening to me rant about this book. Thanks for laughing when I make faces at my characters. Thank you for all your support. Baby girl, I tried to write this story when you were asleep, but sometimes you had to put up with me writing or editing. Thank you for letting me work on this, but I hope you are reading this a very long time from now.

A special thanks to Stephanie Taylor and Rodney Hatfield. You helped make this book the best it could be and get it in front of people. Thank you for all your hard work.

The True Savior

Isaiah 61:1-2
He has sent me to bind up the brokenhearted,
to proclaim freedom for the captives
and release from darkness for the prisoners,
to proclaim the year of the Lord's favor
and the day of vengeance of our God,
to comfort all who mourn,

Jesus would do anything to rescue you from the darkness. The good news is that he already has. He sacrificed his life and took on the punishment we deserved to rescue us from certain death and darkness. He overcame the darkness, so we didn't have to. A day is coming soon when he will avenge his people. It doesn't matter who you are, where you are, or what you've done. You can accept the love and grace that Jesus offers. If you want to know more, visit EvangalinePierce.com/grace

If you or someone you know is contemplating suicide, call the suicide prevention hotline. 1-800-273-8255 or dial 988.

If you have suffered from pregnancy or infant loss, there are people to walk with you through your grief. GatheringHope.net is a non-profit group helping women cope with loss. They offer support and guidance in the difficult process of mourning a loss.

About the Author

Award-winning author, Evangaline wrote her first short story at the age of twelve. She has spent much of her adult life writing papers for college professors. She rekindled her love for storytelling several years later when she published her first book chronicling her family's journey to find a missing person.

Evangaline loves crafting adventures that honor her faith and love of Jesus. Faith, hope, and love within suffering are common themes in her writing. Her main characters often face and overcome overwhelming odds.

She grew up reading Bible stories with her grandpa and always loved supernatural tales. Evangaline combines her love of fantasy with her Christian faith. She draws upon the magic and mystery of the Bible to tell modern stories that engage the reader with biblical truths and Christian themes.

She currently lives in Texas with her husband, daughter, two dogs, and a flock of chickens.

You can follow her on Facebook, where readers can interact with Evangaline and each other. Or get exclusive content via email.

You can connect with me on:

- 🌐 https://evangalinepierce.com
- 🐦 https://twitter.com/evangalinepi
- 📘 https://www.facebook.com/evangalinepierce
- 🔗 https://www.instagram.com/evangalinepierce

Subscribe to my newsletter:

- ✉️ https://www.evangalinepierce.com/contact

Also by Evangaline Pierce

The Sacred Series continues with…

Sacred Mercy

When the skyrocketing crime hits close to home, Alle suspects demons are to blame. Upon further investigation, she discovers cracks in the barrier that threaten to bring it all down. Without the spiritual barrier, nothing is preventing demons from taking over the natural world.

As Alle trains Lani to fight demons, the little girl begins to exhibit some frightening abilities. Although the angels haven't returned, her own personal demon arrives daily to harass her and make offers she can't refuse.

With the mounting burdens, she may have to do the one thing her heart won't be able to handle.

Will this single mom be able to repair what is broken before it's too late? Or will she have to make a deal with the devil?

Made in the USA
Columbia, SC
17 March 2024